Die for Now

BOB HOWARD

ISBN:
ISBN-13: 978-1-945754-33-3

DEDICATION

Writing each book in this series is like taking a journey, and the journeys are always different. It helps to have a guide. What remains constant is the destination. This book is dedicated to my wife and my guide, Dawn. Without her help, I would never reach my destination.

CONTENTS

ACKNOWLEDGMENTS

Writing continues to be an incredible experience. Since I released the second book, I have spoken with many people who say they would like to write a book. To each of them I have said, "Do it. It doesn't matter why you write as long as you are enjoying yourself."

My dedication continues to be for my wife, Dawn. If you have a supportive spouse, you can indulge yourself by spending your time on something you love to do.

Your friends can really influence your ability to feel good about exposing yourself to the world in a creative work, and I would like to thank Cynthia Lara and Leigh Bolick for the way they have supported me. They have encouraged me through all three books.

My daughter, Julie Cowell, formed a writers group about a year ago, and knowing that they have watched my progress continues to motivate me.

My son, Drew Howard, is my constant reminder that hard work is its own reward. Something good always comes from making the effort.

To the readers who have supported me with your kind emails and posts, I can only say I am glad I have found each and every one of you, and thank you for reading my books.

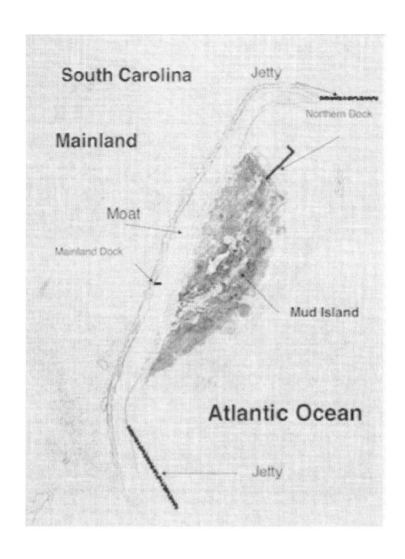

1 YESTERDAY'S GONE

The power grid went down in the middle of the night. We were all asleep, but it was too quiet, and that woke us up just as if someone had turned on the lights and used an air horn. I rolled over onto my back and tried to focus my eyes in the darkness. Jean was already propped up on her elbows trying to figure out what had happened.

"Did you say something?" she asked.

"No," I said, "but I was about to ask you the same thing."

A beam of light was coming down the hall to our left, and it was bobbing up and down. It came into the room, and we could see it was the Chief coming up from the lower levels.

"Good, you're both awake," he said.

The Chief's massive body seemed bigger than the door as he came into the room, and his voice was deep with a serious undertone. He was careful not to shine the light in our eyes, and that was no surprise. The Chief would be considerate in that way, no matter what was happening.

He was a big man, but there wasn't an ounce of fat on his body. He had never told us his age, but judging by his considerable experience and knowledge, he had to be older than he appeared to be. His full, reddish beard and hair didn't give any hints because there wasn't a bit of gray.

Jean sounded half asleep as she mumbled, "What's up, Chief?"

1

"I don't know yet," he answered. "The power is off, and I turned off the emergency generators to conserve fuel until we know what happened outside."

There was just enough light in the room from the Chief's flashlight for me to see Jean's profile under the sheets. At six months she was definitely showing she was pregnant, but she was still petite. She had managed to keep the weight under control even though we had no shortage of food in our shelter and too much free time to fill.

I was amazed by the gradual changes in her body, but I was keenly aware of the determination she showed not to complain about the aches and pains she was having. Jean said it was all about staying part of the team. She had been heard to say more than once she wasn't going to take a back seat to any of us just because she was going to have a baby.

Her recovery from the scratch of an infected dead had been slow, and we were always worried it would cause her to lose the baby. Jean had been captured by the crew of a Russian ship while the rest of us had been away on an extended road trip, and when they made the always fatal mistake of trying to treat crewmen who had been bitten, she showed everybody how tough she could be. She had fought her way to the upper level of the ship where we were able to rescue her. Her escape hadn't been without close calls, though. She was scratched by one of the infected dead, and it had proven to be fairly serious. She had a raging fever for days and was left totally drained and weak after it finally broke.

I didn't have to be told to get out of bed and get dressed. I retrieved my own flashlight from the nightstand and clicked it on. The Chief went through the other door on my right that led to the main living areas of the shelter, and I hurried to pull on my clothes.

The shelter on Mud Island only had one real bedroom so there wasn't much privacy. It had been given to me and Jean by default when it had been just four of us living in the shelter. The fourth person in our original group of survivors was a former Charleston police officer before the world had given in to a strange infection that had spread death throughout the population. Kathy was an extremely attractive blond, but she could be as deadly as she was beautiful.

Before I could get my shoes on, she passed through our room followed closely by the rest of the adults in our group. Tom, Allison, and Dr. Bus all said good morning as they went by. Molly, the only child, was probably still asleep.

Jean was struggling to reach her feet and get into her own shoes. I risked hearing her say she could do it herself and gave her a hand. As soon as we had her shoes tied we followed the others down the corridor that ended at the dining area and kitchen. By the time we got there, the Chief had turned on a few of the battery powered emergency lights and was examining all of the breakers in a hidden panel. The others were waiting for his verdict.

"Everything's good in here," said the Chief. "It has to be a power failure on the mainland. I think we should wait to switch on the emergency generators until after we have to. We all figured this day would come, so let's start conserving now."

The words had barely left the Chief's mouth when we felt the floor of the kitchen shudder. There was a concussive 'thump' from somewhere, and we knew as a group it had to be something that happened outside.

"Forget conserving," said the Chief. "We need the cameras on now."

He ran by us in the direction we had all come from, while the rest of us ran for the living room. As soon as the power came on, I had the camera views appearing on the big monitor. It didn't take a rocket scientist to figure out something big was happening out there.

We had cameras all around the island, and we could use them day or night. They came in really handy when we needed to know if there was trouble nearby.

The infrared views on the ocean side cameras showed a dark beach with a few of the infected dead lying in the sand. It was odd that none of them were standing, but we watched as they struggled to their feet and began staggering in our

3

direction. All of them walked toward the center of the island as if they were being drawn toward something.

"Why were they on the ground, and why are they all coming toward us?" asked Allison.

Allison was Tom's wife, and she was probably the least likely of us all to have survived the infection that had devastated the population of the world. Jean had told me privately that Allison was 'mousey' and she would have been killed a long time ago if not for Dr. Bus and his shelter. Dr. Bus had built a shelter like ours, but it was located in the mountains of north Alabama.

"I don't know," said Tom, "but there are only a few things that can attract the infected like that. I wonder if that thump we heard has anything to do with them coming this way."

"That thump you heard was a whopping big explosion," said the Chief.

We were so intent on what we were seeing on the monitor that we didn't notice when he came up behind us.

"Ed," he continued, "switch the mainland side cameras from infrared to normal vision and then put them on the screen."

"It's pitch black out there, Chief. How are we going to see anything without infrared?" I asked.

"Unless I miss my guess," he said, "there will be plenty of light out there. That's why the infected are all trying to go that way."

Even though I wasn't entirely convinced the Chief was right, I did as he said. The camera views on the mainland side came up on the screen, and they were all much brighter than we expected.

We had three cameras on the island that faced the mainland. For months, they had given us our best views of the Russian naval vessel that was still parked between Mud Island and the mainland. We called the waterway that ran from the north to the south on the mainland side our 'moat'. It kept the infected dead, and the unwelcome living, from walking straight over to Mud Island.

To our surprise, the place where the Russian ship was parked was engulfed in bright light. The Russian ship was burning and beginning to list toward us.

Kathy leaned in closer toward the screens and said, "Someone bombed the ship. The infected on the ocean side of the island are being drawn toward the light. I wonder who did it."

"That's what I think," said the Chief, "and one of the first explosions probably damaged the power lines that cross the moat. That kind of firepower had to be military. They either thought the ship was a hostile, or they knew it was a floating deathtrap, so they hit it hard."

"And it doesn't get much worse than that," I said. "Now we have to go to generator power and hope we can survive off of that."

"It's not all doom and gloom," said the Chief. "We have enough fuel to last two years if we don't run too many appliances at the same time. I imagine Uncle Titus planned on living off of seafood when he built this place, but we just have to find another source of food to replace it."

Uncle Titus was the relative who had left this shelter to me in his will. He died before the apocalypse he was anticipating, but he gave me a chance to survive. I met the rest of the group by accident, and even though I didn't know it yet, I had gotten lonely after only a few days. The Chief, Kathy, and Jean had floated up in a raft, and I couldn't turn them away. That was a good decision because Jean was going to make a father out of me in a few months.

When Titus built the shelter on Mud Island, he had a waterway dredged between it and the mainland. What had once been a marsh was now a deep river that entered an inlet at the northern tip of the island, and because he had the sense to build a jetty at the entrance, the incoming water picked up speed and became a dangerous moat.

We had seen plenty of the infected dead walk into the moat and simply disappear. Some of them were washed out through the southern exit past a second jetty, but as we had learned, most were being caught in nets that crossed the moat in two places. Uncle Titus had probably put the nets there to give a small amount of protection to the power lines that came from the mainland to Mud Island. It wouldn't have surprised him to see fish getting caught in the nets, but nothing could have prepared him for the sight of dead people flailing around trying to get loose.

Just the thought of it gave me the creeps, and for a moment I pictured myself trying to explain it to him.

I thought, "It's like this, Uncle Titus. Some kind of infection caused people to come back to life after they died, but instead of acting like people, they started going around biting other people, even their own families. Then they would die from the bites, come back to life, and then they would find someone else to bite. Next thing you know, there's only a few of us left."

"Ed, are you still with us?" asked the Chief.

I didn't realize the Chief was still talking to everyone about how we were going to get by this latest crisis.

"Sorry, Chief. I was just thinking about how my Uncle Titus would react to all of this. If he would have included zombies in his plans, maybe he would have thought of a way for us to clean the nets, and maybe that Russian ship wouldn't have become a death trap."

The Chief frowned at me, but I saw Kathy trying to hide a grin. He hated it when someone called them zombies. He started to say something, but he stopped himself. He was probably going to say he had told me before why they weren't zombies, but instead he asked, "What did you say?"

I tried to replay everything in my mind, but all I could think of was Uncle Titus didn't include zombies in his plans.

"Which part, Chief? Uncle Titus didn't think about zombies when he built the shelter?" I asked.

He shook his head from side to side. "No, Ed, the part about cleaning the nets. Uncle Titus would have thought about fish getting caught in them, and he most likely considered the possibility of an anchor getting caught in the nets or on the power lines. All we have to do is figure out his backup plan."

Dr. Bus was listening to what we were saying, and we had forgotten he probably knew more about Uncle Titus and his shelter plans than the rest of us combined. When we turned to him to fill in the blanks, he was trying to hide a grin, too.

Jean and Kathy called to us that coffee was ready, and we could all use some to wake up, so we migrated over to the dining area and grabbed a cup. Bus saw we were still waiting for him to say something, and he gave in.

"Okay," he said. "Uncle Titus talked about redundant systems, and we all started working out plans to install secondary power lines in case the main lines were broken. The problem was we couldn't think of a backup power line that was any safer than the first unless it was buried, so we decided to just put something temporary in place until we could bury a cable. At the shelter in Guntersville I used a few political connections to arrange a little diversion from some power lines that ran all the way from a hydroelectric plant."

We all stared at Bus waiting for him to go on, and when he didn't, the Chief said, "Bus, if you don't tell us what the temporary system is, I'm going to make you swim to the mainland with a long extension cord. If you haven't noticed, there aren't any power lines closer than Simmonsville, and I think they were blown up."

Bus answered, "You've got the right idea, Chief, but the extension cord is already on the mainland...or at least close to it. Titus said he was going to put a spare cable under the dock on the mainland. You just have to pull it over from there and plug it in at a special connection near the oyster beds. Once you have it plugged in, you just throw the power switch under the dock, and you're back in business."

Kathy said, "If someone calls me a dumb blonde, I'll make them hold the targets for me while I practice shooting a bow and arrow, but that must be one big cable. You can't just go get it and drag it over here."

"I was going to say the same thing," said the Chief. "Except for the part about being a dumb blond."

7

Kathy pretended to be aiming an arrow at the Chief and pulling back on the shaft.

Bus rubbed his hand across a gray stubble on his chin and said, "Yeah, Titus did mention all he needed was a cable laying boat and he was having a hard time getting one."

"So, he never finished his backup plan?" asked Jean. "Where can we get a cable laying boat?"

The Chief was staring at a spot on the wall and was lost in thought.

"Chief?" said Jean.

He studied our faces one at a time and said, "Why do we have to keep leaving this place?"

We all knew what he meant. It seemed like we would get to stay safe for a while, but then we would have to leave for some reason that always seemed like a good idea at the time. The last time we almost lost Jean.

As soon as I turned toward Jean she said, "Don't say it, Eddie. Crazy Russians on wild horses couldn't drag me out of this shelter. If you haven't noticed, I'm slightly pregnant."

"I wasn't going to remind you," I said, "at least not yet," I said in a lower voice.

"Do you know where to get a cable laying boat?" Kathy asked the Chief.

The Chief must have found the question to be painful because he winced. I had a feeling we weren't going to be too happy about his answer.

"I saw one tied to a dock behind the Atlantic Spirit in Charleston harbor, and it was still there when we went back to get the seaplane."

Kathy, Jean, and I all got the same pained expression as the Chief, and the rest of the group waited for us to explain it to them.

The Chief said, "Tom, you already know some of this, but the rest of you don't. As you know, three of us escaped from Charleston on a cruise ship named the Atlantic Spirit. We found Ed, and he took us in. We got the bright idea to at least try to establish contact with civilization, so we flew the seaplane down to Goose Creek and made contact with the military at the Naval Weapons Station."

"They weren't doing so well," added Kathy.

"As a matter of fact," continued the Chief, "we had it better than they did, but on the way back we had to land the plane and leave it behind. A bullet had clipped a hose in the engine compartment."

"But you went back and got the plane," said Tom. "So, what's the problem? Why can't we go down to Charleston harbor and liberate the cable laying boat?"

Kathy laid a hand on top of Tom's and said, "Charleston was known around the world as a friendly city, but the harbor isn't as friendly as it used to be, Tom. The last time we were like sitting ducks to someone who had control of Fort Sumter. We were lucky to get away."

Tom didn't flinch, but Allison did. Jean and I both saw it and exchanged glances. Since our return from Guntersville, Alabama, we had both seen Kathy try to bury the feelings she had for Tom, but this gesture was a slip on her part. She wasn't the kind of person to try to break up a marriage, but it was no secret Allison had filed for divorce before the infected dead had changed the world. She pulled her hand back, but I didn't think it had occurred to her what she had done. Allison was simmering.

The Chief didn't miss much, but he didn't let on like he noticed. He went ahead and explained the gravity of the situation to Tom and Bus.

"We could probably get into the harbor and get the cable laying boat underway, but they're slower than a snail on a hot sticky road. We couldn't sail it out of the harbor past Fort Sumter, and it would take a lot of fuel to use the route we took the last time. I doubt we would be lucky enough to make it half way."

"Why can't we fly in and land close to it, Chief?" I asked. "You could get it under way while Bus flies the Otter back out. The rest of us could come into the harbor from the Stono River and tow you back to Mud Island."

9

When we had been fired upon from Fort Sumter, we were forced to travel down the coast to the Stono River. It was a longer trip, but it proved to be a safe back door into the harbor. There would be obstacles, but they weren't as bad as getting shot at.

The Chief said, "That's a good idea, Ed, but our boat wouldn't be my first choice for towing a cable laying boat. I'd prefer a tugboat, but I don't think we would have a very easy time liberating one of those."

Dr. Bus asked, "Why don't we just take control of Fort Sumter?"

No one answered him.

Fort Sumter

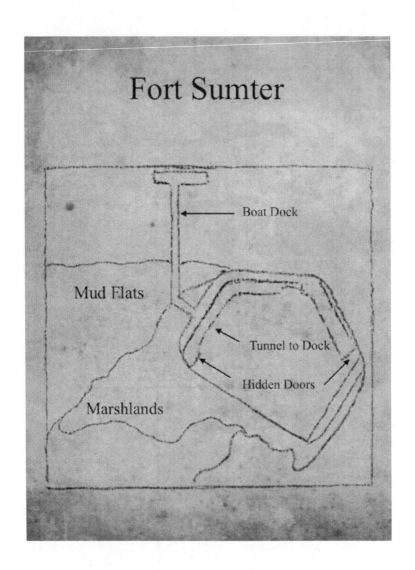

2 FORT SUMTER

Anyone who knows anything at all about the Civil War knows Fort Sumter was the site of the first real battle. It was a Union garrison built to keep the United States from being invaded by a foreign power the way they had in 1812. Construction began in 1829, and it wasn't even finished when South Carolina seceded from the Union in 1860. In 1861 the Confederate army began shelling the fort and it was captured after only one day. Even though it became a national monument and a famous tourist attraction, very few people knew it was the site of another shelter.

Dr. Bus was on the short list of people who knew about the shelters, and he hadn't told us yet where the other shelters were located. When we asked him where they were, he just said he would tell us in due time. When asked why he wouldn't tell us, he said he wanted us to appreciate what we had and not be thinking about the other shelters.

The Chief and I had talked about it several times, and we always came to the same conclusion. Dr. Bus and Uncle Titus were both nuts. They were smart enough to build shelters, but they were nuts.

I asked Dr. Bus once if he knew who built the other shelters, and he just answered, "Of course I do." He didn't volunteer to tell me any names, and I knew he wouldn't tell me if I asked.

This was what Dr. Bus must have meant when he said, "In due time."

"Bus," said the Chief, "the last time we got close to Fort Sumter, we were coasting past it on the Atlantic Spirit. It was populated entirely by the infected dead, and they were walking over the walls trying to reach us. The next time we were in the area, someone took a shot at us from behind those walls. Are you saying whoever that was also has a shelter like ours?"

Before the Chief even finished asking his question, Bus was shaking his head.

"No, Chief," said Bus. "I seriously doubt the shelter was discovered. It couldn't have been too hard for a boatload of men and women with guns to take the fort away from the infected. After that they would have built a small community just like the village above my shelter, and they would have survived until someone got in who had been bitten. By now they are likely to have suffered the same fate you saw when you flew over Green Cavern."

"Or they were using the crabs as a food supply," said Jean. Of everything gross we had seen, that was the one thing that turned her stomach the most.

Kathy asked, "So, you think we could take Fort Sumter to be sure it's safe to sail the line laying boat past it?"

"Exactly," he answered. "We take Fort Sumter, gain entry to the shelter, and when the time is right we can commandeer a tugboat. They couldn't all have made it out of the harbor to safety when the infection spread."

Tom said, "Chief, you could fly over the harbor and check it out first. If Bus is right, we could pull it off in one day."

Allison was clearly uncomfortable listening to us talk about going outside, but she was even more uncomfortable watching Kathy and Tom join in on the planning.

"Why do we even have to do this now?" she asked. "I mean, we could wait another year and still have enough supplies to keep us alive. Maybe if we wait, there won't even be any infected left to worry about."

The Chief knew Allison was afraid. After what they had all seen, there was plenty of reason for all of them to be afraid. She had lost friends and relatives just like the rest of them, and she only survived because Dr. Bus took her in. We all felt sorry for her because she didn't seem to have that instinct for survival we all seemed to have. I couldn't help but think she would have just locked herself inside if she had inherited Mud Island. She would have just locked the doors and lived off of the supplies for the rest of her life.

"Allison, we talked about this before," said Tom. "If this group was made up of the kind of people who would just bury their heads in the sand, Ed would still be here by himself. At the very least, they wouldn't have risked their necks to get me back home to you."

Tom reached for Allison's hand using the same hand Kathy had touched moments before. She folded her arms across her chest and looked at his hand as if it had been contaminated. Tom had experienced her rejection back before the beginning of the infection, and he recognized it again.

The Chief was clearly uncomfortable with the display of emotions at a time when the group needed to focus on fixing a problem, so he was quick to redirect the discussion.

"Listen up, folks. We have several things to figure out. We need to know what or who blew up the Russian ship. I don't like the idea someone even thought it was necessary to blow it up, and we could have used that helicopter. Now that it's done, we have to get that power line across the moat, and there's only one way to make that happen."

"There is some good news," I said.

It wasn't that my input was usually the best. Kathy and the Chief were the real strategists. In this case it was my choice of words. We could all use some good news.

Jean put her arm around my waist and said, "We get to do some shopping in Charleston? Uncle Titus didn't stock the shelter with baby things."

She gave me a smile that could melt me, and I imagined she could have gotten anything out of me with that smile under normal circumstances. I couldn't even guess how we would have found each other if not for the infected dead, but I liked to think it would have happened.

"What do you say, Chief? Any chance we could hit a Walmart while we're in Charleston?" I asked.

Jean reached up with one hand, and before I could stop her, she had grabbed a few chest hairs that were above the collar of my tee shirt. Talk about something that could bring a man to his knees in a hurry.

"Jean," said the Chief, "I believe Ed said there was some good news? I'd like to know if this cloud has a silver lining."

Jean released her grip and gave everyone a satisfied smile. I was rubbing the sore spot on my chest as I said, "When we pull the cable across, we might be able to get it under the hull of the Russian ship to protect it. If we don't, it would just become the world's biggest trip line. There would be all kinds of junk getting snagged on it."

"One thing at a time," said the Chief, "but it's worth keeping in mind. That reminds me, we need to find out if the nets collapsed under the weight of the Russian corvette when it sank, or if the ship stayed close to the surface."

"Why is that important?" asked Kathy.

Bus had apparently been thinking along the same lines, because he answered for the Chief.

"It would be better if it sank and took out the nets with it. There's still a lot of explosive ordinance on that ship, and if it's poking out of the water, there's always a chance someone will be curious about the weapons and munitions."

"For a doctor, you have some interesting ideas," said the Chief.

Bus gave him a sly smile and said, "Chief, I wouldn't be too worried if you told me you knew a few things about surgery."

The Chief returned the smile and said, "Bus, let's put our heads together and figure out how to get that line laying barge up the coast."

Over the next few hours the Chief and Bus discussed a variety of plans. Jean decided to fix us a big breakfast, and Kathy was studying the camera views of the island. She was alternating between the ship and a sudden increase in the number of infected that had found their way onto our side of the moat. The only thing she could come up with that would explain the increase was that they were washing up on shore from something that had happened at sea.

Tom had followed Allison when she sulked away to the lower levels, presumably to talk with her about why she was mad. I got the impression he knew why she was upset, but it didn't do him any good to start by telling her she was overreacting. I had never been an authority on the subject of women, but I was smart enough not to try to defend myself by telling a woman she was overreacting. That was right up there with saying to calm down or relax.

Kathy gave us the news that the ship was starting to disappear below the surface. There's something so morbid about a sinking ship that we all had to stop what we were doing for a few minutes to watch. Maybe it's the finality of it. There's no coming back from it once it disappears from view. It occurred to me it was a lot like watching someone die. You knew it was over, and there was nothing you could do to bring them back.

I watched Jean's face for a few moments and thought to myself how I couldn't bear to ever see that finality. She saw that I wasn't watching the camera view, and I could tell she knew we were thinking the same thing.

The Chief, on the other hand, had a grim expression. When a fellow sailor sees a ship sink, even a Russian ship with a dead crew, they all become shipmates for a few moments. There is a measure of respect passed from the survivors to those who disappear below the surface with the ship.

We gave the Chief the few moments of silence he needed, and when it was over, he said, "We have our answer to one end of the problem, but now we have another one to solve."

Any one of us could have asked him what he meant, but we waited for him to finish his thought.

"How deep did it sink?" he asked. "Did it take the nets with it, or did it get suspended on them? Before we pull the line across the moat we have to know."

Kathy said, "I hope you aren't thinking about going out there again, Chief. If you dive between those nets, you know what you're going to find. Those things can survive under water, and by now there must be hundreds of them."

As if to help Kathy make her point, we saw at least a dozen of the infected dead pass in front of our camera on their way toward the water. They were in varying states of decay, but I saw the dismay on the Chief's face when we recognized the uniforms worn by the US Navy.

The parade of sailors moved unevenly toward the moat where we knew there were submerged oyster beds. They tripped and fell on the razor sharp edges of the shells. They would push themselves back to their feet, leaving parts of their shredded hands and arms behind. They were beyond pain, though, and one by one they walked into the moat toward the sinking Russian ship. It may have already disappeared, but we could imagine the grinding and groaning sounds it was making as the twisted metal released trapped air.

Bus said, "Chief, there's nothing like a thorough visual inspection, but maybe we could try lowering a camera into the water instead of live bait. When I checked the supplies in this shelter, I noticed Titus had included a couple of spare cameras."

"I can live with that, but even if we get the line laying barge back to Mud Island, someone is still going to have to go down there to guide the placement of the new power line."

We could still see air bubbles breaking the surface, but Jean had breakfast ready, and we needed to take our eyes off of the grisly sight of more infected dead walking into the moat. The Chief was the last to sit down at the table, and we all ate in silence for the first time I could remember. Tom joined us in time to get his meal, but he said Allison wasn't hungry. Jean took down plates of food and a cup of chocolate milk for Molly.

When we were finished with our meal, I helped Jean do the dishes while Kathy and Tom joined the Chief and Bus at the table where we usually spread out the charts and maps. Bus was explaining where the entrances had been hidden when the shelter had been dug from the mud and bedrock under Fort Sumter. It was mostly soft earth, so the shelter had to be fortified with steel walls. He explained it had been made airtight just like Mud Island, presumably to withstand the one type of apocalypse everyone had expected.

I heard the Chief ask Bus, "Why Fort Sumter? I can think of dozens of better locations. That place is too open and too easy to hit with almost any kind of weapon."

Bus explained it in simple terms by asking one question, "If you were someone important to the preservation of the US government, and you had to get somewhere really safe and really fast, can you think of a better place?"

Kathy may not have been the first to think of it, but she was the first to ask.

"Did someone important get there Bus, and will they let us in?"

Bus had his eyes on the table as he said in a low voice, "There were at least six political leaders in the line of succession to the Presidency who were attempting to reach the shelter at Fort Sumter. We had a system of coded messages that would tell other leaders and shelter owners who had made it to safety and who was still trying. It took only four days for the coded messages to stop, and there were only a precious few that indicated there were survivors. I listened for a broadcast from Mud Island even though I knew Titus had died."

"What did you hear from Fort Sumter?" asked Kathy.

"Only the messages that people were still trying to reach the shelter. There were some that broke protocol, and in their panic they openly said they were going to try for the shelter. That may have been an incentive for people to go there, and the more people who went there, the more likely it was they would have the infection spread into the fort."

"But the entrance wouldn't have been out in the open where anyone could find it," I said.

"That's right," said Bus. "There are three entrances to the Fort Sumter shelter. Two are the direct entrances they would have used if they had landed a helicopter there. Unconfirmed reports said several political leaders tried that way, and they all ended up the same. Then there's the entrance from Morris Island. It's a door like yours, but it's buried in the sand dunes. It enters into a tunnel that runs the length of Morris Island and then passes underwater for a short distance. The shelter under Fort Sumter is larger than the fort above ground. You would have to know the entrance was there to find it, and it was the primary construction entrance. The Army Corp of Engineers worked with a private company at night so the public wouldn't be aware of what was being done."

"Wait a minute," said the Chief. "Are you trying to tell us the government has been involved with the building of these shelters?"

The question seemed to amuse Bus a little. I liked Dr. Bus, and he had saved Jean, but he was acting like the Chief had asked him a dumb question. The Chief didn't like anyone acting like he was naive, and it showed in his skin color. There was just a bit more red in his complexion than I had ever seen before.

Kathy said, "Bus, if you haven't noticed, the Chief was being serious when he asked you that question."

Since the first time there was more than one person in the shelter on Mud Island, there had only been a sense of belonging. Everyone was important to the group. This was not just the first time I had seen the Chief get really mad. It was also the first time I had seen anyone act like they were superior toward another member of the group.

The tension wasn't lost on Bus, and he helpless under the scrutiny of the Chief.

"Chief, I'm really sorry," he said. "I thought you knew. The cost of the shelters wasn't the biggest barrier to building them. It was getting permission from the government to put them in the safest places. Building the shelter on Mud Island had a tremendous impact on the environment, and Titus had to agree to provide shelter to some important people to get the permits."

"So what happened to them?" I asked. "They weren't exactly beating down my door when the world ended."

"They probably tried to reach you," said Bus, "but there was only a short list of people assigned to each shelter. I guess they just didn't make it."

Jean had been watching the reactions, and she decided it was time to cool the tension. Everyone was still an important member of the group, and we needed to keep it that way.

"Chief, I think Dr. Bus really thought we knew. He apologized, so kiss and make up."

The Chief's head snapped around toward Jean, and she had such a deadpan expression he couldn't stay mad.

"Okay, Bus. I'm sorry I got angry. Was there something that would have given us a clue that an important guest was going to drop in?" he asked.

Bus was lost in thought as he tried to recall and said, "I don't know how you could have known, but Titus knew. I guess he didn't mention it in his will when he left the shelter to Ed."

I thought about it for a minute, but I couldn't think of anything I had missed. The lawyers said I had an island, and that was all there was to it. I started to say as much to Bus and the Chief when Kathy interrupted.

"Guys, check out the camera view where the corvette sank," said Kathy.

We all returned our attention to the screen and saw that the surface was covered in bloated, waterlogged bodies. When the corvette sank it must have shaken the infected dead loose from the nets, and many were being drawn to the surface.

Bus said, "Decaying bodies build up tremendous amounts of gases, and even though they have been remaining animated even after sinking in the moat, they are decaying. After the gases escape, they'll sink again."

Kathy turned a dial on the controls to the camera, and it zoomed in on the mass of bodies coating the surface of the moat. The current was already beginning to pull the logjam of bodies toward the south, but even as they moved out of the way, more bodies replaced those being carried away. To Jean's dismay, they were covered with blue crabs.

"My God," said Tom. "How many would anyone like to guess there are?"

"I don't know," I said, "but maybe hundreds or even a thousand, and that's a good thing. When we run the new power line across the moat, there will be far fewer of them in the nets to worry about."

Jean said, "I'm going to go take a nap."

She left the room before any of us could even answer. Blue crabs had been a favorite seafood to Jean before the infected dead had become a favorite seafood of blue crabs. Seeing them roam over the bloated bodies was almost more than I could stand. It was no surprise that the thought had caused her to turn a funny shade of white every time she saw them feeding.

The Chief asked Bus, "Any idea how much cable is hidden under the dock?"

"Enough to reach the shelter twice," he answered. "Titus said he felt like we should plan to replace the power cables twice. I had a similar supply of cable back at my shelter."

"Okay," said the Chief. "We can live on generator power for a couple of years, or we can fix it now. Does anyone have anything against us taking our fate into our own hands? I mean, that's what we seem to do best."

He surveyed our faces, and I don't know if it was ever in doubt. We nodded our agreement with him, and we all set about the familiar task of planning for another road trip. This time was different because we weren't going to just pass through the Charleston harbor. This time we were going to get out of the boat.

******

21

When I went to check on Jean, she was already deep asleep, so I just pulled a blanket over her and slipped back out of the room to join the others at the dining room table. The Chief was doing his thing again with the high resolution pictures and maps. After Bus had told us that Fort Sumter was a shelter, it only stood to reason that there would be a clue in the wealth of information left behind by Uncle Titus.

There had been clues to the shelter built by Doctor Bus, but we didn't realize they were clues until we actually met the man. One clue had been a building that led us to a supply of aviation fuel, but it had almost cost us our lives when we were trapped between that building and a resort.

I recalled those days when we had flown to Guntersville, Alabama to reunite Tom and Molly with Allison. We had almost lost Jean while we were gone, and that seemed so much more real to me than what had happened to us. First, we were forced into the resort by a pack of hungry dogs, and then we had to escape a horde of the infected dead as they walked out of a lake and up a boat ramp.

After Jean had recovered from the near fatal infection she had gotten from being scratched by a dead Russian sailor, I had told her about our trip to Alabama. She had beamed with pride when I told her about how the Chief had helped the Army evacuate a temporary camp at Fort Jackson, but when I told her about how we had been cornered by a resort full of the infected, she had cried with relief that we had survived. We were both lucky to be back together, but none of the trip seemed real to me. I was too focused on how we had found Jean, feverish and near death in the cabin of the Russian ship.

Since that day, we had vowed repeatedly not to ever leave each other again, but we both knew there would be a time when we would be forced to make the same hard decisions that had been made since the first day when the infection had swept across the world. The Chief, Kathy, and Tom had all told me I should stay behind with Jean if there was ever a reason to leave again.

Bus tried to be neutral whenever the topic came up because Allison felt like Tom should stay behind with her while the rest of us went out and risked our necks to keep her alive. I had heard her say more than once that they would have been better off if they had stayed at the shelter built by Bus at Green Cavern.

I was lost in my thoughts when the Chief said he found something. He showed us an aerial picture of the entire Charleston harbor, and there was a shaded area colored into the sand dunes on Morris Island.

"This must be the location of the hidden entrance to the shelter," he said.

Bus leaned in for a closer look and studied the picture.

"That's about right, Chief. It's directly south of Fort Sumter and about one hundred yards long. I had been told the tunnel was about the length of a football field."

"What are the chances someone else has already found the entrance?" I asked.

"That's doubtful," said Bus. "The entrance is buried under about four feet of sand, and even if you cleared the sand away, it wouldn't appear to be a door. It's disguised as a power junction with warnings on it that say to stay clear due to high voltage."

Kathy shook her head with wonder and said, "So, you say there are twenty-nine more shelters out there, Bus? Wouldn't it be better to just give us a list of them and let us decide what to do with the information?"

"How can I say this?" he said. "For the time being, I'm going to have to think about what I tell you. Some of the shelters would be nothing more than a death trap, and besides, between here and Green Cavern we have enough to survive on. The only reason we have to go to Fort Sumter is to be sure we can control the harbor. We can't have anyone shooting at us from there."

I could tell it still wasn't sitting too well with the Chief. He liked Bus a lot, but he didn't like having someone tell him he was better off being left in the dark because he wasn't capable of making decisions for himself.

"Bus," said the Chief, "one day you may wish you had told us where the other shelters are just because we might need to know in a hurry. This isn't your grandfather's USA anymore. You may feel like you're keeping state secrets or something, but if you haven't noticed, things didn't go down the way the government thought they would."

The Chief was such an easy going man that it was tough to see him be upset. He walked away from the table, and Kathy followed him. If things weren't bad enough Allison chose the same moment to come back into the room and announce that she wanted to go back to Green Cavern, and the way she put it to Tom, it didn't sound like she was inviting the Mud Island group to come along. Things seemed to be unraveling from more than one loose string.

Bus was watching the Chief and Kathy in the living room, and then he turned his attention to Allison and Tom. I was just about to tell him it was time to make up his mind when he did it on his own.

"Chief," he called to the other room. "I was wrong. I don't know why I haven't realized that things aren't ever going to be the same again, but it's time for me to either throw in with you guys or go back to Green Cavern and hunker down forever. And it's an easy choice if you'll forgive me for treating you like adolescents. I'll give you a list of the shelters. If we ever need to bug out from here in a hurry, I may not be able to tell you then."

The Chief visibly relaxed as he walked back into the room.

"I'm glad you came around," he said. "I didn't know how we were going to be able to get along if you didn't show us some trust."

"Tom, did you hear what I said?"

Allison was oblivious to what was happening with the rest of us. She had her arms crossed and assumed a demanding stance squarely at Tom.

Tom had heard what Allison had said, but he didn't pay attention. It didn't sink in until she squared off with him, and even then he wasn't totally comprehending. He looked straight into her face and didn't flinch.

"We're not going back," he said in a tone that left no doubt that he was not going to debate the issue.

Allison must have recognized the finality of his statement because she turned on her heels and disappeared from the room without even making eye contact with anyone else. I expected her to at least say something, and I instinctively watched her leave the room. When she was gone I was surprised to see Tom and Kathy sharing eye contact across the room. I wondered if I had been missing something all along.

While the relationship drama played out, the Chief and Bus had already gotten down to business. They had a map laid out in between them, and Bus was using a red pen to draw stars at different locations. He was also writing the security codes next to each star. I moved into a position where I could get a better look at the map, and I saw the stars were spread out across the country. There was even a star in Alaska.

Bus said, "You'll notice that no one put a shelter anywhere near Washington, DC, and there aren't any located near nuclear power plants. The obvious reason for avoiding those places was the likelihood of a preemptive strike by a foreign power. Those would be targets, so it would be impossible for anyone to reach a shelter in time. It would be better to get out of the area to a place that wouldn't be a target."

The Chief studied the map as Bus added the stars, and he let out a low whistle from time to time. One or two seemed to be more interesting to him than others. A couple of times he regarded the rest of our faces, and he eventually motioned for us to come closer. He pointed at one star and said he thought it was a stupid place to put a shelter. I didn't disagree with him. It was in the Gulf of Mexico and was part of an oil platform.

"If the whole world was wiped out, it might be a good idea," said the Chief, "but it would be a tempting target for almost anyone with a boat."

"Wouldn't that be the same thing as our houseboat or the village above Green Cavern?" asked Kathy. "People could live on an oil platform without ever getting into the shelter."

"Not exactly," said the Chief. "If someone decides to blow up our houseboat, it won't help them get to us. If someone tries to blow up an oil platform, the whole thing will sink."

Despite our loss of electrical power, we were all beginning to appreciate what Uncle Titus had done for us even more than we had before. Mud Island wasn't perfect, but it had been well designed compared to some of the others.

Kathy said, "Some of these have probably been breached already just because of their locations, but we need to find a way to communicate with them to see who made it and who didn't."

"You're right, Kathy, but first things first," said the Chief. "We have to get that power line restored, and that means checking out Fort Sumter."

Tom asked, "When do we leave, Chief?"

"We shouldn't wait," he answered. "I think we should make our move as soon as we can get ready."

As he answered, the Chief studied Tom closely for any hesitation. We weren't sure how Tom was going to react to Allison's demand that they leave, but we didn't think it was going to be a pretty sight when both Tom and Bus told her they weren't leaving for Green Cavern, and it wasn't like Allison could do it on her own.

Tom went to talk with Allison, and there was no doubt in our minds there would be fireworks. What we got was not what we expected. Only a couple of minutes after Tom left the room, Allison stormed in and announced that she was going with us to Charleston harbor.

Kathy was about to say something, which was the last thing she should do, but the Chief beat her to it.

"Allison, there's no need for you to risk your life just to prove you're as tough as the rest of us."

"I am as tough as the rest of you," she said it a loud voice. "I'm not staying behind while the rest of you go out there and fight those things…"

Her voice trailed off as she caught a glimpse of what was happening on the monitors. The mass of bloated bodies, arms and legs moving as the infected continued to reach and push against each other, began drifting with the current. As it did, there was more room for bodies to reach the surface, some so bloated with gases that they broke the surface like cork bobbers.

Allison gasped as a shark tore one away from the rest of them. The face of the infected was expressionless as it disappeared under the surface once again.

I switched on the camera that showed a view of the southern tip of the island. The current was drawing the floating infected through the place where the water exited the moat, and one by one the bodies were washed out to sea. I figured if anything could make Allison want to stay inside the shelter, it would be remembering what was waiting outside.

I thought she was going to be sick, but she put her shoulders back and said, "I'm going along."

It was easy for us to see that her reason for wanting to go was to keep an eye on Kathy, but the truth was that we could always use another gun or just a pair of eyes. Jean could stay behind with Molly, so Allison could come along. Also, none of us were in the mood to argue with her.

"That's settled," said the Chief. "We leave tomorrow at dawn."

3 CHARLESTON REVISITED

Jean and Molly were up before the rest of us the next morning. They wanted to give us a big breakfast as a surprise send off. The smell of coffee and fresh baked bread was enough to get me out of bed, but they had found plenty of other treats to go along with it. The supply room had some wonderful canned food, and the jars of jam and preserves had been a delightful surprise.

One by one we gathered around the table and dug in, but it wasn't the usual excitement we normally felt before leaving the shelter. This time felt different, and it was probably because Allison wasn't a good fit.

Regardless, we were all ears when the Chief explained that the best approach to the harbor was going to be from the south, and it would be by plane. He could land close enough to Fort Sumter for us to beach the plane and then walk to the hidden entrance to the tunnel. The high resolution photographs of Morris Island gave us enough detail to see that there were low places between the dunes that couldn't be seen from the fort. If someone was still in control there, they would undoubtedly have one or two people standing watch in case they were attacked from land.

"If I were in charge of a group of survivors at Fort Sumter," said the Chief, "I would try to post a watch somewhere outside the fort on the island. I hope they don't have enough people or weapons to do that."

Bus asked, "Wouldn't it be a good idea to wait one more day? We could fly over it at night and see if we can spot any campfires."

"We can't risk it," said the Chief. "If they hear the plane, they may increase their security for a few days."

Tom had just been listening and wanted to be careful of what he said because Molly was in the room. She was cheerfully dishing out food, trying to do her part. Allison was sullen, as usual, but she didn't want the tension to be obvious to Molly.

"I'm a little worried about leaving the plane on the beach," said Tom. "These pictures show that the beaches are totally exposed with nothing to use for cover. Even if we pulled camouflaged tarps over the plane it would still stick out like a sore thumb."

"What do you suggest?" asked the Chief.

Tom rubbed his stubbled cheeks and studied the pictures. "If we leave the plane out in the open and something happens to it, we may be able to get inside the shelter, but how would we ever leave?"

"He has a good point," said Bus. "We have two pilots, so why don't I drop you guys off and then fly the plane back out. Once you're inside the shelter you should be able to find the radio and tell me when to come back to pick you up."

Kathy said, "Chief, you've got more hand to hand combat experience than Bus. We could use you when we get ready to take the fort."

I could tell the Chief didn't like someone else being in the pilot's seat of his Otter seaplane, but even he had to admit it made sense. If they were stranded on Fort Sumter, there wouldn't be a way to get back to Mud Island unless Jean could come get them. The current occupants of Fort Sumter were likely to have at least one boat, but there was no way to guarantee it would be at the fort when it was time to take the fort from them. It was also the most likely place to find an armed guard.

The Chief looked at me since I was the only member of the group going on the mission who hadn't given an opinion. That is, the only member of the group left with an opinion that would count. I didn't think Allison's opinion would count for much.

"I don't know," I said. "On the one hand, the reason we're going during the day is because the sound of the airplane landing would carry a greater distance at night, but the sound of the plane powering up for a take off is going to be plenty loud even in the day time. I think we would need to land a mile or more down the coast to avoid being heard. It would be a longer walk, but it might be worth it."

"What about the idea of beaching the plane or flying it out?" asked Kathy.

I answered, "Well, if someone hears it land, they'll come searching for it, so we'll need to get into the dunes as fast as we can. The beach is so wide along the place where we should land that they would spot it from a long way off. It would be good to have it be gone by the time they start their search."

Jean said, "We don't know what size force you guys are going to find at Fort Sumter, so flying the plane for a take off to the south would make sense, and it shouldn't be on the beach very long."

The Chief said, "So be it. We'll land near the lighthouse at the southern tip of Morris Island and head as far into the dunes as we can. Let's try to be out of the plane so Bus can take off within five minutes of coming to a stop."

With that decision made, everyone got up from the breakfast table and started gathering their gear.

"I wish I was going with you," said Jean as she slid her arms around my waist and laid her head against my chest. It was getting harder for her to do that, but then it would be my turn to bend over to make it easier for her.

"I'll bet you could still handle your machete better than the rest of us," I said.

"Sweet talker," said Jean. "Have you always had such a way with words when you tried to charm a woman, Eddie?"

"I don't think I ever charmed a woman before you," I said.

She got a little impish grin on her face and said, "What makes you think you ever charmed me?"

I lowered my eyes to her belly and said, "Your Honor, I would like to enter Exhibit A into evidence...or would that be Exhibit B for baby?"

Jean laughed and hugged me even tighter.

"Okay, you lovebirds," said Kathy. "Jean, leave the boy alone so he can get his gear ready."

I reluctantly let Jean go and caught up with the others. Our standard list of supplies was enough food and water to last three days. If we were out longer than that, we were probably in some kind of trouble that supplies wouldn't help us get out of. It was better to leave room for more ammunition than more food.

We gathered our gear up near the entrance of the shelter and began our routine for departure. One person always had the job of checking all of the camera angles to see if we had any infected dead roaming around on the island. This time it was Jean because she didn't have to gear up to go outside. She scanned the whole island and gave us the bad news. She said the infected were all over the place. The good news was that they were still moving in the general direction of the moat. We didn't have the ability to hear what was happening, but the hundreds of infected dead in the water were thrashing around so much that the noise had to be incredible.

Jean said some of the infected weren't able to stand and were just squirming around on the beach. I went over to watch with her and saw that the beach was thick with their bloated bodies. The infected that had been caught in the nets were being washed ashore with the incoming tide, and they were like beached fish. They were too waterlogged to support their own weight.

"How's the area around the dock, Jean?" asked the Chief.

"Not as bad as the beach, Chief. There are a few that are trying to cross the path that leads to the dock. You'll have to take them out before you can get to the plane."

Allison looked like she was going to be sick again. She was wearing the heavy duty coveralls we had found in the storerooms, so she was well protected from her neck down, but she was holding her machete at an odd angle, almost as if she had no idea how to use it. I didn't think this could go well.

After one last hug and kiss from Jean, we only had to wait while Molly was reassured by her parents that they would be fine. They took turns hugging her and telling her to be a good girl for Jean. Molly had been cheerful and always trying to help out with chores around the shelter, but she had stayed quiet, generally listening more than talking. She said she would be okay and that she would listen to Jean, but her lower lip was giving away her fears. Still, she managed not to cry when we began slipping out through the big door to the shelter.

I closed the door and blew one last kiss to both of them then ushered Allison away from the entrance onto the path. The Chief, Kathy, and Tom had already begun moving forward, stalking the first of the infected dead that were on the path. Bus hung back closer to Allison. Although he was like a miniature version of the Chief, he wasn't as formidable when it came to killing with a machete. That was fine with us because he had other skills. Besides being really intelligent, he was a good doctor, and there weren't enough of those to go around.

I kept Allison in front of me, partially so I could see if anything came at her from the sides, and partially because of the way she held her machete. I figured she was just clumsy enough to stab me in the back with it. I thought I saw Bus glance back at it himself a few times.

The first infected dead we came to had gotten much closer to the entrance of the shelter than I had ever seen before. The weather had really taken its toll, and more than one creature had been feeding on it. There weren't any blue crabs clinging to its clothes, but there was no doubt there had been.

I had gotten into the habit of not thinking about what I was doing when I would kill another infected dead. I tried to ignore what they were wearing, how old they had been, or their gender. It didn't matter what they had done for a living when they were alive. Some wore uniforms, and some wore business suits. I thanked God there weren't many children.

This one was about as unremarkable as the rest, but it went down easier than usual when the Chief swung his machete. He turned toward us with an expression that said, "Did you see that?" Another stepped from the bushes, and Kathy swung low. The blade took off the left leg at the knee, and it fell helplessly backward into the bushes.

We never really stopped to watch when someone else in our group was busy killing an infected dead because it was while you were watching that you were most likely to be caught off guard. There always seemed to be another after you found one, and sometimes I wondered if they would ever stop coming.

A third infected stumbled onto the path, but this one came from the left where the ground sloped upward a bit. The slope made it stumble straight into Allison. Tom and Kathy were busy with their own infected and didn't know what was going on behind them.

It reached for Allison with uncoordinated, grasping fingers, and her use of the machete for defense was less coordinated than the infected. All I could do was hope I didn't cut Allison by accident as I shoved my own machete between them and then swung it in an uppercut motion. The blade came up across its chest and connected with its underarms both at the same time.

Its arms came off at the shoulders, and my blade went straight up under its chin. I watched it fall and was amazed to see my blade had severed the head from the body. Allison was screaming, undoubtedly attracting every infected dead on Mud Island, but the rest of us were thinking the same thing. The weather was breaking down the bodies of the infected and making them easier to kill.

We all converged on Allison at the same time. Tom tried to get her to at least stop screaming, and the rest of us formed a circle around her facing outward. For the next fifteen minutes, the bushes were constantly being parted as more infected would come through. We didn't take turns because there were too many. We just kept swinging high and low.

At some point in time, Allison let go of her machete and just sat down on the ground. In a way it made it easier for the rest of us because we could cover her better. Tom was also able to help us instead of trying to calm her down.

Eventually there was a calm that settled over the group as no more infected dead came at us. Allison was curled up on the ground covered in more human remains than she would have been if she had stayed on her feet. She was crying softly, but at least she wasn't screaming.

"We have to take her back," said Tom.

"No," she yelled.

All of us made a shushing noise at the same time. She didn't yell again, but she glared at each of us one at a time. We were all just waiting for her to make the next move.

She said in a low voice, "I'm not going back. I'm going with you, and I'm going to help."

Allison glared straight at Kathy and said, "I'm not losing my husband to another woman just because she kills zombies better than me."

There it was, finally out in the open. Kathy seethed with anger because Allison's jealousy had gotten them swarmed by the infected dead. Tom was too dumbfounded to speak, and I heard the Chief mutter, "They aren't zombies."

Despite the tension, Bus said, "One of these days someone is going to explain to me why they aren't zombies."

That made us all relax just in time for the next wave, but this time Allison picked up her machete and started swinging at the infected that came through the bushes near her. She made us all nervous with her wild swings, but at least she was contributing.

When it was all over, she asked us in a softer voice if she had caused that last attack, and we all nodded at her. She put one finger to her lips to show she understood, and we started moving again. From my position at the rear I saw Allison giving Kathy scathing looks, and I saw Kathy ignoring her. That was the difference between a pro and an amateur out here. One knew who the real enemies were.

When we reached our dock, there were several of the infected walking off the flat wooden boards straight into the water. We just stopped and waited for the last of them to fall in. They were apparently still being drawn in the direction of the place where the Russian ship had sunk. Even from this far away we could hear the chorus of groans from the hundreds of infected dead that had surfaced when the ship sank below the water.

"Let's get going," said the Chief.

We all threw our gear into the plane that was tied to the dock and untied the mooring lines while the Chief climbed into the pilot's seat. He always did something to foul the wiring under the instrument panel so no one could steal the plane while we were in the shelter. Whatever it was, he could fix it in a heartbeat, and he had it ready to go before we were done with the lines.

The powerful engine of the de Havilland DHC-3 Otter roared to life. Tom and I gave the plane a hard push and then jumped onto the pontoon and through the open door to the passenger and cargo hold. The Chief let the plane rotate to the starboard until he was pointing away from the dock and then increased the power. He brought the plane around the dock in a hard, sweeping turn to the right as he passed the houseboat tied to the very end of our dock.

I don't know how many times I had seen the houseboat, but I remembered how I had felt the first time. As a matter of fact, I remembered how Jean, Kathy, and the Chief had reacted the first time they saw it. They had been awestruck to be so lucky to have found a place where they could be safe after the infected had swarmed through the cruise liner they were traveling on. Not knowing that I had a buried shelter with all the trimmings, they had been prepared to beg to stay in the houseboat.

I had been the same way when I saw it the first time, but to me it was like a cool place to live. The world hadn't come to an end yet, and I just thought it was going to be my new apartment tied to a remote island. If it had been just a houseboat without the shelter, I probably would have just sold the whole thing because there was no internet. In reality, it was nothing more than a really good decoy. If anyone spotted the houseboat, they wouldn't even think there was also a shelter.

The forward motion changed from a roar and bouncing to the smooth droning of the engine and a gliding feeling. I knew the Chief had lifted the plane free of the water, and we were on our way again.

The Chief and Bus were in the front seats because they were both pilots. There was plenty of room in the passenger section of the plane, but Allison was sitting as close to Tom as she could, and that gave me more room to stretch out. Tom was visibly uncomfortable about Allison's jealousy, but Kathy was acting like it was just another day in South Carolina. She wasn't going to give in to Allison's petty behavior at a time when their lives were at risk. Unlike Allison, Kathy didn't think everything was all about her.

To lighten the mood, I called up front to the Chief and asked him to tell me again why we had to keep leaving the shelter. It worked for me and the Chief because he started laughing.

"I'm glad you asked, Ed," he yelled over his shoulder. "The fact is that we don't have to leave the shelter. We just do it because we're too stupid to know any better."

"I do it because it's the only real entertainment we have," said Kathy.

Not to be outdone, I said, "I do it because I like to meet new people."

"I want to leave the shelter because I don't like the food," said Bus.

Tom was feeling the spirit of the moment and said, "I only do it because the pay is good."

Five of us were laughing until Allison said, "You're all going to die because you don't have the sense to stay safe in the shelter."

I thought Kathy could be scary when I saw her in full-attack mode, but the look she got on her face passed anything I had ever seen.

"Say something like that again, and I'll put you out of this plane before we land," said Kathy. Her voice was calm and controlled, but that anger was not something I ever wanted to see aimed at me.

Allison looked at Tom for help, but the anger on his face wasn't for what Kathy had said.

"Allison, when we get to Morris Island, you fly out with Bus while we go to Fort Sumter," said Tom.

She started to say something back to Tom, but she moved away from him instead. She crossed her arms across her chest and fixed her eyes on a spot on the ceiling of the plane. That was somewhat of a trademark reaction from her when she knew she had gone too far. I half expected to hear her say she would be talking with her lawyer after she got back to Mud Island.

The Chief steered a course straight out to sea. We had all agreed we were less likely to be shot down by Navy ships than by land based shooters. We didn't want to advertise our arrival at Charleston harbor, and we didn't want to take any damage before we got there, so the plan was to fly out far enough to where the plane couldn't be heard from land, then we would fly down the coast until we were southeast of Morris Island.

Bus was scanning the water in front of us with binoculars. Chances were that any military ship we saw would already have us in its crosshairs by the time we saw it, but it would be good to know if we had any company. After all, something had blown the Russian ship to pieces, and the odds were good it had been the US Navy.

He pointed about ten degrees to the left of center, and we strained to see what he had spotted. Bus passed the binoculars to the Chief, and he took a quick look before passing them back to me. It was a military ship, but it was too far away to tell what navy it belonged to. The Chief adjusted our course so we would be heading more to the southeast, and he gave us a bit more speed to increase our distance from the ship a little more quickly. There was no sense in provoking the ship, no matter who they were. If we weren't a threat to them, there would be no need for them to shoot us down.

Sooner than I had expected, the Chief began turning back toward the mainland. It was a beautifully clear spring day, and the view was spectacular. Of course it wouldn't be so spectacular close up. Even though we couldn't see the city streets of Charleston and didn't plan to do any sight-seeing, it wasn't hard to imagine what it must look like. There would be no safe place for a living being to hide.

We were within view of Morris Island in only a few minutes, and the Chief adjusted his course again to bring us more to the south before approaching the island. He also lowered our altitude until we were just a few feet above the water. Atlantic swells aren't as high as Pacific swells, so it was easy for him to keep an eye on them. I had faith that he wouldn't clip the top of a wave and send us into a cartwheel, but at this altitude, the plane seemed to be traveling faster. The water rushed past and the shoreline grew in size.

The Chief steered down the length of Folly Beach and then came in close to shore for the final turn toward the north. It gave us a clear view of the beach houses we had passed when we traveled by boat down to the Stono River. The wide porches of the beach houses weren't occupied this time. There were no zombie watching parties and no decks painted with signs begging for rescue.

The beach was littered with trash and long dead corpses of animals and people. When the end came to the people trapped in their beach houses, it was probably a mixed bag of attempted escapes and failed attempts to keep the infected dead from getting inside.

Kathy pointed at something on the main road behind the beach houses, and we all followed her arm in that direction. Someone was speeding between cars and debris on an ATV. The rider was a well muscled surfer with long hair, and he knew how to handle his four wheel vehicle. He disappeared under a beach house that was on high stilts and emerged again on the beach. We could see tracks in the sand that he appeared to be following, and they led back to another house down the beach.

"Smart," said Kathy. "He's holed up in the last beach house toward the southern end of the island, and he draws the infected away from the house before using the beach to get back to the house."

The Chief said, "While he's drawing them away, someone else either leaves or returns with supplies."

"Should we try to recruit them?" asked Tom.

"We don't know if they're friendly," said the Chief.

We were past the last house too soon for us to see if he had fellow survivors either coming to or leaving from the house. I imagined the scenario was being repeated up and down the coast, and on a less successful scale in the cities.

The lighthouse at the end of Folly Beach passed by at high speed, and the Chief gently lowered the plane to the water. He coasted toward the beach with just enough power to keep us moving forward, but the sound of the engine attracted the attention of several infected dead that appeared from behind the sand dunes.

They had undoubtedly washed ashore on Morris Island because they were of the waterlogged variety. They were almost too heavy with water to reach the crest of the dunes, and when they did, it was more like stop, drop, and roll than an attack. We would have plenty of time to unload our gear and prepare for their arrival on our part of the beach.

As the Chief brought the plane to a stop, he reminded all of us to check the water before jumping off of the pontoons.

There could easily be infected under the surface or stuck in the sand. All I saw was blue crabs scurrying away from the plane, and I thought about Jean.

I was a little less worried about Jean this time than I had been when we left her at the shelter the last time. She had Molly to keep her company, her pregnancy made her less capable of going on any missions, and she had learned some valuable lessons the last time. The Russian ship was gone, but someone had sunk the ship, and they were still out there. Mud Island was also swarming with the infected dead, and she knew it.

Once everyone was out of the plane, Bus started to circle around to the other side to get to the pilot's seat.

The Chief caught his arm as he went by. "Not so fast, Bus," he said. "We need to make a change of plans."

Everyone gathered around the Chief in front of the plane, and we all confused.

"I'm taking Allison back to Mud Island," he said. "The rest of you can locate the tunnel and get inside where you can be safe. I'll only be a couple of hours at the most."

Allison was furious. She thought Tom would give her his support, and she was surprised that she wasn't getting it. I wasn't surprised, and I don't think anyone else was either. She started to say something else, but the Chief stopped her.

He said, "I don't want to hear it, and I should have put you back inside the shelter when I had the chance. I've been watching you on the flight to Charleston, and you're just going to get someone killed."

"You can't tell me what to do," she said defiantly.

"Oh, yes I can," said the Chief, "and you can either get back in the plane or I can put you in. It's your choice."

Allison tried one more time to get Tom's support. He made eye contact with her and held it, but it was clear that he agreed with the Chief.

Kathy had turned away from the group and was watching the approaching infected dead. I had a feeling she wasn't as concerned with them as she was about an open fight with

Allison. There was no question about who would win, but that was the best reason to avoid the fight in the first place.

Bus was the only one to voice an opinion, and he said, "We need to get the plane off the beach anyway, Chief. Why not just have her go with me?"

"I'm not losing you and the plane, Bus. I don't have much faith that her attitude wouldn't get you killed," he said. "That's all I have to say on the subject. Let's go, Allison."

The Chief gave me and Tom a nod that meant he wanted us to rotate the seaplane. He didn't need to use words as he climbed back into the pilot's seat because we had seen the nod before. Allison stood with her arms crossed glaring at him, but even then she looked more like she was defending herself rather than attacking.

The Chief faced her and said, "That's exactly why you're going back, Allison. We can't spend all of our time protecting you. We all need to be able to depend on each other, and while we're all watching your back, who's watching ours? Now, get in the plane."

Allison took one more opportunity to convey distaste at each of us and then got in the plane. All she got to see of Kathy was her back. Tom and I rotated the plane as the Chief started the engine. He quickly turned the plane when it started to float and took it to full power as fast as he could. We watched the plane get smaller as it sped away, lifted off, and banked to the south.

"We should start moving," said Kathy.

I saw her and Tom exchange comments in what could only be called nonverbal communication. I wasn't exactly sure what they were thinking, but Kathy seemed to say, "You could do better," and Tom seemed to say, "I know."

We gathered our gear and headed for the dunes. The infected dead had made it onto the beach, and they were in our way but not being a problem. They held their arms out greedily as we approached, but they were all in the sand and not moving within seconds.

Once we had ended the miserable existence of the infected, we set out as quickly as we could go, using the high resolution pictures to locate the hidden tunnel entrance. It only took about thirty minutes to find the right spot and another ten minutes to uncover the secure door. It was located in the side of a dune and sat at about a forty-five degree angle. Bus dialed in the combination on the lock, and the door opened as if the hinges had been oiled recently.

We quickly stashed our gear inside and then gathered as much loose brush together as we could. I pulled out a huge roll of duct tape, and we began taping the brush to the outside of the door. We even fastened several long strips of tape to the door with large areas of the sticky side facing outward. We threw sand against it and were pleased with the results. When we pulled the door shut from the inside, it had to be hard to spot from a distance.

With the door shut behind us, the four of us dug out our flashlights and got together in a huddle over a hand drawn map.

"While the Chief is gone, there's no reason why we can't scout this tunnel," said Kathy. "I think it would be a good idea to find out if the Fort Sumter shelter has been compromised before we get too comfortable."

"I agree," I said. "We should use flashlights until we're sure it's safe. No talking unless we have to. We don't know how well sound carries in this tunnel."

Kathy said, "Good thinking, Eddie."

She turned to Tom and Bus and went back over basic hand signals we had used before. Then she took the lead as we started down the tunnel.

It was a long tunnel, but the floor was totally dry, and there was no moisture in the air. It didn't smell as if anything had died in the tunnel, so we didn't expect to have anything lurch out of the darkness at us. I felt the walls with my fingertips, and it felt like we were inside a big stainless steel tube. It was probably one of the most expensive tunnels ever made, and it was intended to save the lives of important people, but judging by the undisturbed appearance of the tunnel, it hadn't saved anyone.

It wasn't long before Kathy gave the hand signal to stop, then the signal to get down. We didn't know if there was someone up ahead in the tunnel or if she was just being cautious. She shined her light into the distance then stood up and signaled for us to join her. She was standing next to something that could have been an oversized golf cart.

Bus said, "Of course, why didn't I think of it before. This tunnel is really long, and they wouldn't have wanted important people to walk all the way."

"It's electric," said Kathy, "which means it would be relatively quiet."

"Not quiet enough the way sound carries down here," I said, "but I'd rather ride than walk."

"Me too," said Tom. "Why don't we use it most of the way then walk in the last bit? We could be there in no time."

It wasn't much of a vote since all four of us were in favor. Bus was the designated driver, and the rest of us kept our weapons pointed forward just in case we were being incredibly stupid. The tunnel was illuminated by widely spaced lights, but some were burned out, so we couldn't see well enough to go full speed. We still covered the distance from the tunnel entrance to Fort Sumter in no time, and we didn't stop until Kathy held up her hand again. She hopped out while the cart was stopping and strode forward into the darkness.

We all walked up to stand beside her and found ourselves facing a door just like our main door on Mud Island. I let out a low whistle.

"What?" asked Kathy.

Tom interpreted my low whistle by asking, "There are two doors like that?"

Bus cleared his throat and said, "Thirty-two doors would be a more accurate assessment, Tom, and maybe more. Some of the shelters had a main door and a secondary door. This must be the secondary door."

Bus continued as he walked up to the combination lock, "Each door has a unique combination. I may be one of the only survivors who knows all of the combinations. That's why

I gave them to the Chief. If something happens to me, at least you guys can locate the other shelters and get inside."

Bus dialed in the combination, and we pulled the handle. The door swung open on totally silent, polished steel hinges.

4 FORTRESS

The first room beyond the huge door was much the same as the decontamination room on Mud Island, but it was clearly designed to accommodate more people. There were more hooks with SCUBA gear hanging from them, more showers, and there were rows of lockers. It was obvious from the start that the people who had set up camp in Fort Sumter had not gained access to the hidden shelter because there were far too many supplies in racks along the walls. Everything was neatly stored and appeared to be untouched.

The lighting in the room was bright, and they didn't know if it had come on when they opened the door or if it stayed on. Either way, this shelter clearly had power.

"Shouldn't we wait for the Chief to get back?" I asked.

Kathy studied Tom's face for any sign that he was thinking the same thing. He was clearly weighing what would be best, but in the end he was too curious to wait.

"We still have a long time before the Chief is due back. Let's take a quick tour and then go back to the beach," he said.

Bus went over and opened several of the lockers and checked the boxes of supplies. Our hesitance gave way to curiosity, and we all joined him checking the labels on packages. There were medical supplies, ration packs, and a variety of useful items. I didn't know what the others were thinking, but figured this shelter would be an excellent backup to our already large cache of supplies.

"This may be premature to ask," I said, "but do you guys think this would be a better place to live or a good place to just visit when we need supplies?"

"It's too soon to say," said Tom. "For one thing, we need to find out what the situation is like up above."

"I'll second that," said Kathy, "and we need to think about how exposed Fort Sumter is. As long as people can see it from shore, they're going to think it's a safe place to be."

Bus added, "Fort Sumter may have been occupied several times by now. Whether the occupants died from within because someone was bitten or they were attacked and defeated, someone else will try to use it like our houseboat. It's just too visible from the mainland."

We finished checking the treasure trove of supplies and then gathered at a second door. It wasn't exactly like our shelter, but we fully expected to find the next room on the other side of the door to have its own wealth of things we could use. Kathy opened the door slowly and peeked around a corner.

"Another hallway," she said.

She stepped through the door, and we followed her single file. There were three more doors set in stainless steel walls, and each door was closed. For some reason it didn't feel like anyone had been through those doors in a long time, probably not since the place had been built.

"Did you say the people who were supposed to use this shelter died trying to get here, Bus?" I asked.

"So I heard when everything started to happen," he said. "Shortwave radio sources started checking in as shelters were occupied, but no one heard from this one."

The closest door was logically the first one to check, so Kathy opened it. The interior was a theater that could seat about three or four hundred people. It wasn't what any of us had expected, so three of us waited for Bus to give an explanation.

He shrugged his shoulders. "Your guess is as good as mine," he said. "My guess would be that important people need a stage to stand on, and they need people to make speeches to."

The realization hit me that this shelter would have some of the more sophisticated communications equipment if it was going to be some kind of command and control center. I squeezed past Kathy in the doorway and hurried down an aisle that had a slight downward slope. I passed rows of empty seats that had never been used until I came to the steps that led to the stage. A row of switches were on the wall by the steps, and I put them all to the on position.

Lights came on around the room and curtains parted from the center of the stage outward. There was a podium set off to one side of a massive TV screen, and I was sure I would find the power button in the podium.

Kathy, Tom, and Bus were all trailing behind me, but instead of coming up on the stage, they filed onto the first row as if they were going to sit in the front row of a movie.

I went around behind the podium, and like a true computer geek, I was immediately in my element with the controls. I pressed the familiar button with a partial circle on it, and I could hear a hard drive spinning up. At the same time the huge monitor began to glow with a faint bluish tint. I was so excited that I didn't realize at first that the image forming on the screen was a panoramic view of Charleston harbor. The others stood transfixed by the beautiful sight of the Ravenel Bridge that connected the peninsular city of Charleston on the left to Mt. Pleasant on the right.

From the bridge, tourists would point at Fort Sumter and marvel at the sight of the first shots of the Civil War. From the ramparts of Fort Sumter, tourists would marvel at the beauty of the Arthur Ravenel Bridge. Even now there were probably people with binoculars on both sides eyeballing each other suspiciously.

The others all came up onto the stage and stood right in front of the screen. It was so big and so high resolution that it was like standing in front of a big plate glass window. I pointed over to the left side of the screen. It was partially blocked from view because the camera feeding this big screen must have been hidden somewhere along one of the walls. There was a piece of a wall in the foreground.

"Isn't that where your cruise ship was docked, Kathy?" I said.

"As a matter of fact, Eddie, it is." She stared at the spot remembering that frantic day when she had coordinated the efforts of a few people to help her put up a blockade along the dock that led to the cruise ship terminal. Then came the escape of the Atlantic Spirit from the terminal and out of the harbor to the open sea.

Kathy remembered passing by Fort Sumter and how the infected dead were walking off of the walls that now stood directly above her. Thousands upon thousands of people had died on that ship and in the city, and she had survived because of sheer, stupid luck. She had met the Chief and Jean on the Atlantic Spirit, and then she had met Ed when they had been forced to abandon ship.

Now she stood with Ed and two new friends across the harbor from the place where it had all begun for her. The difference was that there were no signs of life. There were no cars or people moving on the bridge or at any of the familiar landmarks of the city she had called home.

As a Charleston City Police Officer, Kathy had been along the waterfront areas to her left many times. She had crossed that bridge and visited the Patriots Point Maritime Museum where the World War II aircraft carrier, USS Yorktown, was parked. She stood there just soaking in the beauty of it all, totally unaware of the speck that had entered the view in the upper right hand corner of the screen.

"What's that?" asked Bus, as he pointed at the speck.

It was so small at first that standing too close to the screen made it look more like a fly walking across the panorama spread out before us. We instinctively stepped back from the screen to get a better view, and the speck grew a little larger.

There are some days that you never forget, and for those people who were standing in front of their television sets watching as the second plane hit the World Trade Center in New York, one thing many of them had in common was a feeling that they weren't watching something as it happened. It was slow to sink in that they were not watching a replay. We experienced something similar to that.

As the speck grew larger we could see that it was a plane, and not just any plane. It was the Chief's de Havilland DHC-3 Otter. I couldn't speak for the others, but they were all staring at the screen as if it was a movie. None of us was speculating out loud about why the Chief's plane was flying straight into Charleston harbor.

It wasn't coming toward Fort Sumter. It was on a course straight for the State Ports Authority over by the cruise ship terminal, and as it started to pass closer to Fort Sumter, we could see smoke trailing out from behind it. It was not coming in for a controlled landing on the water. It was on a collision course with the city, and it appeared that the Chief was aiming at the patch of water between the bridge and the docks. We watched in open mouthed horror as the plane tilted to the right, showing us its bottom side. It was also missing one of the landing pontoons.

The piece of wall sitting in front of the camera kept us from seeing what happened, but the plane did not emerge from the other side of the wall. Maybe that was the best way for it to happen. I don't know if any of us could have dealt with the sight of our beloved friend crashing into the water.

Kathy had tears streaming down her cheeks. She wasn't making a sound, but her eyes were big and round, and she was just trying to hold it together.

Tom's face was a mixture of confusion and pain. He kept checking the time on his watch and then going back at the screen. It finally dawned on me that he was trying to decide if the Chief had been returning to Fort Sumter on schedule. That would mean Allison was safe back on Mud Island. He would eventually figure out that the plane was returning too soon. The Chief couldn't have flown back to Mud Island, gotten Allison to the shelter almost a mile inland, returned to the plane, and flown back to Charleston in such a short amount of time. Something had happened, and the Chief had tried to make it back to Fort Sumter.

It was Bus who brought us all back to reality. He had been as stunned as any of us by seeing his good friend die in a plane crash, and Allison was Molly's mother. Whatever else happened, it was unbearable for him to think Molly had lost her mother.

"There's still plenty of daylight left," said Bus. "If there's any chance of finding either of them alive, we're going to have to get moving. We need to see what we have running around on top of Fort Sumter, and then we need to find a boat."

That snapped us all back into motion, and we followed Kathy as she turned on her heels and ran for the door of the theater. She didn't worry if there was anything behind doors two and three. She just wanted to get to the Chief like Bus had said.

We went through the door into the hallway at a full run, and Kathy didn't even slow down as she ran through the second door. I felt like I was back in Guntersville…not at the shelter in Green Cavern, but at the country club.

A corridor went to the left, and there were doors on both sides. The floors had plush carpeting, and there were ornate decorations. Bus had a different impression.

"I went on a White House tour once. It was a lot like this," he said.

Directly ahead was a pair of doors that stood open, and beyond them we could see a banquet hall. Tables were set as if there was going to be a large gathering.

"This is no help," said Kathy. "We need to get to the area above the shelter while there's still time."

There was a service entrance at one end of the dining hall, and we guessed the kitchen and food supplies would be the only areas beyond that door. That left us with door number three. We backtracked to where we entered door number two and hurried for the last door, and it had everything we needed.

The main console of a control room blinked with digital readouts giving everything from outside temperature to wind speeds. There was a map of the east coast with different colored lights at various locations, and one of the lights was situated directly over Fort Sumter. It was red.

I traced a path up the coast to a tiny island that had a green light on it. It was Mud Island. I considered the possibility there would be something automated on Mud Island that sent a signal to this console. It was intended to let someone know that Mud Island shelter was alive and well, but there was never anyone here who got the signal.

Kathy and Tom had zeroed in on a terminal that controlled an impressive number of cameras and monitors. They were scanning each monitor as fast as they could to see if we were going to be able to go up to the surface and find a boat. What they found was not encouraging.

Some of the cameras were either partially or completely blocked, and none of them had a clear view to where the Otter had crashed except a smaller version of the big view in the auditorium. The cameras that weren't blocked showed enough of the old fortress to know that it was occupied by people, and they didn't seem like people we would want to meet.

One camera view showed what they did to people they didn't like. They had prisoners. Some were in cages, and some were tied by their arms and legs to makeshift crosses. They appeared to be alive, but the four we could see wouldn't be alive much longer.

On closer inspection, most of the cages appeared to be full of women. Kathy found the controls and zoomed in closer. They were mostly young, and Kathy could guess why they were being held captive.

Kathy saw that the controls would also allow her to pan the cameras and began to rotate the one we had been using. Bus reached over and put his hand on top of hers.

"Kathy, that camera may be well hidden, but moving it may be visible to them. We won't know until we see them for ourselves."

"Okay," she said, "but I need to see more of what's happening out there. I need to get one camera turned far enough to see the other side of the harbor, and I won't know which one does that without trying."

She was still trying to fight back tears, but I could tell that more than anything, Kathy was really, really angry. Seeing we couldn't go out to the surface and at least find a boat was bad enough, but seeing caged women and tortured men was causing her to want to get even.

"I'll take it really slow, Bus. One camera at a time until we know everything we need to know."

Tom was as angry as Kathy, but he was keeping it under control. He positioned himself between Kathy and the monitors.

"If the sun hits one camera lens, Kathy, there's a chance someone will see it. The sun is far enough in the west where that shouldn't happen, but that also means you can't leave any pointing west when you're done. The plane went down just slightly northwest of here, so just take it nice and slow."

Kathy glared at Tom for a moment and then softened a bit. It might have occurred to her that Tom had a reason to be angry, too.

"I'll be careful," she said.

She pressed her lips together in a grimace of half smile and half pain.

Tom stepped out of her way, and Kathy began to pan the camera view very slowly to the left. The cages disappeared from view to the right, and then we were seeing the inside wall of Fort Sumter. It was clear that this camera was going to be of little use to them because it was practically at ground level, well below the walls. She kept rotating it until something began to fill the entire field of vision.

The autofocus feature on the camera made the lens sharpen the image of something big and olive green. Whatever it was, there was no worry about the sun reflecting from the camera lens because it was practically on top of the camera.

Bus said, "Kathy, how far back can you focus?"

Kathy reversed the zoom as far as it would go, and a symbol took shape on the field of green that was blocking their view. It was an eagle with its wings spread wide, and it was perched on a globe that had an anchor right through the middle of it.

"What is that?" asked Kathy. "I've seen it before, but I don't remember where."

"Try a different camera," I said. "I think I know what it is, but I want to be sure."

There were more cameras than we had on Mud Island, perhaps because Fort Sumter was more conspicuous, or maybe because there was more to see from the fort. All you could really see from Mud Island was trees and water. From Fort Sumter you had a three hundred and sixty degree view of cities, islands, sand dunes, bridges, ships, and countless other things to see. The disadvantage was that there could be any number of things close enough to see you.

"Here it is," I said. "This camera should pan far enough to show us what's blocking the other camera."

The camera I had found was located somewhere on the wall facing the ocean and Morris Island. If someone had been watching this monitor earlier, they might have seen us landing near the southern tip. I began to rotate it slowly, and it gradually focused on the prisoners from the opposite side of their cages.

I began to see the edges of the massive shape that was blocking the other camera, and it quickly revealed its origin by the lettering on the side.

"Kathy," I said, "that eagle sitting on the globe and anchor is the symbol of the Marine Corps, and that's a helicopter."

"That's not just any helicopter," said Bus. "Do you see the big white letters on the side back by the tail?"

We couldn't see the whole thing, but we could see enough to know it said, "United States of America."

Bus added, "The White House had several of them at Andrews Air Force Base. In the event of a catastrophe, they could get the President and his family away from Washington, DC in a hurry."

Tom said, "You mean that's the President's helicopter?"

"There's no telling if he was on it or not, Tom. It could have been the Vice President, his family, the Secretary of State, or any number of other important people. They would have picked up whoever made it to the White House lawn, and then they would have tried to make it to different shelters. They wouldn't have tried to bring all of them here. They would have tried to spread out their chain of succession."

"Keep switching cameras, Eddie. We need to get back to finding where the Chief went down," said Kathy.

Every camera I found that was capable of viewing the docks near where we saw the plane crash had the same problem. The wall had blocked our view when it crashed, but now other obstructions were in the way. The most promising view had Castle Pinckney directly between the camera and the crash site. We also learned that the current occupants of Fort Sumter had seen the Otter crash into the harbor, and they were standing along the walls waving their rifles in the air and cheering.

They were a ragged bunch, and they were the kind of people who survived by preying on others. The plane crashing into the harbor was nothing more than entertainment to them. The loss of our friends had made their day. As a matter of fact, they were enjoying themselves so much that some of them were waving in the direction of the crash site, and some were shooting their rifles in the air.

I could tell Kathy was too mad for words, and for a moment I thought she was going to find an exit to the surface and go out guns blazing. I was standing off to her right just in the corner of her eye, and I was watching for her to give me a sign about how she was going to react. Tom had a confused expression on his face that was more defeated than Kathy's expression, and Bus just seemed like he had aged right before our eyes. It had taken something out of all of us, but as much as I wanted to punish the people on the walls, there were just too many of them.

"Don't worry, Eddie. I'm not going to do something stupid," said Kathy.

"I don't know what we're going to do right now," I said. "We're hurt, we're angry, but we're also stranded. If I had to bet anyone could survive a plane crash like that, I would bet on the Chief, but we have to think of ourselves right now."

"Plan A," said Tom. "We have to figure out a way to eliminate the trash on the surface of the fort, and it wouldn't hurt if we could save the people in the cages at the same time. We aren't leaving this place until we deal with them."

Hearing Tom use one of the Chief's phrases galvanized us. It was like a spark of energy for all of us. If we made a plan for eliminating the threat outside, then we could take it to the next step and find a way to at least cross the harbor to see if the Chief and Allison had survived the crash.

"Let's get started with that plan," said Kathy.

5 CITY STREETS

The Chief knew the seaplane was never going to land on water again. It had to come down sooner or later, but it wasn't going to be a landing. From his window he saw the struts sticking straight down, and there was no pontoon fastened to the ends. He would have preferred to lose both pontoons so he could put the plane down on its belly, but you couldn't pick your damage.

They hadn't flown even half of the distance back to Mud Island when the small gunboat had opened fire on them. He had no idea who they were or why they even cared enough to open fire on their plane. The boat was nothing more than a small river craft like the boats that third world countries use for their navies, but it had a fifty caliber machine gun on its bow and a gunner with good aim. He had shredded the pontoon, and something in the engine had been critically damaged. The Chief didn't know how the plane even stayed in the air.

Allison had been alternating between yelling at the Chief and sulking when it happened, and the Chief honestly couldn't tell the difference between when she was mad and scared. She was sulking when the first rounds hit the plane, and when she started yelling it sounded like she was blaming him.

To get away from the boat, the Chief had put the plane over into a steep bank toward the coast. The gunner must have been experienced with moving targets because he led the plane with his aim instead of firing straight at it. The Chief heard the bullets punching holes in the plane even when he thought they should be out of range.

The Chief wrestled with the steering yolk to keep control of the plane, but the remaining pontoon was putting drag on the right side while the engine was sputtering and trying to keep them in the air. The Chief was also cursing himself for not watching for exactly this kind of trouble. He couldn't count the number of times they had kept one eye out for people cruising the shorelines for something to shoot at. Whether it was for piracy or sport, it was bound to happen sooner or later.

The effort to keep the plane in the air was so demanding that the Chief was surprised when he spotted the Ravenel Bridge and then the Yorktown on the left. Allison was screaming in his ear that she didn't want to die, and she wanted him to land the plane. He didn't have the time to explain to her that landing wasn't really an option. He reached over and grabbed her seat belt just to be sure she was wearing it as tight as possible.

As the distance between them and his target began to get shorter, the Chief saw that he only had one choice. They were going to hit hard, and there was no doubt they were more likely to be killed than to survive, but it wasn't in him to just give up. He knew that he had to try to pull up at the last second, cut the engine, and try to do a controlled fall. If they were lucky the fall would kill them instantly, but if they were really lucky it would just hurt like hell.

They passed over a small bit of land that jutted out from under the bridge, and the huge cranes that loomed over the docks seemed to be rushing toward them. At the last second the Chief did his maneuver. He pulled up and banked as if trying to make a turn and shut off the engine at the same time. He heard Allison screaming the entire time, but the sound of the plane's belly hitting the water was ear shattering.

The Chief was disoriented at first, especially because of the silence that engulfed him. When his eyes opened, he saw that he was in the water. The plane had come apart, and he was sinking while still strapped to his seat.

Years on the ocean had given the Chief the unique ability to feel totally at home in the water. So much so that there wasn't the slightest bit of panic as he unbuckled his seatbelt and began his ascent toward the surface. It was also zero visibility in this part of the Cooper River. He couldn't see his hand in front of his face, and he knew he had to make it to the surface before he could even think about what had happened to Allison.

It was probably because he didn't have any hope that he could locate Allison that he was so surprised when he bumped into her. She was free from her seat but unconscious, and she was drifting downward as he swam upward. The current made it difficult to swim and hang onto her, but he had to get her ashore as quickly as possible.

The fact that Allison was drifting downward was either good news or bad news, but the Chief wouldn't know which it was until she was on dry land. A submariner had told the Chief that unconscious people had a better chance of not drowning than conscious people. If she was unconscious before going under the water, then she was drifting downward because she wasn't making an effort to stay afloat. If she was awake when she went under, then she was drifting down because she had inhaled water. He hoped she had been unconscious, and he hoped that submariner hadn't been just telling him a sea story.

When the Chief broke the surface with Allison in tow he began scanning the area for the nearest place to get out of the water. The dock was closer than the end of the island that jutted out from under the bridge, but he didn't know if the docks were occupied. He quickly decided the land that was hardly more than a mud plain with scrub bushes growing on it would at least be safe long enough for him to try to save

Allison. He started swimming as hard as he could away from the docks.

Allison was totally limp when he pulled her body onto the sand, but there were no external signs of injury other than a bump on her head that was probably responsible for her being out cold. The Chief also didn't see any obvious signs of broken bones. He did a quick visible inspection of her scalp, neck, rib cage, arms, and legs then began doing CPR.

Despite the nasty bump, Allison coughed and began spitting up water almost immediately. She would be sore, but unless she had an internal injury, she would survive. The Chief finally had a chance to take stock of his own condition. He took in a really deep breath of air to test his own ribs, and he moved his arms and legs around to be sure he hadn't just been moving without pain due to adrenaline.

Satisfied that he was just going to be sore himself, he checked their surroundings. The docks were only about one hundred yards away, and there was no movement. He was a bit cold, and even though the day was pleasant, being wet and exposed was not the best thing for either of them.

Allison was still gasping and wasn't sure where she was. It was a good thing they were both wearing the Navy blue denim outfits they had found in all sizes in their shelter. The sun would dry them more quickly, and they blocked the breeze better than most clothing.

"Are you okay, Allison?" the Chief asked as gently as he could.

He wanted her to feel safe, but the only thing safe about their predicament was that they weren't being attacked by a swarm of infected dead. Even though there hadn't been an explosion, the sound of an airplane smacking the surface of the water was noisy, and the Chief kept checking the docks to see if they had attracted any attention.

The longer the Chief looked at the docks the more he expected to see them coming their way, but it suddenly occurred to him that there was no safety railing along the concrete loading docks of the State Ports Authority. These were commercial docks for loading container ships, and the people who worked these docks would have seen a safety railing as a nuisance that was in their way as they worked. If there had been any infected dead on these docks, they would have walked off the edges a long time ago. The current was so swift most of the time that they would have washed out to sea or become fish food, and if any had walked up onto this narrow spit of land, they would have just walked right back into the water again.

Allison was finally able to speak in a raspy voice. Salt water down the throat could really burn.

"Where are we? We're alive?" she asked.

The Chief said, "It's a miracle, but yes, we are alive. Better than alive for now, but we need to get to the mainland and find a boat. First things first, though. We need to find a way to get from here over to there. Do you think you can swim if I help you?"

"I don't even know where we are, Chief. This isn't Fort Sumter?"

"No, Allison, Fort Sumter is over there." The Chief pointed at the other side of the harbor where the Ashley River and the Cooper River joined into one wide passageway for the huge container ships.

As soon as he pointed at Fort Sumter he realized it was a mistake. Even from a distance without binoculars he could see the tiny bits of color moving on the walls of Fort Sumter were people. If one of them was using binoculars to watch the Chief and Allison, they would be in a position to cross the harbor if they had a boat. By the Chief's logic, if they held Fort Sumter they must have boats in order to keep it supplied.

The Chief had a trained eye, and with the sun in the west he was able to catch the reflected light as several of the figures on the wall lifted their binoculars. It was like being naked in the middle of a football field, and it was a sell-out crowd. There was nowhere to hide, and the men or women with the binoculars could study them both closely.

Allison turned toward the fort, and before the Chief could stop her, she waved excitedly in that direction. A few of them started waving back and shooting their rifles in the air.

The Chief wasn't going to wait to see if the fort people took Allison's wave as an invitation to come get them, and he wasn't going to play twenty questions with her about whether or not she could swim. She hadn't even thanked him for saving both of their lives, and she was already putting them in more danger by waving at the people in the fort.

Without warning the Chief scooped Allison up off of the sand and ran into the water toward the docks. He was stronger than most men on dry land, but he was almost stronger in the water. He knew it would be a race to swim one hundred yards and get to safety on land before the people in Fort Sumter could get there with a boat. He didn't doubt the order had already been given by someone in authority over there.

Allison screamed at the Chief the way she had in the seaplane, and he was at least a little tempted to swim underwater. He resisted the temptation because he didn't have time to do CPR again if there was a boat heading their way.

With powerful strokes the Chief crossed the docks and aimed for a steel ladder that was bolted to the concrete and extended below the surface of the water. Allison had no choice but to hang on until he put her within reach of the first rungs. She didn't have to be told to climb, and she was waiting for him at the top just to give him a piece of her mind.

The Chief didn't give her a chance. Before she could get out more than four words, he had her over his shoulder and was running for cover. A quick glance toward the harbor told him he had won the race because the boat was only half way across, but that was just the water part of the race. If they were armed and had been coming to the mainland for supplies, then they knew this terrain well. There was no place to hide that those people hadn't already been, so the Chief decided he wouldn't try to hide until they were away from the waterfront. That meant they would be forced to cross the downtown part of the city. It was either that or try to cross the Ravenel Bridge, and there was no doubt in his mind that they couldn't be more exposed if they had targets painted on their backs.

Allison was struggling enough to be slowing them down, and he had to stop for a minute. As soon as her feet were on the ground and she started to verbally assault him, he pulled back his right arm with his massive fist where she could see it. Her eyes went wide, but she stopped talking.

Chief Joshua Barnes had never hit a woman in his life, and he wasn't going to start now, but he needed her to pay attention long enough to understand what kind of trouble they were in, and they were really short on time.

"Do I have your attention, Allison?"

She nodded her head, but her eyes stayed glued to the fist.

The Chief lowered his arm and took her hands in his. His grip was urgent but reassuring at the same time.

"Allison, those people at Fort Sumter are dangerous. They weren't excited because we survived the crash. They were excited because they saw a pretty woman waving at them. They're coming after us, not coming to rescue us."

The Chief's words were well put for such a short amount of time, and Allison understood they were in really big trouble. She glanced toward the harbor and could see there were now two boats crossing the water. Her head turned back the other way and she saw that they were surrounded by cargo containers, and they would run out of hiding places in a hurry.

"What are we going to do?" she asked barely above a whisper.

"First we run," said the Chief. "Then we need to make it out of the cargo storage areas and cross the city. Our only hope of getting out of here alive is to get a boat, and the nearest place I know of where we can find one that isn't in their clear view is the Coast Guard base. If there isn't one there, we have to make it to the city marina."

Allison was afraid of the city that was beyond the tall chain link fence surrounding the cargo containers. She hadn't known its beauty before it fell to the infected. It was an old city dating back to the original settlement in 1663, but even though it was old, it was always a shiny kind of old. It was clean and colorful. Now, after long months with no loving care from its residents it seemed old and worn, and it was foreboding. The buildings were dirty, and more than one fire had ravaged entire neighborhoods. Smoke was still drifting upward from somewhere not too far away, and they could smell something in the air that could only be decay.

"We have to go, Allison. There's no time to think about it. We have to be on the other side of that fence before they reach the docks."

Although they knew what would be in the city, the alternative left no choice. The people in the boats had weapons, while the infected dead had to get up close and personal. They would have to take their chances in the city.

This time the Chief didn't need to carry Allison, and they both broke into an all out run through the containers. It was during that run when the Chief remembered they had very little in the way of weapons. They both had large hunting knives on their belts, but the guns and machetes had gone down with the plane. He took the lead from Allison just in case there were any infected still within the perimeter. There was always a chance that there was a hole in the fence somewhere.

He led Allison on a diagonal path that would take them to the fence. He reasoned that the people coming from Fort Sumter would probably tie up at the docks where they saw them climb the ladder. If he was right, that would put them at a greater distance from their pursuers, but he also wanted to move as far along the city as they could before they no longer had the protection of the fence. Once they got past the fence, they would face an unknown number of the infected.

They zigzagged through row after row of stacked containers. Some stood open, and the contents were spread around the open doors. Colorful containers full of electronics shipped to stores like Best Buy and Target were mostly full, but containers of packaged foods like Ramen Noodles were almost stripped bare. It was no surprise that this had become the private shopping center of the people in Fort Sumter. There were probably skirmishes with other groups that were holed up in other places, so this wasn't the safest place for them to be even if there were no infected.

The Chief saw the first of the infected dead only about twenty yards beyond the fence. It had already spotted them and was weaving in their general direction. At first the Chief figured they would just outrun it, but one groaning infected would attract the attention of others, and it wouldn't be long before they were noticed by their pursuers.

The Chief pulled his hunting knife from its sheath and ran straight toward the noisy infected. Allison stopped and watched with disbelief on her face, but it became obvious what the Chief was doing when she saw his knife was already in his hand. It didn't take more than that for the infected dead to rush up against the fence. The Chief quickly silenced the groaning with his blade and just as quickly began running again.

As he passed Allison he said in an urgent voice, "The reason there aren't any infected on this side of the fence is because those people cleared them out and then secured the fence. We won't find any holes to escape through, so we have to find a good place to climb."

"I was raised around tall trees, Chief. I can climb just as good as you."

Somehow the Chief doubted that, but he wasn't going to argue with her about it. He at least needed for her to believe she could climb as well as him. It would be a good thing if she could climb that well.

They reached the border of the container storage area and came to the tall fence that stood between them and the city. The fence didn't end at a perfect corner but in a long curve that went around a power junction like the one Tom had told them he had encountered near Simmonsville. A police officer from Conway, South Carolina had heroically destroyed hundreds of the infected dead by drawing them into the fenced perimeter of the power junction and then blowing it up while he was still inside. If not for him, Tom and Molly might not have survived.

"No explosions today," thought the Chief. "Today everybody lives." The sign on the nearest corner said they were at the intersection of Charlotte and Washington Street. That meant they were already parallel to East Bay Street, the main street that would take them most of the way to the Coast Guard station.

The Chief mentally clicked off the main streets in his mind and estimated that they were about twenty blocks from White Point Garden, otherwise known as the Battery. Then they would have to go west for another eight blocks to reach the Coast Guard station. He could try to take a more direct route by turning onto Tradd Street and going straight for the Coast Guard base, but the houses were too close together, and the street was too narrow in places. He didn't see how they could avoid getting caught by the hordes of infected dead he knew were wandering through the city the way they had been in the woods near Mud Island.

He also considered the possibility that there would be a boat at one of the many small docks along Concord Street, but that would have been the most likely place for the inhabitants of Fort Sumter to have gotten their boats in the first place. Even if boats had docked there from somewhere else, those docks were all too visible from Fort Sumter. They would be spotted by either the people in the fort or the people who had crossed the harbor in pursuit of them, and even if they weren't, there was no guarantee that a boat would be just sitting there waiting for them to take.

The Chief had also considered the possibility that there would be no boats at the Coast Guard station. If there weren't any working boats there they were still close to the Charleston City Marina, and they wouldn't be in clear view of Fort Sumter.

Allison hit the chain link fence faster than the Chief expected. He thought she would need a leg up, but she went up the fence like a squirrel on a tree. She was half way to the top before he even got started. They managed to keep from falling over and breaking a leg, and they both ran stooped over to the other side of Charlotte Street where a few trees provided some cover. The trees were up against another fence that surrounded another power junction area. They were far enough ahead of the people from Fort Sumter to be safe, but now they had to cross a dead city to find a boat, and they had to do it before it got dark.

The Chief checked the position of the sun and didn't like what he saw. If they could just walk along the sidewalks to the Coast Guard station, they could do it easily within an hour, but the last thing he expected was deserted streets or that they would be able to just walk. He expected a lot of running. If it took too long, they would have to find a place to be safe for the night. There were plenty of houses, but thousands of people had tried to stay inside when the infection spread, and that was where they had died. Finding an occupied house was going to be as easy as finding the infected dead out along the streets. Empty houses were more likely to be rare.

"So, how do we do this, Chief? Are we going to run down streets or climb fences the whole way?"

"Some of both, I'm afraid," answered the Chief. "I was just thinking we should keep an eye out for a safe place to spend the night."

Allison said, "If there is such a place."

At first the Chief felt angry at Allison's pessimism, but in her simplistic way she had summed up how hard it would be to find a safe place in downtown Charleston. The infection had spread quickly throughout the city. People on the streets were attacked, and if they died on the streets, they rose up and attacked more people. If they made it to safety inside, they most likely carried the infection inside with them.

"For the first time today, Allison, I'm inclined to agree with you. We can only keep moving and run faster than whatever we find out here. Let's try to take the shortest path as often as we can."

The Chief pointed toward the nearest corner and said, "That's Washington Street. Let's get this party started."

Keeping low and close to the trees they crept along Charlotte Street until they reached the intersection. The Chief peered around the corner of the trees and fence, and he was surprised to see so many of the infected dead. There were dozens along the first city block. The closest was only a few feet away, and it appeared to be focused on something that was running along the street. A large rat came over the curb running straight at them, and Allison couldn't stifle the scream in time. The infected dead down the entire block heard it, and there was no telling how many had heard it on other streets.

The Chief grabbed Allison by the hand and started running hard for the intersection in the opposite direction. It was a long block, and by the time they reached the corner, a quick look back was all they needed to see that the scream had gotten a lot of attention. The first of the infected was only barely able to follow them, but it was making such a racket with its groaning that it was bound to be attracting everything at least a block away in all directions.

The Chief let go of Allison's hand as they got closer to Concord Street and said, "Get ready."

She didn't know what he meant until she saw him pull out his hunting knife. She drew her own knife from its sheath and held it out in front of her. If they were lucky she would run into something hard enough to at least knock it down.

They reached the corner and saw that it was bad but not as bad as the last street. The first infected was coming straight at them because it was being drawn by the noise a block behind the Chief and Allison. The Chief shoved the hunting knife upward into the bottom of its chin, and the infected fell backward out of his way. The next one was at least twenty feet away, and the Chief had time to prepare for the attack.

Allison was just tagging along at this point, but she wasn't screaming, and she was watching how the Chief made short work of his targets. She saw that the Chief was letting the knife and his momentum do all of the work. He would run straight at the infected, and he didn't extend his arm with the knife until he was within an arm's length.

The Chief was moving toward a pair of the infected that were walking side by side at their typical shambling pace. It was going to be tricky because he would have to stab one and then immediately get the other. The problem was that they were so close together that one would be able to grab at him while he was taking care of the other.

To say the least, the Chief was surprised when he went for the one on the left, and Allison stepped confidently into the one on the right. She neatly pushed her blade upward just as she had seen the Chief do, and the infected dead dropped to the pavement.

Allison had made the decision to help when she saw there were two of the infected too close to each other. There wasn't time to ask the Chief which of them she should try to eliminate, so she watched from a half step back to see which one he would take first. As soon as he committed to the left, she stepped forward and aimed at the soft spot below the chin.

Their timing was so good that both of the infected dead dropped to the street at virtually the same moment. Even though they didn't have a second to waste, the Chief hooked him right arm around Allison's neck and pulled her into a hug.

He thought, "Maybe this is what she needed to get herself to feel like part of the group. The way she had insisted on coming along couldn't have all been because of Tom."

Allison was pleased with herself and gave the Chief a big smile. They turned together and charged the next of the infected that were coming their way. As soon as those were down, they moved on to the next ones.

Eventually Allison and the Chief reached the next intersection on Concord Street. The sign on the corner said it was Aquarium Wharf, and the Chief saw an opportunity to gain some advantage.

The infected that had been drawn to Allison's scream had been attracted to Charlotte Street, and it had ironically provided just enough of a diversion for them to escape around the other end of the block. Since they were unable to think through a problem the way a living person could, the infected were still drawn to the spot where the scream had come from. It was almost as if they were determined to reach that spot while the Chief and Allison escaped around the other end of the block.

The opportunity the Chief saw was a park that occupied the entire block just ahead and to their left. It had a heavy growth of trees surrounding it, and they would be able to run an entire block without having to leave the cover of those trees. He caught Allison by the sleeve of her denim jumpsuit and led her to the left into the trees.

They were able to drop to their knees out of sight long enough for Allison to catch her breath. It wasn't that she was out of shape. She just wasn't used to having her adrenaline so high for this long. She had survived a plane crash and was having to run an obstacle course within the same hour. The Chief had to give her credit for eventually coming around, and it made him regret deciding to take her back to Mud Island.

"Well, you can't live in the past," he said.

"What was that, Chief?" Allison asked in a low voice.

She was either too winded to be loud, or she really was starting to understand how bad things were for them. He didn't have the heart to tell her, but the chances of them living long enough to get a boat were slim. It just wasn't in his nature not to try. On her own Allison had a zero percent chance of living. With him, the Chief figured they had about a ten percent chance at best.

"Nothing, Allison. You did good back there. You keep that up, and we might just clean out the whole town and move here."

He gave her his big, broad smile and she visibly appeared to be ready to go the distance.

"Let's get going and see if we can't have you safe with Tom sometime tonight."

They stayed in the trees until they reached the end of the small park, and then they took a chance and crossed the middle of the street to get to a much larger park. It didn't have much cover at all, but it gave them the advantage of being able to see what was ahead. By crossing the wide open area, they would be able to cover the distance of three city blocks more quickly. Plus, the park was so wide that any infected that saw them would be so far away that they could change course long before the infected could reach them.

The streets around the aquarium and the park were relatively clear considering what the Chief had seen so far in other cities, but the more distance they covered, the closer they were getting to the more heavily populated part of Charleston. There were more cars in the streets, more damage to buildings, and more human remains. Everything was changing the way he had expected it to. Overgrown patches of grass and weeds choked the sidewalks, and the city was as dead as it could be. He doubted that any survivor groups had managed to reclaim any part of the city.

The Chief could see something beyond the park that was familiar, and he felt like he had come full circle. If he was right, it was a place he had seen before but from the other side. It was the Charleston cruise ship terminal where the Atlantic Spirit had been docked during the outbreak of the infection. If he was correct, the cable laying barge would be at anchor just up ahead and to the left down Laurens Street. It would be great to see it still there, but he knew they wouldn't be able to get it under way and past Fort Sumter.

For a moment he allowed himself the luxury of thinking about his friends who had hopefully gone into the tunnel on Morris Island. He also hoped they had gone ahead to Fort

Sumter and found that the new inhabitants of the fort hadn't discovered the shelter. If that was true, the Chief didn't doubt that they would find a way to liberate the fort as they had planned. With Kathy leading them, they could be a dangerous group of people.

When they reached the corner of Concord and Laurens Street, there was a nice little hiding spot among some trees where they were able to plan their next move. They were also able to see the docks at the end of Laurens Street, and the cable laying barge was still there.

"That was half of the plan right there, Allison."

"What do you mean, Chief?"

"Well, if the cable laying barge was gone, all of this would have been for nothing," he said.

Allison thought it over it over for a second, and she said, "I hate to tell you this, Chief, but we lost the plane, and getting that boat back to Mud Island is going to be a tough job if that jerk that shot us down is still out there."

"I have a score to settle with him, Allison. If he's still out there, I'm going to make him sorry for what he did. I liked that plane."

Allison got a chance to see the side of the Chief she had been missing all along, because for a moment he had her going. He had fooled her by reacting the way most people would have, but when she saw his face more closely she caught the faintest of grins at the corners of his mouth.

"Chief," she said, "were you just pulling my leg?"

The grin spread a little wider.

"What makes you think that, Allison?"

"You know what I mean, Chief. You're not the kind of person who would go after someone out of revenge."

"You figured me out, Allison. The fact is, we can get another plane, and those guys in the boat will probably be crab food within a year. You ready to get moving again?"

She nodded, and he pointed at the huge paved areas south of Laurens Street. There were burned out trucks and cars everywhere, but he didn't see any infected moving around between them.

"We're going to cross that mess until we get past the cruise ship terminal. There were a lot of people here when the attacks started, and a lot of people tried to escape through here, but it wasn't really a populated area. Most of the infected would have found a way to walk into the water by now, so it shouldn't get bad until we reach Market Street." He left off the part about expecting Market Street to be crowded with the infected.

6 PLAN B

Not much had gone the way I had expected on this trip. Plan A was totally changed when the Chief left with Allison, and Plan B was still lacking answers. I could tell Kathy was still holding out hope that the Chief was alive. I'm sure she was including Allison in those hopes, but if she had to pick one who she thought would survive, it would be the Chief. He was just wired that way.

We watched the people who were living in the fort above us, and they were not the kind of people who should survive, but sometimes the ones who just take what they want are the ones who do survive. After watching for a while, we decided there was no clear purpose to much of what they did with their time. Most of them just laid around all afternoon. Some of them got into fights for no reason at all, and some of them just sat around talking.

We had managed to get another camera to rotate far enough to show a view of the long dock where tour boats tied up when they came out to the fort. There was a large number of boats there now, but we had watched as several had pulled away after the plane crashed. We assumed they had decided it was worth investigating. Some returned a couple of hours later with nothing to show for the trip. There had been some arm waving by one guy who we thought might be in charge.

Another camera angle had revealed more cages with prisoners. We tried to work out a plan that would include their rescue, but there were just too many people with guns up there. The best idea we could come up with was to wait until dark, sneak out and kill as many as we could, and then retreat back into our shelter.

More than once we talked about what we were forced to become in order to survive. We had all killed, for lack of a better term, the infected dead, but killing a living person was something new. The problem was that they stood between us and getting the cable laying barge back to Mud Island. They also stood between us and knowing for sure if the Chief and Allison were still alive.

As the afternoon passed, it became more and more obvious that the only answer was to find a way to kill all of them. We decided to take a break from watching their moronic behavior and find something to eat. We also still needed to find the hidden entrance to the shelter that would allow access to the surface.

The food was easy enough to take care of. There was a tremendous supply of flash frozen foods and MRE's. Over our meal we talked about how we could take the fort, and I suggested it would be great if we could just ask them to leave. Of course all three of them voted that I could be the one to go ask them, but Kathy stopped in mid-sentence.

"Wait a minute, Eddie. I think you might be onto something. What if we can find a way to make them want to leave?"

Neither Tom nor Bus understood what I had said that made Kathy think there was a way to make them want to leave. The blank expressions meant they were both clueless, so they turned to me for an answer. I was just as clueless.

I said, "Kathy, I was just kidding. I didn't seriously think we could ask them to leave."

"I know," she said, "and I wasn't planning on asking them. I said we could make them want to leave. What makes anyone want to leave somewhere these days?"

We three men were being dense, because the only thing I could think of was why we left Mud Island so often. Tom and Bus weren't doing any better.

Kathy shook her head and asked, "What's that thing you said once about being dropped on your head when you were a baby, Eddie?"

The light suddenly went on over my head and I asked, "What would they do if there were infected dead wandering around in the fort? Especially in the middle of the night?"

"They might want to leave," said Kathy. "It might take a few days, but once we get the ball rolling, we can let them kill each other or leave."

One thing we had discussed plenty of times was how this whole thing got started in the first place. We knew from my experience that there was a wild attack at a fast food restaurant, but I never assumed it started there. We all had similar experiences in the first few days, and almost every time it was because someone had been bitten by someone who was infected. We all agreed that a bite was the means of transmission, but where did they all come from in the first place.

It was Bus who had the answer for us because his communications network at the beginning had been much better than what the rest of us had. He told us he had received reports from friends who had first hand information about unbitten people coming back from the dead. As crazy as it sounded to us at first, we had to admit, that wasn't really crazier than coming back from the dead after being bitten. Both were crazy, but we had only seen it happen when people were bitten.

Bus said there was plenty of speculation about how it could happen, but the part that made the most sense was the virus that was causing people to come back from the dead could be transmitted in more than one way. Viruses often mutated to find other methods of transmission. The bite was just proving to be the most lethal way that it was transmitted, and it caused such a destructive infection that it sped up the death of the person who was bitten. Bus pointed out that Jean's illness after being scratched was a clue that the bite is fatal because the virus is carried by bodily fluids. There were no bodily fluids under the fingernails of the infected dead that scratched Jean, so she just got sick. Since Bus was a doctor, he could explain it in a way that really made sense.

"Do people still salivate after they're dead, Bus?" asked Kathy.

"The glands that produce saliva stop making it, but there's going to be saliva in the ducts for a long time after you die," he said.

"So," said Tom, "you're saying it isn't necessarily the bite that's killing everyone. The bite is just something that the infected do after they come back to life. And you're saying anyone that dies is going to have the infection, and when they get back up they're going to start biting?"

"That's a fair summary," said Bus.

Kathy said, "Let me get this straight, Doc. If we sneak up there at night and kill one of them, he would turn into an infected dead and start biting people?"

"Seems to me that we might have a plan B after all," said Kathy. "We don't have to kill everyone. We just have to get it started. Now let's find the door that opens to the surface."

******

There were two hidden doors leading from the shelter to the surface. Not surprisingly, they were both located in the rooms behind the doors in the corridor that had reminded Bus of the White House. When we went down the corridor, it just looked like a series of doors, ten on each side. That was why it looked so much like a hotel to me. The surprise was that each room opened into a much larger room, and each of them had ten more doors. When I did the math, it was two hundred rooms.

We were worried at first when we saw so many doors. Some opened into storage rooms, and some into living quarters. I opened one door and found myself in a stairwell that went downward. I didn't bother to go down because I knew I was just going to find more rooms. It was a maze of doors and rooms, and it could take days to search them all.

Kathy said she was going to go back to the control room to see if she could come up with a floor plan of the shelter. She caught up with the rest of us only thirty minutes later, and she had a printout for each of us.

"Keep these so you don't get lost," said Kathy. "The exits go to the surface through secure areas. There are checkpoints and living quarters for the Secret Service just inside each of the checkpoints."

We each took one, and we were amazed by the number of rooms. The government apparently thought there would be more time to establish a command and control center in this shelter.

"Why do you suppose they didn't make it here?" asked Tom.

Bus said, "When the infection started to spread, did you think the stories were true?"

"No, not really," said Tom. "I kept saying to myself the military would get it all under control. I guess the military kept saying the same thing."

"Exactly," said Bus. "And the government thought the military would stop it, too. I can't say I really blame them, either. Can you imagine if the Joint Chiefs of Staff had sat down around a table and one of them suggested they develop an emergency response plan for zombies?"

As soon as Bus said it he regretted it. It made them all think of the Chief.

Kathy said, "If it makes you feel any better, I'll go ahead and say it for the Chief, Bus. They aren't zombies."

In a weird sort of way it did make me feel better. As the Chief had explained to us numerous times, zombies are under the control of someone, and the infected dead were reanimated by an infectious virus. No one really knew enough about it to say how it worked, but it certainly wasn't giving someone control over the infected dead.

"Back to your point," said Kathy, "if someone had proposed to the President of the United States that the government needed to be prepared to deal with a virus spread by dead people biting healthy people, that person would have found themselves working in a small government office at the South Pole. So, when everything hit the fan, they kept looking at the military expecting them to stop it."

Bus said, "It's a time honored tradition in the military that no man will be left behind. It's not hard to guess what that means. They had wounded men and women who they tried to treat, and that spread the infection behind the military lines."

"You're assuming they were able to establish lines of defense that were effective," I said. "Remember those broadcasts I watched from the shelter? They weren't able to strike back after they set up their lines of defense. Eventually they were overrun or ran out of supplies. At the very least, they weren't able to coordinate with other military groups or bases."

Tom said, "I guess that explains why they didn't make it to here, but do you think any of the government made it to safety?"

"Certainly," said Bus. "The President is undoubtedly in a secure location. I wouldn't be surprised if they moved him from one safe place to another by now."

"Which brings up an interesting point," I said. "If this was one of their primary shelters, is the military going to show up here? Better yet, why haven't they shown up yet?"

The realization that dawned on us was an unattractive thought. This thing had not only crippled our land forces, it had cut deeply into our ability to respond from the sea and the air. Our assets couldn't keep supply lines open long enough to be able to mount any kind of resistance.

"If it was up to me," said Kathy, "I wouldn't even consider moving the President to a ship. After what we saw on the Atlantic Spirit and on the Russian corvette, I don't think a ship is a safe place to be."

Kathy said, "I think it's time for us to stop worrying about why the military couldn't stop this thing. We still have a goal, and even though it won't stop the infected dead from running the whole world, it will keep us alive a while longer, and who knows? It may even give us a chance to find out if the Chief survived that crash."

"So, what's the plan?" I asked.

Kathy said, "It's really simple, Eddie. We pop out of the hidden doors and take out a few of them as quietly as we can. We don't do any head injury. Then we get back into hiding and hope they start biting people before sunrise. If it's dark enough out there, those guys will be so spooked they'll be shooting anybody who smiles enough to show teeth."

That got a laugh out of us, and we could feel the tension dropping as we laid out our plan. We decided to go out in pairs because there were two hidden doors that were also clearly out of the immediate view from the people above. We had also spent a few minutes in front of the video monitors to see if we could tell if the morons were posting watches. We saw that there were only two places we would see people always hanging around, and the only time there were two people at either spot was straight up on the hour. Somebody had a working clock, and those were most likely to be our guards.

The doors to those hidden exits could be reached from escape hatches that went up through steep tunnels. Each tunnel had three ladders down the curved walls, and was about the size of an elevator shaft. When we found the rooms where the tunnels began, we could see that they were intended to get dignitaries in and out quickly. The three ladders would allow for protective forces to be with the VIPs at all times. There was also the same type of harness that was used on rescue helicopters and a line that went up the shaft. If we needed to move fast, that would come in handy. A flashlight up the tunnel revealed that we were about three stories below the surface, and we could see a platform at the top of the ladders. A quick climb to the top was all we needed to see that the doors were nearly vertical, so we could open them and step through instead of having to climb up through them.

The rooms were far enough from each other that we had to synchronize our watches. I had stopped wearing one, but both Tom and Bus found it harder to break the habit. We decided to go out at 9:15 PM. Sunset would be just after 8:30 PM, and the guard would change at 9:00. The guard going off duty seldom hung around more than a couple of minutes, and it was our guess the guard leaving at 9:00 would be ready to go faster than the ones during the day.

I paired up with Tom, and we started our climb well in advance of the time to go out. The plan was simple. We would go out through the tunnel, come up from behind the guard and bag him. The storeroom held a large quantity of supplies, and there were some really strong plastic bags that would be perfect.

When we had gotten to the part about how we would kill someone, none of us wanted to treat the living the way we had the infected. They were already dead, and even though it wasn't an easy thing for us to get used to, we had been able to do it because we were forced to. In this case, the guard would start yelling, and then we would have to kill more than one or two people.

That got us around to a variety of suggestions. Cutting their throats was one way to kill them without having them yelling their heads off, but all of us had a problem with that. I guess we were still human after all. Someone suggested hitting them over the head hard enough to knock them out, but no one knew just how hard that had to be. Tom told us that he had seen baseball players hit in the head hard enough to knock them down but not out, and that was with a fastball going over ninety miles per hour.

It was our good doctor who came up with the most humane idea, and Bus said he hated the idea that his medical training was what made him think of it.

Bus explained that we only needed to control the guards long enough to give them a lethal injection. He said he had done an inventory of the surgical suite located in the Fort Sumter shelter and had found that they could do almost any surgery they wanted because they had everything they needed for anesthesia. He said he could mix a cocktail of propofol and morphine that would stop someone's heart in seconds. All we would have to do is keep the person quiet long enough to give him the injection.

Since Tom had been a baseball player, my physical strength was no comparison to his, and he was much taller. He was the obvious choice to be the bag-man, and I was the obvious choice to give the shot. He jokingly said he would appreciate it if he didn't feel a needle going into his arm by accident.

That didn't produce any laughs, and we decided we had what we needed to do some practice runs first. He brought down Kathy with a pretend bag because we were sure he was strong enough. My goal was to give the shot into the neck, and I used a syringe without a needle for practice.

Tom was right. The first time we did it, he didn't pull his hand back enough, and I plunged the syringe straight into it. We did it at least a dozen more times, and I got the neck every time. Then we had Bus give it a try. Even though he was a doctor, he got Kathy's hand on the third try after missing it twice. He got to do it a dozen more times, but the most valuable lesson was that Tom and Kathy had to pull back harder on the side where the needle would go in.

Kathy and Bus had gone to their tunnel at the same time as us. We were all eager to get it over with. At 9:15 Tom gave me the signal, and we shut off the lights in the tunnel then eased the door open. There was a small shower of dirt, but the hinges on the door were silent.

There was enough light outside the door for us to see the guard standing about twenty feet away. His rifle was leaning against a brick wall and he was doing something with his hands that we couldn't see. After standing watch on this old fort many times, he was totally relaxed and complacent.

As we eased closer to him, light flared on the other side of his head. He had been lighting a cigarette, and ironically this cigarette would kill him faster than if he hadn't been smoking. He inhaled deeply, and Tom pulled the plastic bag over his head before he could exhale. The guard was so desperately trying to breathe that he didn't even try hard to struggle. I had the cap off of the syringe and easily hit my target. The man slumped over and his legs went limp.

Tom held the plastic bag in place for about a minute while I watched for signs that anyone else was heading our way. He was just about sure it had been long enough when I noticed our door was really close to one of the cages we had seen on the security camera. It wasn't more than ten feet beyond our door, and there appeared to be only one person inside it. It was like the type of cage divers used to safely study sharks.

I whispered, "Tom, can we get that cage open?"

Tom lowered the guard the rest of the way to the ground and pulled the bag off of his head. He felt for a pulse and told me to start timing how long it took for the guard to become an undead version of himself. I checked the time while Tom side stepped over to the cage. The lone figure inside moved away to the farthest corner.

"It's just tied shut, Ed. I can cut it."

He started cutting at the rope while I went to the side of the cage. I saw that the woman inside was an African American, and she was scared.

"Don't be afraid," I said. "Just come with us, and we'll get you to someplace safe."

Tom made short work of the rope and opened the door. The woman didn't move at first, obviously trying to decide if she was just going from the frying pan into the fire. Tom didn't approach her. He just held out his hand. That did it for her, and she held out her own hand. Tom took it gently and led her out of the cage.

I got to the door ahead of them and held it open for them to go through.

"Be careful on the platform," I said. "I'll turn the lights on as soon as I have the door shut."

Tom helped the woman through the door and then guided her hand to the railing on the platform. I squeezed through with them and closed the door.

I turned toward the woman and said, "I'm going to turn on the lights, and you're going to find you are standing at the top of a tunnel about three stories high. I don't want you to get scared and scream when you see how high up we are."

I seriously doubted anyone could hear her even if she did scream, but I also didn't want her to be that surprised by the height of the tunnel. I was glad I warned her because when the lights came on, she recoiled from the side of the platform so hard she almost rammed into the door.

"Are you okay?" asked Tom. "Do you think you can climb down a ladder?"

In the light I could see just how afraid she was, but she appeared to be unhurt. She was wearing blue jeans, running shoes, and a burgundy sweatshirt from the College of Charleston, but she had been rolled around in the dirt a few times.

She nodded at Tom and then at me and went to the ladder on her own. Tom and I went to the other two ladders and started climbing down quickly. I wanted to see how Kathy and Bus had done with their guard and be at the monitors in time to see how fast the guards would be back on their feet.

When we reached the bottom of the ladders, I told the woman we had rescued that we would explain everything later. We told her our names, and she just stared in numb silence as we reached out to shake her hand. Her reaction must have been how we would have felt if at one moment we were in a cage, and the next moment we had fallen down the rabbit hole into safety.

"Olivia. My name is Olivia Rutledge," she said.

"Pleased to meet you, Olivia," said Tom. "I know you have a thousand questions, but right now we have something important to do. Just follow us, and when it's all over we can have a long talk."

It was my guess that Olivia was somewhere between thirty-five and forty years old, and she kept herself in good shape. She nodded again like she did at the top of the tunnel, but she still couldn't believe what was happening, so she wasn't ready to talk. It occurred to me that there was something I could say that might shake her loose from her catatonic state.

In a soft voice I asked her if she used to believe in zombies. She thought about it for a moment and then shook her head from side to side. Then I asked her if she does now. This time she nodded her head.

I said, "Then you shouldn't have a hard time believing that we're real or that you're safe now. This is all real, and those men can't get to you anymore."

"Let's go," said Tom. "It could be starting already."

By the time Tom and I got to the control room, Kathy and Bus were already there. Our new friend came in with us, and it was still too much for it to all sink in, but I saw her smile a couple of times as we crossed some of the more impressive rooms. She stopped for a moment as we passed the dining room, and I told myself not to make her wait too long before we fed her.

Kathy and Bus didn't seem totally surprised when they saw Olivia, and they said a quick hello when I introduced them.

Olivia said, "Hi," in a barely audible voice, and made a little halfhearted wave with one hand.

Kathy smiled at her and said, "It's okay, Olivia. You're with friends now. Give us a few minutes and we'll take you to the kitchen for something to eat."

It was already more than Olivia could absorb, and she very slowly started to shake and cry. She needed someone to hold her, and Kathy was quick to get to her side. She helped Olivia into a chair and explained to her that we were really the good guys, and that she was going to be okay. Then she told her we had to take care of some business and asked if she would be all right by herself. Olivia nodded, so Kathy gave her a hug and then came back to the monitors.

"How did things go with you guys?" I asked.

"We didn't rescue anyone," said Bus, "but taking out the guard was a breeze. The guy got comfortable for a nap as soon as the last guard was out of sight."

"We were paired off right," I said. "Our guard was bigger and stronger, but Tom's timing was perfect. He caught him right in the middle of lighting up a cigarette."

"It's starting," said Kathy. "Check out the guard you guys took out."

In the monitor we could see the guard slumped over against a wall, but his legs were starting to twitch. It was faint at first, but then it became more pronounced. It was like his feet knew where they were supposed to go, but they weren't sure how to get there.

Olivia slowly came over to the monitors as if she wasn't sure if she was allowed to. Kathy put one arm around her and brought her into our little fold so she could see the same things we were seeing.

Kathy said, "This isn't going to be pretty, folks."

On another monitor the guard that was taken out by Kathy and Bus rolled over onto his stomach and then pushed himself to his knees. He did it so naturally that at first he looked like he was just shaking off the effects of being drugged, but then he face planted right where he was.

Almost as if nothing had happened, he pushed himself up for a second time, and he didn't stop until he was standing upright. Then we could tell he was really dead, and he was starting to be attracted to the other noises in the camp.

Our guard was also making an effort to get his feet under him. He fell over backwards and was lost from our camera view for a minute. When he showed up again, he was shuffling off in the direction of a group of men who were arguing about something. We couldn't hear what they were saying, but two of them were pushing each other and pointing fingers.

We watched the dead guard shuffle up to them unnoticed until it was too late. He came up behind one of the men and firmly gripped his teeth into the muscle between the neck and shoulder. The bitten man screamed. Even though we couldn't hear it, we could imagine the gut wrenching pain as the infected dead tore away a mouthful of flesh.

The fighting men froze in mid-finger pointing to see why the man was screaming and then went right back to arguing.

"What could be so important that those guys don't know what's going on?" asked Bus.

Kathy said, "I don't know how many times I saw that kind of thing in the short time I was a cop. People get so mad they become oblivious to what's happening around them."

The bitten man went down face first into the dirt. It was either the bleeding or the shock, but the bite had been deep enough to kill him. He was getting back up on his feet even before the first infected dead had a chance to close the gap between it and the arguing men. It was our first time witnessing that some people died and got back up faster than others. It was much quicker than the ones we had drugged to death.

Over on the other side of the fort, the previously sleepy guard had found a tent where some of the men had turned in early. The infected dead clumsily pushed through the flap of the tent and disappeared.

Seconds later the walls of the tent started getting pushed outward in a random pattern, going from one side to the other as people were trying to keep from being bitten. A man fell out of the front of the tent and then jumped to his feet and ran. He was holding a badly bloodied hand against his body.

We watched in fascinated horror at the process we had started. We had all seen this scenario play out when the infection first appeared, but this was like watching it in a lab, like it was some controlled domino effect. One by one people went down, and one by one people got back up as infected dead and then went in search of new victims.

Tom said, "Check out the view by the boats."

We all looked and saw there were boats pushing away from the docks, and some of the men being left behind were mad enough to shoot at the people in the boats. Needless to say, the people in the boats were shooting back, and since no one was trying to take cover, everyone was getting shot. It wasn't long before the boats and the dock were a horde of infected dead. Newcomers to the dock who were trying to get to a boat were being attacked and bitten as soon as they arrived.

"That's Larson," said Olivia. "He's the crazy boss of those misfits who had me put in a cage."

She pointed at a monitor, and we saw a group of men walking defiantly through the melee shooting people in the head. There were about eight men in the group, but it was easy to tell who was in charge. He was the one in front, but he had enough people flanking him to keep from being bitten. At least that's what he thought.

He was leading his band straight toward the dock as if there would be a boat being readied for him. I knew it was going to be worth watching, especially because he didn't even notice when two of his entourage were taken down from behind.

Larson was wearing an ankle length black coat and had long black hair. He had to be younger than most of the men, but his ruthless look gave him the appearance of a crazy man with a gun. He kept raising his gun and firing even though some of the people he shot didn't appear to have been bitten yet. He was oblivious to the fact that more of his men were dead than alive.

He only had three men with him when he passed through the entrance of the fort and walked onto the dock. Many of the infected dead had walked over the edge and fallen into the water, and several empty boats with their engines idling had drifted out of reach. He stopped, and for the first time he surveyed the scene as if he was really understanding his predicament. He turned toward his bodyguards and was visibly shocked to see how many were there. We watched him stretch to his full height to see over the infected on the dock as if he expected the rest of his bodyguards to show up at any time.

"This is entertainment," said Olivia. She was getting redemption and total satisfaction. "The man's an animal, and he deserves to go out like one."

Larson and his three remaining men put their backs together and began shooting outward, but it was too little and too late. The gunfire was attracting the attention of every infected dead in the fort, and they began swarming the dock. The four men shot the infected that were blocking their way toward the end of the dock and began moving in that direction.

From our camera angle we could see that there were no more boats at the end of the dock, but in the dark it must have looked to them like it was their only means of escape because they hurried to get there. Larson pointed at a boat that was idling about ten feet from the dock, and one of his men dove into the water to retrieve it. Halfway there he was pulled under.

As the last of Larson's men went down, he disappeared under a mass of the infected dead.

"I don't know about the rest of you," I said, "but I'm eating a bullet if that happens to me."

Our group nodded in agreement, but Olivia said, "Since this all started I've heard people say that would be the coward's way out, but in Larson's case, he was too big of a coward to even show himself a little mercy."

Kathy said, "Whatever he did to you, Olivia, it's over now. He can't hurt you anymore."

Kathy started panning the cameras around the fort to see if anyone had managed to survive. We saw plenty of men trying to hide, but that wasn't working out so well for them. They were all found by the infected sooner or later, and then they too were out searching for victims to bite. Some were jumping over the wall into the shallow water close to the fort, but we were only seeing infected dead inside the walls. Night time in the water of Charleston harbor was not a safe place to be even without the infected dead. We doubted we would see any of the men who escaped trying to get back into the fort. Then we saw the other cages.

"Olivia, how many people were in the cages?" asked Kathy.

"I don't know," she said, "but Larson killed most of them just a few hours ago. He just started going around shooting into the cages. I think he killed some in each cage and then let them turn into those monsters so they could attack the others."

Olivia was thoughtful for a moment and then giggled.

"That's kind of what you people just did to him, isn't it? You used the fort like it was one big cage," she said.

I hadn't thought of it like that, but she was right. We did do the same thing he did, but we didn't do it for fun. That at least kept us from feeling like we were the same as him.

Olivia realized what she had said, and she immediately felt bad.

"Oh, no," she said, "I didn't mean it that way. You people did a good thing. That man was a monster, and if you had come along a day later I wouldn't be standing here with you. I can't thank you enough."

She was crying, both from relief and from thinking she had offended us. She didn't know us, and she didn't know if we would think badly of her for comparing us to Larson.

"Olivia," said Kathy, "we know the difference. Larson put them in those cages in the first place. Then he killed them. We didn't put Larson and his men in a cage. They even had a chance of escaping if they had cared enough about each other."

Kathy took Olivia by the hand and said, "Come with me. When was the last time you had a good meal and a bath?" She led her away from the monitors leaving the three of us to watch the rest of the carnage that was taking place above us.

Most of what we were seeing was deep in shadows. There were flood lights around the inside and outside of the fort, but they weren't on, and they could have been broken or they could have been simply switched off. Whatever the reason for the lights being off, the campfires were beginning to burn out, and the fort was growing too dark to see. We agreed that it was time to call it a day, because Plan B was a tremendous success. The Chief would have been proud of us.

7 NIGHT IN THE CITY

The Chief and Allison didn't make it too far before they almost got trapped. The parking garage was an open invitation to get off the streets, but the Chief didn't like the idea of having to go up to get away from the infected when there was bound to be a top floor sooner or later.

It started when they tried to cut across the inside of the parking lot on the first floor. There was a large group of the infected dead that had been unable to find an exit. After bumping into concrete walls and cars for several months, they had done what they tended to do, and that was to stand around waiting for the next thing to draw their attention in a different direction. The sound of Allison landing too hard on the concrete when she climbed the low wall was all they needed.

Allison instinctively tried for higher ground and went up one level before the Chief could stop her. He caught up with her, but the ramp behind him was already full of the infected. The Chief spotted the stairwell in a far corner of the second level. He pulled Allison toward it and whispered to her as they ran that they had to go down and out before they got trapped. They dodged the cars that had been abandoned by their owners when the logjam of cars had become so bad that no one could drive out of the garage.

He said, "Never go high unless you have to or if you have an escape route."

When they reached the stairwell and pulled open the door, they saw they had made another terrible mistake. There were already infected dead on the other side of the door. The Chief put everything he had into pushing the door shut again, which was far more than most men could do, but the weight of the infected had already opened the door too far. He let go of the door, and they fell out in a pile.

This time there was no choice but to go up another level, and there were more infected waiting on the third floor. Realizing they couldn't keep going up until they ran out of places to go, the Chief began checking cars.

"What are you doing, Chief?"

Allison wasn't quite ready to cry, but she sounded like she was ready to panic.

"I'm hoping for anything with the keys and a forty-eight month battery in it." The Chief had opened one car's trunk and snatched up the lug wrench.

"We can't drive out of here, Chief. There are too many cars blocking the way." Allison was definitely getting a frantic edge to her voice as the infected were coming down from above and up from below.

The Chief found a white Charger with the doors shut and the keys in the ignition. It was parked along the outside wall of the garage. He called for Allison to catch up with him, and as soon as she arrived, he broke the window on the driver's side. The car alarm immediately started its ear splitting wail. He shoved the lug wrench through his belt. He was sure it would be the best weapon he would find for a while.

With Allison in tow for a second time in one day, the Chief dragged her away from the Charger toward the center of the garage. He lifted her easily over the railing and practically tossed her down to the second level, then he climbed over and jumped. They hid behind the cars parked along the inner row and watched as a steady parade of the infected walked by on their way to the car alarm.

"We have to move fast because infected outside the garage are going to be drawn to the sound, too," he said.

Allison was beginning to catch on to the plan because she turned and checked the first level that was now behind and below her. She didn't wait for the Chief to toss her over the railing. This time she jumped and moved quickly to hide behind a car. The Chief smiled and followed her.

Being back on the first level, the Chief and Allison were able to hop the low wall as far from the exits as they could get. Even as they moved away from the garage they were stunned speechless by the sheer numbers of the infected dead being summoned by the car alarm on the third floor. What had started out as a death trap turned into a way for them to remove large numbers of the infected from their path, but what frightened them was how easy it was to become cornered.

They still had most of the peninsular city to cross, and that meant countless streets that were unknown to them. All it would take was to go down the wrong alley and they could find themselves trapped with nowhere to go. When they decided to cut across the garage, they would have been safe if they had run for the other side and jumped over the wall on the ground level. Even Allison's mistake didn't seem like the end of the world, but it certainly could have been.

The Chief had to admit to himself that he was a bit more impressed with Allison since the plane crash, and he had even started to like her more because she was at least trying to act like a survivor, but her blunder when she panicked and ran up the ramp made the Chief wonder if she was capable of consistently making the right decisions.

Over the last six months or so, the Chief had seen good decisions and bad. The worst decisions seemed to be made by people he didn't know. Jean's decision to leave the shelter a few months ago had been a bad one. It nearly cost her life when she was captured by the crew of a Russian ship, but not because they were bad people. It was what they became after the infection had spread through their crew.

Even though that was a bad decision, Jean showed she was capable of making sustained good judgement calls, and she survived the ordeal largely on her own. The Chief told himself that he didn't think Allison would have survived the same ordeal, and he wasn't so sure she could survive this one, even with him along to protect her. He decided that the best place for her would be somewhere behind him until they were safe again.

The Chief motioned with a finger to his lips not to speak and then gently guided her into position behind him. She seemed to understand.

The trees along the side of the garage gave them enough cover to make it to the next street, and the infected that were being drawn toward the parking garage were mainly using the paved areas and sidewalks. It wasn't that the infected had the mental powers to stay on the road and then use the entrance of the garage. It was a case of taking the path of least resistance and then banging into things that were in the way until they eventually got around something. The trees surrounding the grassy area next to the parking garage served as a natural barrier that deflected the infected dead back onto the road, and with the exception of a half dozen or so infected that were stuck on a bicycle rack, most of them were past the place where the Chief and Allison had to leave the cover of the trees.

For about the hundredth time the Chief checked the position of the sun. For about the hundredth time the Chief checked the position of the sun. He knew it would worry his good friends, who were hopefully in the Fort Sumter shelter by now, but there was no doubt they would be spending the night in Charleston. He wondered if it would be possible to find a place that still had some supplies or if they should just settle for something that wasn't a death trap.

On his signal, he and Allison made a run for the other side of the street. Other than the infected that were stuck on the bicycle rack, they seemed to go unnoticed, and that group didn't pose any threat. If anything, they were useful because their groaning was distracting some of the infected toward them.

They edged along the wall of a building until they reached an intersection that said they were on East Bay Street. The Chief remembered that East Bay Street was the road that would take them all the way to the Coast Guard base if they took the longer route. It was safer in one way. After reaching White Point Garden, there would be water on one side and buildings on the other. If they got trapped, they could jump over the railing into the water and swim far enough out to be safe. He didn't think Allison would be too happy with getting wet, but the alternative was far less attractive.

The Chief leaned around the corner and studied the next couple of blocks. There was a parking lot on the left and homes on the right. Most of the homes were turned sideways to the street, which was a common form of architecture in the city. He leaned out a bit more to see what kind of building was connected to the parking lot, and he could just make out a few shopping carts mixed in with the cars that had been randomly abandoned at the store. Shopping carts meant supplies if the building hadn't already been looted. Judging by the number of infected that had swarmed the parking garage after the car alarm began blaring, not many people made it out of this area, and not many people would have chosen to come here for supplies. The Chief certainly wouldn't have chosen this place.

"Allison, there's some kind of store about a block from here. Judging by the number of shopping carts it might be a grocery store. If we have to fight our way out of trouble, don't let yourself get cornered. Try to stay on the ground if you have to run, and try to stay in the area by circling back on this spot. Got it?"

"Yeah, I got it, Chief," she said. "What if I see a chance to get inside the building?"

"That's what I'm hoping for, Allison. If you see a way in, let me know so we can go in together. There's likely to be something bad roaming around in there that hasn't been able to find its own way out, so we're going to help it find another way out."

Strangely enough, Allison's question gave the Chief an idea.

"Allison, you're a genius," he said.

"Seriously, Chief?" She couldn't believe he had chosen the wrong time to be kidding around about her abilities.

"Seriously," he answered. "We need to get around behind the store. I can't think of many stores that have their loading bays at ground level. If we can get into the storage areas, we can find a way to attract the attention of the infected out the back door. They'll eventually fall off of the loading dock, and they won't be able to get back in."

"That was my idea, Chief?" asked Allison.

He smiled at her and said, "Not directly, but your question about getting inside the building made me think we aren't likely to be able to walk right in the front door, and if you had seen this area when the whole world went to hell, you would know that there wasn't time to loot for food, water, and batteries. The infection spread through here like wildfire."

"Do you think they had a chance to lock the doors?" she asked.

"There's a possibility of that, but if the store was really modern, the doors could have also been automatic. Once power failed, they would shut, and I don't know if the infected would have had a reason to push them open, but I know they aren't smart enough to pull them open. Let's circle around behind the store and see if we can get in through the loading dock."

They stayed close to the wall and went to the end of the street. Not far away the horn continued to call to all of the infected dead in the streets. Hopefully, they would all find their way up to the third level of the parking garage before the battery finally died.

When they circled the block of buildings and were able to see the back of the building, they also saw that large numbers of people had tried to escape using the street behind the grocery store. It really wasn't a street, and with the exception of the place where trucks could back up to the loading dock, it was only one lane. Most of that lane was filled with cars, dumpsters, and human remains.

There were no infected wandering around behind the building, and what few may have been in the front parking lot were being drawn down the street to the parking garage.

"Allison, if not for the plane crash, I'd say you have some unbelievably good luck. Even running up the ramp inside the garage turned into a good thing."

"I planned that all along," she answered.

The Chief gave her a sideways glance to see if she was serious and caught just a hint of her grin.

"Let's go," he said, "and here's the plan. If we can go in the back door, we have to make sure the front doors are closed tight, and then we have to get all of the infected to walk out the back door. The main problem is getting trapped inside somewhere between the front and back doors with infected blocking our exit."

Allison thought it over and said, "Chief, I was in line at a Walmart once. You know, one of those times when it's really packed but they only have two registers open. I was about twelve carts from the front when they announced something was on sale at the back of the store. I wouldn't have given up my place in line if it had been free, but almost everyone in front of me took off."

"What are you talking about, Allison? Not that I would seriously think you're suggesting a sale announcement would get them all out, but I don't see what you're saying."

"I'm just saying, Chief, that no matter how good the sale is, you're not going to get all of them to come out the back door. Some are going to stay right where they are, or they're going to go in a completely different direction."

The Chief understood what Allison meant. It was likely that they would have to flush out as many as they could, but then they would still have to dispose of some inside the building.

They reached the loading dock and found the steps that led up onto the platform. On the opposite end was a ramp that was used to drive a forklift up onto the loading dock. The concrete loading dock itself was close to six feet from the payment below.

The Chief studied the layout and said, "I think they had to have a higher loading dock than normal because of the possibility of flooding. We're only a block from the river, and a surge through here would wipe out a lot of inventory. They must've used the forklift to unload trucks and then drive up the ramp."

Even though they would have to find a way to block the ramp and the stairs, they were happy with the height of the loading dock. Anything that went over the edge wasn't going to make it back up onto the same level as them. Because the horn in the garage had worked so well, they also had the time to get the stairs and ramp blocked without having to deal with infected dead coming at them from those two directions.

The Chief went over to the large door of the loading dock and checked to see if it was locked. When it wouldn't move he resigned himself to the fact that he would have to go inside to unlock it. He checked the solid metal door to the right of the big door, and the handle moved easily to the open position. Since he couldn't see inside the door, he put his ear against the cool metal and listened...not a sound.

Allison had been standing off at a distance watching how carefully the Chief was doing everything, and she didn't see they had company. Three of the infected walked up the forklift ramp without a sound and were practically on her before the Chief even turned in her direction. All she saw was his reaction and the way he bolted at her, and for just a moment she thought he was attacking her.

That was probably what saved her life. The Chief was big when he was standing still. He appeared to be even bigger when he was charging at you like a bull. Allison turned and started to run from him all in one motion, and she collided with the three infected dead that were right behind her. The first one was already reaching for her, so Allison got a face full of stinking, rotting hands as her momentum carried her directly into them.

The infected dead could still reach, grab, and bite, but they couldn't react quickly, especially those that had been decaying for a long time. Those that had died at the beginning were even likely to pull apart like an over cooked roast. Allison's sudden reaction knocked them backward and over the edge of the loading dock, and the Chief grabbed Allison just in time to keep her from going over with them. He pulled her back from the edge and held her in a big bear hug as she shook uncontrollably for what seemed like an hour.

When the Chief finally knew he could let her go, he held her out at arms length and checked her face.

"Were you bitten or scratched?" he asked.

She shook her head and he saw that the tears were pouring down her cheeks.

"Are you sure?"

She nodded but said, "One of them stuck its finger in my mouth, and I think I'm going to be sick."

Allison turned and went to her knees and started retching so hard the Chief thought she would tear a muscle in her abdomen. Breakfast had been a long time ago, so it was mostly dry heaving, but the taste had to be awful. The Chief knew he had to get inside the building and find her something to kill the taste, and probably even some hydrogen peroxide to rinse the germs out of her mouth.

The Chief checked along both ends of the building and saw there were no more infected coming their way, so he helped Allison to her feet and half carried her across the loading dock to the farthest corner. If any came along while he was inside, they weren't likely to see her where she was sitting.

"Allison, you need to stay really quiet until I get back. The forklift is most likely inside the door, so I'm going to go find out. I'll get you some mouthwash and see if I can find a way to deal with whatever's inside the building. If you have to get away from anything while I'm gone, come inside and find me. Do you understand?"

Allison nodded that she understood, so the Chief went back to the door and eased it open. It was pitch black inside, but there were no sounds of movement so he slipped inside and closed the door shut behind him.

The smell inside was awful, but without power and a few months to rot, there was plenty inside the store that could smell bad. Even worse, it was an unimaginable cocktail of odors from many different sources. Standing in the darkness the Chief thought it over and came to the conclusion that the front doors must be shut, and the windows must be intact, or the place would have had time for the odors to dissipate.

The Chief waited for his eyes to adjust to the darkness before moving from his place by the door. He was happy when he saw there were two forklifts instead of one. That meant he could block the stairs and the ramp, and if the front doors were really secure, they would at least have a safe place to spend the night.

The double doors that led from the storerooms to the main floor of the grocery store were directly in front of him. Each door had a circular glass window in it, and there was enough light coming from the store for him to see if it was safe. As he stepped closer he saw a sign that reminded all Harris Teeter employees to wash their hands before returning to work.

He thought to himself, "That won't be a problem anymore."

From his vantage point, he could see down two aisles, and he thought it could be worse. Shelves were in disarray, and the floors were covered with boxes and cans, but it was obvious that no survivors had been able to resupply from this store. The littered aisles were evidence that there had been struggles, probably when the infection started, and there had been or still were infected dead blundering around inside the store.

A crashing sound somewhere far off in the store confirmed the theory that something, whether living or dead, was in the store. The only question was how many. The Chief slipped the lug wrench from his belt and moved without a sound through the doors. It was like stepping back into daylight because there were skylights as well as windows. Something was moving on an aisle to the left. He could tell because it kept bumping into items that had been knocked from the shelves.

From the sounds he could tell the infected was moving toward the back of the store, and it was nearing the end of the aisle. His best choice was to wait for it to come around the corner where it would either turn away from him or toward him. Because he would have a longer reach with the lug wrench, he raised it above his head and waited.

He heard the slow, shuffling sound of the infected only a few feet away. It was still moving, but it didn't appear at his corner. A quick look around the corner revealed the infected had made a right turn and was heading for the next aisle. The Chief took one long step to close the gap and brought the lug wrench down on the back of the infected dead's skull.

Even as it went down, the Chief realized he had just stepped into clear view down the next aisle without checking to see if it was clear first. A glance to his right showed an empty aisle, but the fine hairs on the back of his neck had already caused a shiver to race across his scalp and down his back. He had seen too many infected dead bite outstretched arms, and his were extended as far as they could be. He made a mental note that he must be getting tired if he was going to make that mistake, and he made himself a promise that it would be the last time. It had been a long day.

The Chief stepped into the aisle so he wouldn't be so exposed and began listening again. There were sounds coming from several locations now. Maybe the sound of the infected hitting the floor was louder than he had thought. He tilted his head to one side and tried to focus on the most distinct sounds, hoping they were also the closest. He also saw that the shelves that were lit by the light from skylights were now a bit more in the shadows. That meant the sun was going to go down before he could clear the entire store unless he got moving. He needed to take the hunt to the infected instead of waiting for them to come to him.

With that decided, the Chief also decided it was more likely to find the infected spread out rather than in a group. A smile crossed his face as he thought to himself there was no rational reason to believe such a thing, and maybe it was just what he hoped. There was also his gut, and he trusted his gut feelings to keep him alive better than almost anything else. His gut was telling him to get on with it, and it was telling him to get back to Allison before it was too late.

The Chief went back to the corner where he had dropped the first infected. He turned his head both ways and saw he was only on aisle three. It seemed logical to him to clear aisles one and two before the rest of the store, so he marched with resolve to his left onto aisle two. There was one infected walking slowly away from him and one on the floor. It was dragging useless legs behind it. The upright infected was closer, and the Chief unceremoniously did the same thing to it as he had the first one. He didn't wait for the one on the floor to start groaning, which would draw other infected toward him in the store. He stepped on its back in the middle of its shoulder blades and brought down the full weight of the lug wrench as it tried to turn under his foot.

Without waiting, the Chief stepped into full view at the end of the aisle. A glance to his right showed he was clear that way, and a longer inspection down the front of the store revealed at least three more infected dead. One was walking along the front aisle just as one was turning out of view on row eight. The third was a former employee of the store who was stuck behind the enclosed area where cigarettes were sold. That was more evidence that this store hadn't seen any living people in a long time, because the cigarette counter would have been looted by now.

Figuring it would be safe enough to clear aisle one before going after the three infected dead he saw, the Chief spotted what he needed for Allison. There was a pharmacy along the back wall of the aisle, and it had a cage pulled across its entire length. That didn't matter because the Chief saw bottles of Scope arranged haphazardly on a shelf, and not far away was hydrogen peroxide. He grabbed one bottle of each and went through the back door without being spotted by the infected that were deeper inside the store.

He found Allison curled up in a ball right where he had left her, but she was lying on her side and holding her stomach.

When she realized he was there she said, "It hurts bad, Chief."

The Chief sat her upright and uncapped both bottles. This was something new to him, so he didn't think to get anything for stomach cramps. He wasn't even sure what would work for her. He had her take a mouthful of peroxide first, and he made sure she understood to hold it in her mouth for as long as she could and then spit it out. He had her repeat the process until the bottle was empty, then he switched to the Scope.

"Let's see if we can't do something about that nasty taste," he said.

Between rinses she managed to gasp out that it was helping, but her stomach still hurt. She told him to get something called Phenergan. She said it was also called Promethazine, and every mother knew it would help with nausea. As she finished saying it, she accented the point by doubling over and dry heaving again.

The Chief got her to rinse a couple more times before going back in. He considered taking her inside and leaving her by the fork lifts, but then he remembered the smell. He seriously doubted she could get over her stomach pains in there, and the air outside was still cool enough to help.

"I'll be back as soon as I can," he whispered.

This time the Chief moved with more purpose because it didn't appear that the store was overrun with the infected. When he went through the doors into the store he went straight to aisle four. Since it was clear he checked five then six. He saw the infected he had spotted walking away from him along the front aisle, and it saw him. The groan it made seemed louder than any the Chief had heard, and it was going to draw plenty of attention.

The Chief didn't charge at the infected because there was more concern for slipping on the messy floor than there was for being cornered. He just walked straight at it, and as it raised both arms to reach for him, he knocked its arms to one side using the lug wrench and then immediately brought his hand back the other way, delivering a blow to the side of its head. It was like a tennis forehand and backhand at high speed.

Even before the infected crashed to the floor, the Chief met the next infected as he turned the corner to aisle seven. It was a repeat performance on that aisle, but he had to be more careful with aisle eight. There were three infected coming his way, and they had somehow managed to get into a tight group.

If there was a lot of room to move, the Chief preferred that they would be more spread out, but if it was in a close area such as a grocery aisle, he preferred to get them into a group just like this. The one on the Chief's right was leading the pack, so the Chief used the lug wrench to knock its arms to the left, but this time instead of following with the backhand swing, he stepped in closer and used his hands to spin the infected around to face its two friends. The Chief gave it a shove, and the infected flew into the outstretched arms of the other two. All three went down in a heap, and the Chief stepped over them to deliver three fast blows to their heads.

In only a matter of minutes the Chief had cleared every aisle and found himself standing in the wide produce department. It didn't resemble any produce department he had ever seen before because the long ago displays of fruit and vegetables had gone through their stages of complete decay. There were no more infected, so he went up to the front of the store and down to the cigarette counter.

Despite feeling little emotion over the many infected dead he had put to final rest, this one he felt sorry for. Because the former employee was wearing a store jacket with the company logo on it, he knew she had simply shown up for work on a day when she might have lived if she had just stayed home. From what he had seen, though, staying home hadn't done people much good either. He just couldn't help wondering if she would have been a different story.

She leaned as far over the counter toward him as she could, and he put an end to her imprisonment. Then the Chief stood still and just listened to the silence. Out of the corner of his eye he saw motion in the parking lot out front. He couldn't hear the car alarm in the garage from this far away, but if it was still doing its job, the infected passing by outside would keep going. He didn't think they could see him inside, but to be safe he decided to use the aisle that ran along the back of the store to get to the pharmacy.

It didn't take a minute to get there, and he studied the cage that ran the length of the counter. It made the pharmacy the safest place to spend the night once he was sure he had blocked off the access to the loading dock. He went around to the door that went directly into the pharmacy and found it wasn't as secure as the cage. He only had to use the end of the lug wrench to pry open the lock.

It took a few minutes to find Promethazine, but the Chief didn't waste any time getting back to Allison. She was on her side again, so he had to sit her up again and help her take the pill.

"One or two?" he asked.

She grimaced at him like he was out of his mind.

"Do me a favor, Chief. If you ever have to give Molly some medicine, let someone else do it. One will do just fine, but hang onto the bottle."

After a few sips of water, she said she felt well enough to go inside and asked him to help her up, but he said he had one more thing for her. He slipped a hospital style mask onto her face and stretched the band over her head.

"This won't block out the smell completely, but it will help you get used to it."

"Thanks, Chief. There's hope for you yet," she said.

He couldn't help but laugh, but there was still work to do, so he took her into the store and led her straight to the pharmacy. He got her comfortable with a box of saltine crackers that had probably gone stale and then tied the door shut with bungee cords he found in the hardware aisle. He wouldn't be gone long, but he had to be sure he hadn't missed anything.

The Chief also found some flashlights and candles because the sun was about to set. For what had to be the hundredth time he thought about his friends at Fort Sumter. They had to be worried by now, and if they saw the plane go down, they must have thought he died in the crash. They had no way of knowing that his last second maneuver was something he had seen done by other pilots, and they all walked away from the crash.

The loading bay doors were electric powered, but all overhead doors had the capability of being opened manually. Especially if the person opening them was strong enough to lift them by himself. He used a flashlight to find the release that would separate the door from the electric motor, then he pulled the cable that raised the door until it was high enough to allow the forklift to pass through. There was a battery cart with the forklifts, and it could jump start them if their batteries were dead, but luck was on his side. The first forklift started easily, and he drove it out onto the loading dock and across to the ramp. The ramp was wider than the forklift, so he wedged it across the ramp at an angle.

The second forklift needed a jump start, but it didn't take more than two or three minutes to get it done. Then he drove it over to the steps on the other side and easily parked it so nothing could get by. Knowing that nothing could get in was half of the goal. The other half was knowing they could get out without a problem.

With their safety greatly improved, the Chief got a small shopping basket and went through the store selecting a few canned goods that were likely to still be good. When he returned to the pharmacy and secured the door, he found Allison sound asleep where he had left her. He got comfortable next to her and helped himself to a cold but satisfying meal.

******

Rain started to fall on the dark city of Charleston, and the sound was enough to wake the Chief from a light sleep. At first he thought it was someone tapping on the glass doors at the front of the store. He raised himself just enough to see over the counter, and he could see that it was completely dark outside. He listened for the sound and zeroed in on the skylights up above. He couldn't see it, but he imagined the water running down the glass in little streams. It did sound like tapping when he thought about it.

Allison was still sound asleep, so he took a flashlight and went to find something else he needed. He had something specific in mind and wasn't sure why he hadn't thought of it sooner. He didn't need his flashlight until he was out on the main floor, and he didn't want to mess up his night vision, so he found his way to the aisle that had party supplies for things like birthdays. He found what he was searching for and tore open a bag of balloons. He dumped them on a shelf and sorted through them until he was sure he found the red one. It was hard to tell colors in the dark. He stretched it over the end of his flashlight, and keeping his body between it and the front of the store, he clicked it on. He was satisfied with the results as the flashlight gave him enough light without advertising his position.

The Chief went into the loading bay and opened the back door. The loading dock was still empty, but he could see a few of the infected stumbling aimlessly through the tangle of cars. The horn in the parking garage had long since gone silent, so they didn't have anything to attract their attention. He backed into the dark loading bay and locked the door.

With the forklifts outside, the Chief had a better view of the entire storage area. At the far end in a corner he saw what he was hoping to find. A ladder went up the wall to a metal door set in the ceiling. It could only be the maintenance access to the roof. When he stood directly beneath it he could see there was a padlock on it. He had expected the padlock to be there, and doubted he would find the keys, but he really wanted to get up on the roof to see if he could survey the area. He needed to be able to tell if they had a chance of reaching the other side of the city.

He was just about to go back into the main part of the store to search for the office area when it occurred to him to check the lock first. He grabbed the ladder and climbed upward.

When he reached the top, his suspicions were confirmed. In a modern age of security cameras and magnetic locking devices, there were still people who just plain trusted their employees instead of spending a few dollars to keep the employees honest. For whatever reason, the person in charge of locking this door had simply slipped the lock through the ring but didn't close the hasp over it first. Maybe it was his way of coming back into the store at night, or maybe it was his way of hiding during his shift. It didn't matter because it was the Chief's best way to see what was happening in the streets.

The Chief pulled himself up onto the roof and found he had more than adequate cover to hide behind. The facade of the building, in keeping with local architecture, had a waist high wall around the roof of the building to keep the power and cooling units hidden from view. It was easy to navigate around the roof of the building until he was satisfied with their route. He was still content with staying on a course parallel to East Bay Street, but he wondered if it was possible to try for a boat at the dock used by the harbor pilots. If he could get a boat there, he would still circle the Battery and go to the Coast Guard base because they needed weapons. If they were confronted by the men who had come after them when the plane crashed, he couldn't expect to beat them with a lug wrench and a knife.

Without binoculars the Chief couldn't tell for sure if the harbor pilots had left any boats at their dock. For now he just had to be content with watching the streets to gauge the amount of infected in the area. Fort Sumter was just a dark spot on the water in the distance, and he couldn't tell from his rooftop if there was even any activity there.

At least he was sure his friends were safe. When he thought about it, he felt like they were safer than the inhabitants of the surface part of the fort. Not only did they have the infected dead to contend with, they had a hidden enemy beneath them. The Chief thought to himself that he wouldn't be surprised to find they had already figured out a way to take the fort away from its current occupants.

When the Chief got back to Allison, he found her sitting up and eating a can of Vienna sausages. Thanks to the Chief remembering to get a can opener from the kitchen utensils aisle, she was also working on a can of beans. He handed her a warm bottle of beer, and she gratefully accepted.

"The worst part about Promethazine is waking up hungry. I'm glad you left me a picnic basket, or I would've been stumbling around out there in the canned foods section," she said.

"If you're going to eat that whole can of beans, I'm sleeping out there," said the Chief. "Are you feeling better?"

She giggled at his comment about the beans, but then she got stone cold serious.

"I was really sick, Chief. What does that tell us about getting any part of them in our mouths?"

"I wasn't planning on cannibalizing them if that's what you mean," said the Chief.

Allison visibly shivered at the thought.

She said, "I was thinking more along the lines of what happened to me, Chief. Or what if one of us gets some bodily fluid in our eyes? We know what that scratch did to Jean, but I just got a finger in my mouth, and yuck! That was enough to make me throw up for hours."

"Well, now that we know, we just have to be careful. Maybe we can find you a motorcycle helmet or something."

Allison sort of brushed off the idea and asked, "Where did you go for so long?"

"I was up on the roof planning our next move. I don't think we can make it all the way to the Coast Guard base on foot. The harbor pilots dock is closer, and if there aren't any boats there, we might be able to get one at the Carolina Yacht Club."

They both froze at the sound of tapping on the glass. At first the Chief wondered if it wasn't the sound of rain again, but this was louder and came in sequences of threes. Tap, tap, tap…pause. Tap, tap, tap.

"Stay down," whispered the Chief.

He raised his head only as high as he needed to and pulled it back down just in time as a bright beam of light passed over the pharmacy. He had seen enough to know there were two dummies outside the main windows at the front door. One was tapping on the glass with the barrel of a rifle to see if it would draw any infected dead into the open, and the other was using a big flashlight to scan the interior of the store. The Chief didn't doubt that they had been the people who had come from Fort Sumter on the boats, but he was amazed they were this dumb.

The tapping changed from a sequence to a hard bang. The Chief raised his head again and saw the one who had been tapping the glass was drawing back his rifle and hitting the glass in the same spot. The other idiot was helping his friend by shining his light where the rifle was hitting. Both of them were so intent on what they were doing that they weren't paying a bit of attention to the shadows moving behind them in the parking lot.

The Chief said, "These guys are either on drugs or they haven't been on the mainland for a long time. Get ready to move with me."

They kept low and followed the counter to the pharmacy door. The Chief untied the bungee cords and slowly opened the door. The Chief could see the men clearly from where he and Allison were crouched, and if the one with the flashlight aimed his beam in their direction, they would be like deer stuck in headlights of a car.

The glass started to crack along a curved line, and the sound took on a higher pitch. The Chief knew it would all collapse in a noisy pile at any moment, and he didn't want to be stuck inside when it did. He grabbed Allison by the hand and together they ran practically right in front of the two men.

The one with the flashlight was so startled he aimed it at the pair as they ran across the store. The second guy didn't know if he should aim the barrel of the rifle at them or keep hitting the window. What he wound up doing was something in between as he swung the rifle around and hit the window with the metal barrel. The glass rained down with as much noise as the Chief expected, but by that time they were going through the back doors into the loading bay.

The falling glass made the two men instinctively jump back from the window, and the man with the rifle found himself being embraced by an infected dead. He only had a split second to get out one word before the teeth bit into the back of his neck. The one word turned to a scream.

More infected were crowding into the area between the cars and the window, but somehow the other man dodged them and reached the corner of the building. With his flashlight still on, he ran as fast as he could for the back road behind the grocery store and then straight for the parking lot of a restaurant that featured dining along the river. As he crossed the road, Allison and the Chief were climbing through the driver seat of the forklift to go down the steps. The idiot with the flashlight ran right past them without slowing down.

The Chief said, "He's going for a boat."

He didn't need to tell her what to do, and they both started running behind the man.

At one point the man turned to see what was behind him, and he must have thought the infected could run. He saw the Chief and screamed for help just as the Chief hit him with his best diving tackle. Allison ran past them and retrieved the flashlight. She turned it off just as the Chief managed to get the much smaller man beneath him to stop squirming. The Chief also had a big hand firmly clamped over the man's mouth.

"Shut up," the Chief said in a low, menacing voice.

The Chief could have sworn the man was relieved as he went completely limp.

He said, "I'm going to take my hand off of your mouth, and you're going to tell me where you left your boat. If you say anything else, I'll snap your neck and leave you here. Do you understand?"

The man could hardly move his head under the weight of the Chief's hand, but he moved it enough to indicate he understood. The Chief lifted his hand, and the man took in a deep breath of air.

"The restaurant," he said. "The boat is tied up at the restaurant. There's a dock on the other side."

The Chief faced in the direction of the restaurant, and it was clear of the infected at the moment. He stood up and pulled the man with him. The size difference between the two of them was so incredible that it could have been a man shaking a rag doll. He put the man's feet on the ground and told him to lead the way but stay quiet. The man nodded, his eyes big and round as he marveled at the size of the Chief.

It didn't take long for the three of them to cross the parking lot to the restaurant. There were a few cars in the lot, but the restaurant must not have been open when everything began to go haywire. They were only about a hundred yards from the cruise ship terminal, and the Chief remembered that this area had been a mass of people. Some were screaming as they ran from their attackers. Most ran from one attacker straight into the arms of another. The people who had been in the parking lot of this restaurant were the same people that Kathy was forced to abandon when she organized a blockade of the pier that led to the cruise ship terminal.

The man leading the way reached for the door to the restaurant, but the Chief stopped him.

"Do we have to go inside the restaurant to reach the dock? We can't go around?" he asked.

The man halfheartedly pointed at the door and said, "It's the only way."

"Did you clear it first?" asked the Chief.

The man stared at him as if he didn't understand for several moments then said, "Sure. Sure we did. There's nothin' inside."

The Chief didn't have much faith in the man's ability to clear a room, let alone an entire building, but he didn't have much choice at the moment. He reached back and gave Allison a reassuring squeeze on her arm then motioned for the man to open the door.

It was almost pitch black when they stepped inside. Like most restaurants there was a small area up front where patrons could wait for their table, and off to the right was the totally dark entrance to the bar. The Chief took the flashlight from Allison and shone the beam into the ink black rooms. There were barstools on their sides on the floor, and that meant there had been infected inside the building at some point in time, or that people had rushed around in a panic. When he pointed the flashlight to the left, he saw the main dining area, and it extended all the way to a long wall of windows facing the river.

"The kitchen must be somewhere behind the bar," he said in a low voice.

But it wasn't low enough because the groans started as soon as he spoke, and they were coming from somewhere on their right in the totally dark bar.

Allison was the closest one to the safety of the boat, and the Chief pushed her in that direction. He was next, and he followed closely on her heels. The little man had stepped too close to the dark door to the bar, and something was pulling him inside by his shirt sleeve. He was pulling back as hard as he could but kept sliding toward the darkness. When he screamed the Chief stopped for just a moment, but it was too dark to see what happened. The scream went higher and then just stopped at its peak.

They found themselves on a veranda with tables lined up along a rail. Each table still had a folded umbrella sticking up from the middle as if waiting for the next group of customers to be seated. At the center of the railing was an opening that led to a narrow ramp. It dropped down to a floating dock, and tied to the dock was a fairly decent boat with twin outboard engines. The Chief had a fleeting thought that it was too much boat for the two idiots who had left it there, but with sturdy sea-legs used to the motion of the water, he bounced down the ramp into the boat with a practiced ease.

The ramp was steep, and Allison had a hard time keeping her balance as she followed the Chief. The floating dock at the bottom caused the ramp to rise and fall with swells coming in from the river, and each of her steps was measured as she tried to guess which way it was going to move. The Chief started back across the dock to help her but was only in time to see a hand reach out from under the ramp and pull her by the ankle hard enough to make her fall head first down the ramp.

Allison started to get up on her own, at first just a little dazed and with a scrape on her right cheek, but the pain was written on her face and the scream that erupted from deep in her soul was unmistakable. The infected that had tripped her was biting into the soft flesh of her calf. It would hurt even if it didn't break through the thick denim she was wearing, but the sound of her screaming made him expect the worst.

The Chief shoved his knife through the side of the head that was buried against Allison's leg, and even though it was instantly destroyed, the jaws were still clamped firmly in place. The Chief pulled his knife free and immediately used it to pry the teeth apart. Allison had stopped screaming and was biting down hard on the heavy material of her own sleeve.

When the head dropped away from her leg, the body of the infected rolled out from under the ramp. The Chief knew he had passed right over it, and he had moved much more quickly than Allison. It would have been him face down on the dock if he had not been so sure footed. The infected had probably even reached for him first.

The Chief grabbed Allison's leg and saw the big red patch of blood that had already soaked into the material. Allison didn't even lift her head to see how bad it was. She just kept biting down and softly crying.

They both knew what it meant, and as ready as the Chief had been many times to feel the teeth piercing into his own skin, he wasn't ready to see it happen to someone else... even someone who had been such a spiteful thorn in his side less than a day ago. He started to say something, but he wasn't able to make the words come out of his mouth.

Allison said, "You have to leave me, Chief. You know what's going to happen." She managed to get the words out through gasps of pain and crying.

"How could I face Tom?" he asked. "At least let me get you back to him before the end."

Allison finally moved from flat on her stomach to face the Chief. She stared down at her leg like it had to be a mistake. Like it had to belong to someone else. She shook her head.

"We've talked about this, Chief. You know what I'm going to become. You have to take care of this for me. You can't leave me here alive, and you can't take me back with you. Tom will understand."

"And how will I face Molly? How will I be able to look at her and not think about it?"

The Chief wasn't able to cry, but he felt a powerful rage building up inside of him. He wanted to kill every infected dead on the planet. In his mind he was saying to them all, "Bring it on."

His rage made him begin to move. He still felt helpless because there was nothing he could do to save Allison, but he had to do something, even if it was the very thing they had all talked about. If someone gets bitten, loved ones would try to keep them alive for as long as possible. The desire to keep a loved one alive could be stronger than self-preservation.

The Chief scooped Allison up from the dock and stepped easily over the side rails into the boat. Allison was protesting the entire time, insisting that the Chief should do the right thing.

"Chief, please. You have to do it. If you take me back I'll be dangerous to all of you, and I don't want to cause any of you to die."

The Chief put Allison on a comfortable bench seat that wrapped around the stern and then cast off the lines. He started the powerful twin outboards and pulled away from the dock in a hard turn. He hoped his friends had taken care of business on Fort Sumter because he was going to drive right up to the front door and ring the bell.

The water churned behind the boat as the Chief opened the engines up as far as they would go. It crossed his mind that Allison had stopped arguing. He was glad because he was afraid he would have to tie her up to get her back to Fort Sumter. He looked over his shoulder and saw that she had passed out and was lying peacefully on the seats.

As many times as he had heard Jean say it, he couldn't bring himself to just leave Allison, and he couldn't kill her. Jean had said to the Chief a long time ago that she would end it herself rather than to become one of them.

He remembered how close she had come to being bitten when they had been disposing of a bite victim on the cruise ship. The best thing they could think of to get rid of the people who died was to drop them overboard from a floating dock. As they were about to push a body over the side, it had reached out and grabbed Jean, tearing her sleeve but missing with a bite. Jean told us then that she would have jumped in with the infected dead before she would have gone through the agony of dying and then coming back like that.

He knew Allison felt the same way as Jean, but he was trying to tell himself there had to be another way. There had to be something they had never thought of to save someone after they were bitten.

Away from the shore and in near total darkness, the Chief focused his eyes on the channel while his back was to Allison. In the past there had been harbor lights and the lights from the city itself to guide a boat across the black water. The Yorktown and Patriots Point would be bathing the river with light from the other side, and a boat ran little risk of straying into shallow water.

The Chief had gone so far into his thoughts and the feeling of total desperation that he almost forgot he wasn't alone. The hairs on the back of his neck stood up with the sick realization that Allison was right behind him, and he spun around to defend himself. The move almost made him lose his balance, and the boat turned into its own wake, but Allison was on the bench seat where he had left her. He had become spooked by his own imagination.

Being tired was nothing new to the Chief. He had made a career of pushing himself beyond the limits of normal people, and then he would push himself even harder. But this was different. For the first time he felt mentally and physically like he couldn't take more from the world. He had failed a member of his own group, and he wasn't used to failing.

With his shoulders slightly lower, he turned back to the wheel and brought the boat back on course. He couldn't remember ever being wrong when his senses told him danger was near. He was sure he was going to find Allison dead but coming for him with her teeth bared.

It was while he was readjusting both his course as well as his state of mind that Allison rose on the seat, studied the Chief standing at the wheel, and then pushed herself to a standing position. She had lost a tremendous amount of blood, and her skin was so pale she seemed to give off light in the stern of the boat.

The shell that had been Allison was unsteady with the damaged leg, and a slight course correction and a bump from a small wave was just enough to cause her to fall toward the rail. Uncoordinated hands clutched at a damp metal railing, and Allison was gone. If the Chief or anyone else had been watching, they wouldn't have been entirely sure if it had been a living person or an infected dead that had gone over the side. Even the fact that there was no scream for help was not a clue. Allison wanted to jump from the moving boat and had been waiting for the opportunity as she slipped closer to unconsciousness. She was only vaguely aware that he had turned toward her for a moment, acting as if she was already standing. It was at that moment that the lights had gone out behind her eyes.

8 RESURRECTION

While Kathy was taking care of Olivia's needs, Tom and Bus decided to try to get some rest. I took the first watch on the monitors and played with the different camera angles. The campfires were all but burned out, but they were still too bright for me to think about switching to night vision. I also explored the other switches and controls until I found the power for the floodlights. I thought about turning them on, but then decided against it. In the absence of the Chief, I wasn't able to decide if it was a good idea or not.

Part of me was saying to leave the lights off in case more of the people from the surface came back. They would see the infected dead and either reclaim control of the fort or they would leave. Another part of me was saying to turn the lights on in case the Chief was alive. If he could see the fort and the walls blazing with light, he would know we had taken control. Of course there was another possibility. The light would be easily seen by anyone else who might be watching the harbor.

In the end it was my curiosity that made me hit the switch, and I couldn't have been less prepared for what I saw. There were dozens of infected dead that had given up trying to find more flesh to bite, but when the lights came on, every living being in the fort was immediately exposed.

Some ran for the walls and jumped into the water, but most were cornered.

Not far from the cage where we had found Olivia, there was another cage, and the infected dead were gathered around it, reaching through the bars. I couldn't see much of what was happening, but I caught a glimpse of a man in the center of the cage, and he was trying to stay out of the reach of the dead. The cage would keep the dead from getting in, but the man didn't have an inch to spare in any direction.

I scanned the control panel where I had found the light switch and found the right button. It was an intercom and it would let me call for the others to come back to the control room. I found the microphone and keyed the switch.

"Kathy, Tom, Bus...if you can hear me, please come back to the control room."

The scene around the cage turned into chaos. The intercom was on the surface as well as inside, and the infected dead went into a frenzy like I hadn't seen since the first day when they had attacked so violently. Some attacked the cage even harder while others broke away from the crowd and tried to find the source of the voice.

Kathy was the first to arrive. Olivia wasn't with her, and Kathy answered my question before I could ask.

"Olivia was wiped out. A hot bath and a little bit of warm food was enough to put her to sleep. I doubt that we'll see her again tonight. What's up?"

I gestured at the monitors, and Kathy leaned in closer.

"Let me guess. The intercom system also broadcasts to the surface. You really got them shook up."

"Not only that," I said. "Check this out." I pointed at the man in the cage. "Any chance we could help him out?"

"Oh, wow," said Kathy.

Tom and Bus came in and saw all the bright lights and the commotion around the cage. They moved in closer, but no one said anything. It wasn't that we didn't feel a sense of urgency. We simply didn't know how we could help the man.

Bus asked, "Could we go up through the tunnels and then get to a safe spot where we can pick them off one at a time?"

"That would be my best idea," said Kathy, "but none of us has a clue where a safe spot would be. There are so many of the infected up there that we wouldn't be any better off than those other people were. We can't just run around until we find a safe spot."

"I have an idea," I said. "Watch this."

I keyed the intercom switch and then tapped three times on the microphone. Almost every infected dead turned in the same direction. I keyed the switch and tapped again, and the rest of them turned toward the sound. Some began to move toward the right side of the screen.

Kathy said, "You're a genius, Eddie. I'm going to go get Olivia. We can have her talk into the intercom while the rest of us go out through the tunnel. That cage is close to the exit down by the docks. I think we can get up on top of the walls where the infected won't be able to reach us. After we've cleared enough of them, we can get that guy out of the cage."

"That reminds me," I said. "Did you check Olivia for bites?"

"She understood completely," said Kathy. "I talked with her while she ate, and when we went to get her cleaned up, she insisted that I check her. She said she didn't want you guys doing it." Kathy smirked just enough to make us all a bit uncomfortable.

"Let's get going," said Tom. "I'd rather do this in the daylight, but I can't stand the thought of that poor guy out there."

Kathy went to get Olivia while the rest of us got our weapons ready. We didn't have a large amount of firepower, mostly just surplus M-16's. We all preferred them over the more powerful rifles because the ammunition was so small. We were able to bring more with us on this trip, and it would be easier to take more up the ladders to the exit.

When Kathy got back with Olivia, dressed in navy blue coveralls just like ours, she showed her what we had seen on the monitor. Olivia was sleepy but woke up fast when she saw the brightly lit fort and all of the infected dead walking around. She woke up even more when she saw the man in the cage. With fewer of the infected surrounding it, we could tell it was an African American man, and there was no mistaking that he was scared out of his mind.

"That's Chase," said Olivia. Her voice sounded pained. "Oh, my Lord, that's Chase Kennedy. I saw him around the College of Charleston and talked with him a couple of times. He's a nice boy. We've got to help him."

Olivia looked at us with pleading eyes. Even though we had already rescued her, she didn't know us well enough to know that we weren't the kind of people who could just ignore someone who was in trouble.

"That's why Kathy woke you up, Olivia. We need you on the microphone so we can have four guns up there instead of three. You ready to help your friend?"

Olivia enthusiastically got herself situated in the chair at the console and listened when Kathy explained the plan. We wouldn't need more than fifteen minutes to climb up to the landing by the door, so we synchronized our watches with Olivia and told her when to begin talking to the infected dead. We would wait five more minutes to allow her to get them all moving away from the cage, and then we would do our thing.

Our goal was simple. We would try to remain out of sight until we got to the top of the walls, and then we would start shooting. Hopefully, we wouldn't run out of ammunition before we ran out of targets, but we had packed our bags with everything we could carry.

We left Olivia at the microphone and ran off at a trot for the tunnel to the surface. As we expected it didn't take us long to climb up to the landing at the door. I could hear my heart pumping in my ears as we got ready to go outside for the second time.

When fifteen minutes passed, Olivia began talking into the microphone. We didn't know for sure what was happening on the other side of the door, but we were hoping the infected had begun moving toward the sound of her voice.

Five more minutes went by, and Kathy opened the door. Tom had his rifle up to be able to shoot quickly if there was anything at the door when Kathy opened it. It was considerably brighter on the surface with the floodlights on, and we could see a set of worn steps that went to the top of the ramparts. They were steep enough and didn't have a railing, so anything that might follow us up there would be easy to knock back down.

Kathy pointed at the steps, and after closing the door, we moved in single file. We had to pass the opening to the main entrance, and as we went by we caught a glimpse of the dock where the tour boats used to arrive. It was deserted now. The boats had either left or drifted away, and the infected had wandered around until they fell over the sides.

As we climbed up the steps, we heard Olivia more clearly over the speakers on the other side of the fort. The infected were being drawn away toward the sound that promised them more living people to attack.

"Everyone spread out along the wall," said Kathy. "Single shots only, and try to work your areas so we don't double up on one. We need to make the ammunition last, so let the others know if you begin to run low. Ed, you have the steps. Keep one eye in that direction and watch for anything trying to come up here with us."

As we were getting into our positions, Tom said, "I wonder why none of the people in this fort tried to make a stand up here."

Bus said, "I think I know why. They were shooting each other. In the dark they were shooting anything that moved. When they got done shooting each other, they got back up and began biting the ones who were still alive. If we had turned the lights on sooner, they may have been able to defend themselves against the infected."

"Okay, everybody pick your targets and make your shots count," said Kathy. "Get the ones that are closest first and then wait for the others to replace them."

The first volley of shots was almost one sound, and it dropped four of the infected. After that the shots were spaced out, and it sounded like a string of firecrackers. The infected dead began turning from the sound of Olivia's voice and coming back toward us. There was no way to tell how many there were, but it was like the first days of the apocalypse when I had watched the television feed that showed their steady advance toward the fenced in radio station. The big difference was that back then they would be replaced as they fell, but inside the fort they would have no replacements.

I kept glancing to my right to be sure none were coming up the steps, but they weren't getting that close yet. We were all hitting our targets, but I think we all had a bad moment when it felt like there were too many for us to kill them all. They may not have had replacements coming from some hidden army of infected dead, but it sure did seem like it.

Olivia helped by yelling into the microphone. Some of the infected turned back toward the speakers in search of the voice, and that helped to thin out the crowd that was advancing toward us.

We had a bit of a problem when they began passing the cage where Chase was trapped. Even though we were being careful with our shots, we didn't want any mistakes to be too close to him.

"Shoot anything that's moving in the direction of the cage," yelled Kathy. "Let anything that's already in line with the cage get closer until you're almost shooting down at it."

We switched our targets as Kathy said and began preventing more of the infected from getting close to the cage. The ones that had already passed it were getting closer to our position, but we would deal with them when we had to.

******

The Chief saw Fort Sumter light up like a Christmas tree, but against the black sky behind it, the lights were even brighter. He slowed the forward motion of the boat until he was just coasting. A pair of binoculars would at least allow him to figure out if the lights were turned on by friends or by the occupants of the fort. At this distance he couldn't tell what was happening.

The boat bobbed on the water as the Chief tried to spot any activity. He thought he saw someone jump over the wall and fall to the rocks below, but he wasn't sure. He knew he had to get closer, but he didn't want the wrong people to hear the boat approaching.

The feeling that he was alone came over him slowly at first, but then there was a feeling of certainty. The Chief turned toward the stern and saw the empty bench seat. There was a short set of steps that led down to a tiny cabin in the bow, but he knew without checking that she couldn't have gone down there. He knew the only place she could be was in the water. He turned the wheel and let the idling engine just rotate the boat in one spot.

The Chief didn't need a degree in Psychology to know what he had done. He only needed to know how people think when they're in denial. He had deliberately kept his back to Allison for a long time, and he knew he had done it to give her the opportunity to take matters into her own hands. She knew there was no going back either way. If she went to Fort Sumter, she still wouldn't live long enough to see her daughter again. In the mean time, she would be a danger to her friends. She also knew there would be no going back if she jumped into the dark water while the Chief was speeding across the harbor. He wouldn't have been able to help her even if he spotted her in time, but at least she would eliminate the threat she would become.

He stopped idling in a circle and faced back toward the city of Charleston. Somewhere back along the path he had taken, Allison had done what any of them should do if they were bitten. Love wasn't enough to beat this infection, but it was enough to keep others from being bitten. The Chief silently hoped Allison had the chance to show her love for her family and friends by doing it herself, but he would never know for sure. He thought of the many bumps over swells and quick turns on the wheel and knew she could have fallen over the side whether she was alive or dead, and he also knew if she hadn't done it on her own, he would have eventually done it for her. Either way, it was done.

The Chief didn't know how long he stayed in one spot. The wind was calm, so he sat in the boat and let the feel of the swells comfort him. He was always more at home on the water, and for at least a while he needed to feel at home. No infected dead, no people, and no responsibility for a few minutes. He only gradually became aware of the popping sounds from the fort that had to be made by guns. He had no way of knowing if it was good news or bad news, but he couldn't stay where he was if his friends needed his help. He turned the boat toward the fort and increased his speed.

As the Chief drew closer to the fort he could see that the dock was abandoned. Whoever was doing the shooting inside didn't have a means of transportation once the shooting was done. That meant his boat had just gone up in value.

******

The infected were mostly coming our way. They either lost interest in Olivia's voice, or they were more attracted to the sound of gunfire. It didn't matter which it was to us as long as we were able to keep dropping them fast enough. We were practically shooting straight down, and the infected had been passing the cage without showing the least bit of interest in Chase. To his credit, he was smart enough to get low to the ground and to stay very still.

Olivia could see that she had lost her audience, and she was shouting four letter insults at the infected as if it would make a difference. She even tried singing to them, and when that didn't work, she switched to ugly mother jokes. Under different circumstances she would have had us all in stitches.

The bodies were piling up in front of us so fast that we had created a barrier, and the infected were having to crawl over them. As we shot the ones that were crawling, it became more and more difficult for the ones in back to advance. The result was that they began spreading toward the edges of the horde. I saw the infected dead that were going around the left end where Tom was shooting, but for some reason I didn't think the same was happening to the right. I just kept alternating from shooting the crawling infected to shooting the infected going around Tom's end.

There was a groaning sound to my right that reminded me of the very first time I had heard that sound. I had spent the night in a tree, and it seemed like the infected dead had spent the night waiting under the tree.

I was in a prone shooter position sighting on the head of an infected dead that was trying desperately to reach the top of the pile of bodies when I heard the groan, and it was too close. I saw my mistake immediately, and the infected was already reaching for me while my rifle was pointed in the wrong direction. It had gone around the pile of bodies on the right side and managed not to fall over the edge when it came up the steps. I heard Kathy screaming for me to move, but there was no way any of my friends were going to be able to bring their rifles around fast enough to save me.

I tried to roll away from the grotesque creature that was so close that it was literally going to fall on top of me, and I tried in desperation to bring my feet up into its stomach as it fell forward. I guess I planned on hurling it backwards, but these were recently dead people. They weren't emaciated and paper thin like most of the infected dead we had seen recently.

When my feet made contact, and the infected dead began to fall with its full weight against me, it felt like it weighed a ton. My legs bent at the knees as its face came straight at mine. Then the weight was gone.

I didn't even realize the force of it landing on me had made me shut my eyes for a split second. It had driven my feet so far into me that my knees had knocked the air out of my lungs. My eyes were shut for a split second, but when they opened, I thought the infected dead had learned how to fly. I watched with fascination as it seemed to rise in the air on its own power.

There was a second flashback in that moment. I remembered when I had finally come down out of the tree on that first day, I had become tangled in the thick bushes along with an infected dead. Neither of us could move, and it was trying its best to reach me. Just when it managed to free itself and moved in for the kill, an alligator had grabbed it from behind and dragged it away.

I had a split second expectation that an alligator had grabbed the heavy infected dead and pulled it off of me, but the last thing I expected was to see a mountain of a man dressed in Navy coveralls holding the infected dead straight up in the air. The Chief only rotated slightly at the hips and threw the infected so far that it landed beyond the barrier of bodies. It immediately began to crawl back toward us.

"If you aren't using that rifle let me borrow it for a minute," said the Chief.

I heard Kathy, Tom, and Bus cheering behind me, but I was so dumbfounded I just held my rifle out to him. The Chief gave me that big smile we all loved to see and turned back to the stairs. He pulled the trigger several times, and the result was a pile of bodies at the bottom of the steps.

There are few words to describe what it felt like seeing the man I had come to know standing above me taking aim at the infected dead below. It was a crowd, but it was growing smaller in size with every shot. He had effectively blocked the steps with bodies, so those that came around the main kill zone to the steps were no longer a problem.

My other friends resumed firing, but as I reloaded their magazines for them, I saw they were as wide-eyed as I was. All except Tom. I noticed he kept glancing over his shoulder toward the long dock that extended away from Fort Sumter.

From the wall where we had made our stand, we could see the entire dock, and there was one boat tied up at the very end. We could also see there were no other passengers in the boat. Wherever Allison was, she had not arrived with the Chief.

Kathy would shoot three or four times and then glance quickly at the Chief. I saw her eyes were wet and she appeared to be holding her breath. Bus hadn't made the connection yet about Allison not being there, but he would soon enough. He loved her as if she was his own daughter, and he was likely to think the Chief brought her back in one piece. He stayed focused on his targets, but he wanted to laugh because he was so happy.

The Chief caught me glancing at him with the unspoken question, and his smile was still there, but I caught the brief nod he gave me. It was a silent acknowledgement of the obvious. Allison didn't make it. I returned the nod, and the Chief went back to work.

Olivia's voice continued to taunt the infected dead even as the last of them were falling. The popping shots from the rifles decreased until no one could find another target, and then it was quiet except for the voice. Olivia couldn't see anything moving anymore, so the speakers went silent, too.

Below us and across the entire area of the fort were bodies. If we could see the rocks along the walls down by the waves that splashed against Fort Sumter, we would see a similar scene. The gang that had controlled the surface of the fort had been far more numerous than we had known, and that was why we had won.

A smaller force might have been able to kill the infected that had appeared amongst them, but the large force was so congested that it had quickly become a raging mob of bitten victims. They turned quickly because they were attacked by so many of their comrades at once. There were no lingering deaths to allow the living to strike back in time. The arrogant leader of the gang had learned he was no more safe than his followers, and with no one to rally them into a defensive stance, they were as feeble as sheep inside a fence.

All of us gradually stood from our places along the wall to face the Chief. Kathy almost knocked me over getting to him. She passed her rifle to me, not even waiting to see if I had taken it and was hugging the Chief with everything she had. I could tell from behind her that she was sobbing because of the way her back was heaving between her shoulder blades.

There wasn't much room for us all to stand next to each other on top of the wall, but I managed to get the Chief's huge hand in my own and shake it behind Kathy's back. Tom and Bus both needed their turn, so I eased past them along the wall to let them by. Bus shook his hand and gave him a sad smile, and I could tell Bus had come to the same realization that Tom had earlier. He stepped back around Tom to where I was standing, and gave Tom room to face the Chief.

The Chief gave Kathy a final squeeze and a kiss on the cheek. When they made close eye contact with each other, she saw the sadness in his eyes and the smile that wasn't quite what it should be. We could see the words form on her lips, "Oh, no."

Tom stepped up to the Chief, and as Kathy backed away to give him room, he stepped in close to the Chief. They embraced each other as real friends do, and I saw Tom whisper something to the Chief. I didn't know what it was, but the Chief just nodded and said something that made Tom appear satisfied. I would learn later talking with the Chief that Tom had simply said to him that he was glad the Chief had survived the plane crash, and he was glad that Allison had not. Tom told him it was far better that she died that way rather than by being bitten and to become one of the infected dead.

The Chief told me later that Tom told him which truth he wanted to hear, so he had told Tom the crash caused Allison to suffer a head injury. She didn't suffer, and she didn't turn into one of the infected.

9 JEAN & MOLLY

Jean didn't think she would ever get used to being left behind, but at least this time she had Molly. They worked out a daily schedule that included meals, time on the radio, watching the security cameras, movies, and even homework. They both kept hoping there would be radio contact with their friends, but there was still nothing. If it did happen, it would be in some cryptic way that wouldn't divulge the secret of Mud Island.

Jean didn't really know how to set up classes for an eleven year old, but she hadn't gotten through college and nursing school by luck or beauty, even though she felt like she had plenty of both. So, she taught Molly what she knew...medicine.

Molly was more than interested, and she soaked up the lessons like a sponge. She didn't understand some of the math, but there were plenty of books and computer programs in the shelter to practice such things as mixing prescriptions and drawing the proper dosages into a syringe. She was especially good at remembering anatomical terms. She had a long way to go before she could do surgery, but Jean had no doubt about Molly when it came to stitches or bandaging wounds.

Jean didn't think about the long term implications at first, but she gradually realized Molly was part of the future.

Somewhere south of Mud Island, her friends and the father of her unborn child were trying to solidify that future. They could hole up for a couple of years in the Mud Island shelter and then move to another one, but from what she could tell, Mud Island was still the safest shelter of them all. Eddie's uncle had made a good choice when he decided on this location.

She watched Molly who was taking a break from her studies and sitting at the old style shortwave radio that had proven its value many times over. She was undoubtedly hoping to hear a broadcast that included the voices of her mother and father. It was one of her evening routines she enjoyed the most. The headphones would always seem too big on her, but in a few months she would be twelve years old.

Then there would be puberty, but without the normal distractions of the pre-infected world, it would be interesting to see what would be a crisis and what would be something for her to be excited about. There were no more young rock stars for her to daydream about, no best friends her own age, no boys to pass notes about, and no outfits to die for.

Jean thought about that phrase and what it had meant a year ago. It was said by millions of young people every day, but now dying for something was exactly that. It even meant dying so someone else could survive. Now it meant sacrifice.

The cameras spread around on the island were next up on Jean's list of things to do. She got herself comfortable at the controls of the console that operated the cameras and monitors and scanned the surface. It was too dark for normal vision, so she switched the night vision on.

Her thoughts were on Eddie as she surveyed the surroundings of Mud Island, and she couldn't help but laugh. She remembered when she pulled her shirt over her head to show him she didn't have any bite marks, and she thought he was going to fall out of his boat. She would deny it to her dying day if he ever guessed it, but all of the near death experiences she had been going through in the days leading up to meeting Eddie had left her a bit vulnerable, and she needed to feel alive again. She felt alive when she had shown her bare body to him, and he had reacted. He reacted pitifully, but he had reacted. The memory made her smile.

The camera on the southern tip of the island was acting odd. Instead of rotating slowly from left to right, it stopped in the middle of its turn and changed to a view of the sky. Jean was just beginning to wonder if the camera had fallen over when a face appeared on the monitor.

She almost turned the camera off, irrationally feeling like the face could see her if it was on, but Jean composed herself, understanding that she should get as much information as possible about the man. She didn't know if he was alive or if he was an infected dead, but the infected didn't tend to be interested in the cameras.

"Molly, are you getting any traffic on the radio?"

Molly used both hands to pull the headphones from her ears and said, "There's someone out there talking in Spanish. I don't know what he's saying, but he's just broadcasting and listening. I don't think anyone has been answering him."

"Don't talk with him. I think someone just found one of the cameras, and he could be Hispanic."

In the days and weeks of her recovery from a nasty infection she had gotten from being scratched by an infected dead, the men had kept themselves busy by installing more cameras around the island. Since they were wireless, there was nothing to hide but the cameras. They had found a case of them in the supply rooms under the living quarters, and even though they were primarily intended to use as backups for the existing security network, they had decided it would be useful to have cameras located in places that would allow them to look back at themselves.

Jean activated a camera they had put on the other side of the moat, the waterway that served as their protection from the mainland. It was a bit grainy because of the darkness and the night vision, but it was good enough. She slowly panned it straight at the place where the other camera had been aimed into the face of the rough complexion of a dark skinned man. From behind she could see there were two men now. They were wearing camouflaged uniforms of some kind, and each of them had AK-47 automatic rifles slung across their backs.

There was a boat partially in the view with them, so Jean rotated the camera slightly to get a better look. She couldn't really identify the weapon mounted on the bow, but she knew it was some type of heavy machine gun. It was almost like something from an old movie she had seen about Vietnam, and she thought it might be a fifty caliber machine gun. She remembered something from the movie about how the bow and stern mounted guns could be as deadly as a Rocket Propelled Grenade when they were working right.

The men both turned at the same time, and for the second time Jean felt like they could see her watching them, but this time the view wasn't blocked by a living face. An infected dead shambled into view and walked away from the camera toward the two men.

With the moat separating the mainland from the two men, they showed little interest in the nuisance that only wanted to bite them. Most of what Jean could see for a few moments was the back of the infected dead. The shirt it was wearing was probably tacky before its owner had become a victim of the infection. It had probably been a tourist from Myrtle Beach, about forty miles up the coast. It was wearing socks with sandals and Bermuda shorts, and an already bad hair style had gotten even worse.

The two men in uniform paid it no attention until it reached the water. As soon as it was a few feet out from shore, it dropped into the deeper water, and the stiff current began pulling it out to sea. The men turned and waved at the infected as it was swept away, almost as if it was going to wave back. Jean couldn't be sure, but she thought one of the men pretended to be hurt when the infected didn't return the courtesy of a wave, then the two of them started laughing.

Jean moved the camera back to the boat, and she saw a third man lounging at the stern. He appeared to be totally bored, but he was in no hurry for his shipmates to come back. He was swatting at mosquitoes and had a bright lantern on top of a small camping table. Jean switched to normal light because the lantern was like a hot flare. When her eyes adjusted and let her distinguish colors again, she noticed a patch on the sleeve of his uniform, and she zoomed in on it. It was red, white, and blue, but it wasn't an American flag.

"Molly, do you know the flags of different countries?"

Molly grinned at Jean and nodded. She was always so happy when she was able to contribute to the group.

"Okay, then help me out with this one. There are three blue bars, two white bars, and a triangle on its side with a white star in the middle of it."

Molly said, "That's an easy one, Aunt Jean. That's a Cuban flag."

Jean thought, "Great. Just what we need."

10 CHASE KENNEDY

Getting down from the wall by using the steps was almost impossible, but the Chief led the way as he dumped bodies over the side. We were all being careful of the possibility that one or more of the infected dead were in need of another bullet, and from time to time someone would say, "Live one". Then a shot would ring out. We hadn't forgotten that they were not alive, but there wasn't really anything else we could call them that would get everyone's attention.

When we got down to the end of the long barrier of bodies, we circled around and began working our way over to the cage where Chase was still curled up in a fetal position in the center. He had his arms wrapped around his head and wasn't moving.

Kathy got down on one knee and spoke to him softly.

"Chase? Chase, can you hear me? My name is Kathy. We're here to get you out of there."

When Chase finally moved his arms away from his face, he only stared at Kathy. It was still a bit dark despite the lights, so his features weren't clear. He didn't appear to be hurt, but he was still in shock and was clearly expecting to die.

The rest of us were standing behind Kathy, and it may have appeared as if she was being backed up by a gang of her own, but all of us were wearing the same coveralls, so we were different from the people who had put him in the cage. They had been a ragged bunch that sneered at him and threatened him at every opportunity. At least when he studied us with curious eyes, he saw a group of people who were waiting for him to answer instead of ordering him to speak.

"It's okay, Chase. We're friends. Nobody's going to hurt you now. Give us just a minute to get this thing open, and then we're going to go somewhere safe."

He still didn't move until there was a new voice behind us, but even then it was barely more than lifting his head from the ground.

"Chase, it's me, Olivia."

Olivia sounded out of breath, and her voice was higher than normal. She had apparently run from the control room to the tunnels and then climbed the ladder as fast as she could.

"They're friends, Chase. They saved me, and now we're getting you out of there, too."

The lock that held the door shut wasn't much trouble, but even with the door open Chase stayed where he was. He was still not sure of what was happening around him. Olivia motioned for us to stay back while she went in to him.

I didn't know how old Olivia was, maybe just under forty, but she had the appearance of an athlete much the same as Kathy. She was attractive and moved in a smooth way that said she took care of her health, too. She moved to Chase's side and gently placed her hand on his shoulder. He flinched and pulled his arms back over his face again.

She kept talking to him as she slowly lifted his arms away from his eyes. He watched her closely, and I think we all felt like he was going to spring into action and attack her at any moment. He blinked his eyes a few times, and through a parched throat he tired to speak.

"Olivia? Is that you?"

"Yes, Baby, it's me. It's Olivia, and we've got some friends here to help us. You can trust them."

Olivia gradually got Chase to sit up and face her, and he could see us over her shoulders. I think we all tried to appear harmless to him, but that's hard to do when one member of your group is as big as the Chief. Still, his size was somehow tempered by the kindness of his face, and Chase studied us with curiosity instead of fear. He pushed himself to a standing position and allowed himself to be led out of the cage by Olivia.

Kathy told Chase there would be time for introductions later, and that we should all go somewhere safe. It was still too dark outside to be standing around in the open with spotlights shining on us. If there was anyone we had missed, dead or alive, we were far too exposed.

Tom took the lead as we navigated through the bodies back to the hidden tunnel entrance. We filed through one at a time, and then I sealed the door. By the time I got down the ladder everyone was already in the main corridor that went to the shelter. I saw Chase up ahead with the same wide eyed amazement on his face I must have had the first time I saw my shelter on Mud Island. Of course I wasn't being rescued from a locked cage and hadn't been brutalized by a gang of survivors.

I had walked into my shelter when things were normal and had seen the shelter as something fun to own, not something that would keep me safe from harm. As a matter of fact, I didn't think it was perfect because there were no video games. I seriously doubted that Chase would criticize the shelter for any reason, especially the lack of video games.

Olivia was helping Chase walk down the main corridor, and it suddenly struck me that he had a serious limp.

"Hold up just a second," I said.

Everyone stopped, not just because I said to, but because the tone of my voice was different from what they normally heard. I think we had all become that way since the first day when we had met. There was a way to talk that meant more than what was being said. Sometimes it was joking around, and sometimes it was so serious it could stop everyone in their tracks. That's what happened this time.

"What is it, Ed?" asked the Chief.

"I hate to ruin the party, but Doctor Bus should examine his leg."

I gestured toward Chase, and everyone instinctively withdrew a short distance from him.

"I haven't been bit," he said with a little too much defiance.

"No one says you have been," said Kathy, "but ask Olivia. We have to check everyone just in case."

Olivia took Chase by the shoulders and pinned his eyes with her own. I wasn't sure, but I thought I saw some attraction Olivia had toward the younger man when she got that close to his face. He was about twenty-five years old, and even though Olivia was ten to fifteen years older than him, he seemed to enjoy her attention.

"Listen to me, Chase," she said. "These people saved my life, and now they saved yours. They did it because they're good people, so what more do they need to do before you really begin to trust them?"

Chase's defiance melted. He leaned against the smooth wall of the corridor and let himself slide down to the floor. He pulled up the leg of his pants and showed us a nasty raw area that went completely around his ankle.

"Rope burn," he said. "They tied a rope around my ankle and dragged me behind a boat when they brought me here."

Doctor Bus got down on the floor and examined the red wound.

"This should have been treated days ago," he said, "but it should heal well once I clean it out. It's not infected yet."

To show him there were no hard feelings, I offered him a hand to help him get up.

Doctor Bus said, "Let's get him to the infirmary, but I'm just going to clean the wound. I think a hot bath and some food are what he needs right now."

Bus and I took Chase from Olivia and supported him the rest of the way to the surgical suite. We could see that he was beginning to loosen up around us, but I couldn't really blame him for wondering if he hadn't gone from one cage to another. He had seen what Larson and his men had done to the other prisoners, and he had fully expected to be a victim of their treatment, too.

The Chief took Tom aside and whispered a few words. They walked off together with their heads aimed toward the floor. My guess was that he wanted to talk with him about Allison, and it was a conversation that needed to be private.

Kathy and Olivia took another turn in the corridor and headed for the kitchen. I could hear the excitement in Olivia's voice as she talked about putting together a big meal for the men. Kathy had been around us long enough to know we would eat anything, but Chase was probably who Olivia was trying to impress.

Bus helped Chase up onto an examining table and cut away his jeans with a pair of scissors. The antiseptic he used made Chase wince, but it was obvious that he knew he was being helped, and his attitude toward us began to soften.

"Who are you guys anyway," he asked, "and where are we?"

"I'm Ed, and this is Doctor Bus," I said, "and you're in a bunker under Fort Sumter. A bunker that was supposed to save any high ranking politicians who could reach it in the event of a major disaster. But I don't think they planned on zombies."

"They aren't zombies," he said. "Zombies are controlled by people. Those things aren't controlled by anybody."

Bus and I exchanged shocked expressions that asked, "Did I hear him say that?"

"Run that by me again, Chase. Did you just say they aren't zombies?"

He started to repeat what he had said, but I put up a hand and stopped him.

"Never mind," I said. "You and the Chief are going to get along with each other just fine."

Over the next hour while I helped Chase get to one of the many private rooms where he could get a hot bath, I learned that he was from Atlanta and had moved to Charleston to go to college. He had seen Olivia around campus, and had a crush on her. He knew she was a lot older than him, but he had been trying to work up the nerve to ask her out when the infection began.

I told him about our group, and in particular about how I had met Jean and knew what it was like to fall head over heels in love with someone in a short time. I told him not to wait until it was too late to let her know how he felt. It was funny, but that simple comment seemed to make us feel like old friends. The defiance and fear out in the corridor when I saw him limping just seemed to melt away.

After his first bath in longer than he could remember, I found Chase a set of coveralls that fit his body but also made him fit right in with the rest of the group. The supplies in the bunkers were remarkably similar when it came to clothing and weapons, so we stayed with what worked, and the thick denim of the coveralls afforded some small protection from the teeth of the infected dead. Of course I didn't know yet that it had failed Allison.

Where the similarities between the shelters ended was in the quality of the food and other amenities, such as liquor and desserts. By the time Chase and I arrived in the dining hall, Kathy and Olivia had prepared a meal fit for kings. Chase hadn't eaten a decent meal in weeks, so hotdogs and hamburgers would have satisfied him, but the deep freeze units in the kitchen had vacuum sealed cuts of beef that thawed quickly in the microwave. Whoever was supposed to stay here was also supposed to eat well. I thought Chase was going to cry when the smells hit him, and the rest of us were also starving.

I noticed that the Chief made sure Tom was sitting next to Kathy, and there seemed to be an agreement not to talk about Allison yet. The last thing the Chief wanted to see was Tom distancing himself from her because he had feelings for Kathy before Allison died. Kathy was being more or less forced into normal behavior by Olivia who couldn't get enough of having another female around and getting the attention of a handsome younger man. It wasn't long before the smiles became infectious, and even Tom began to feel the effects of good company.

We told our stories to each other. I told about how I came to have a shelter that was perfect in so many ways, and I explained to Olivia and Chase how Kathy, the Chief, and Jean came into my life.

When we told them about some of our trips away from Mud Island, Olivia asked, "If it's so safe there, why do you keep leaving?"

"I think we leave Mud Island because surviving isn't enough," I said. "Surviving is also fighting back, and it's also finding a way to make it last. You know, the future isn't just being alive. It's knowing that you will still be alive next year and the year after that."

"Well put," said the Chief. "This time we need to get power restored to Mud Island, and after that, believe it or not, we have to find another backup system and put it in place. We can't just go on believing the power supply will last forever."

The discussion went around the table until it got to Bus. Olivia and Chase were really wrapped up in his story because he was an insider of sorts. Someone had given him the knowledge about the other shelters, and he had shared it all with the Chief. As long as there was another shelter to go to, there would be a place for them to be safe.

"Have you considered giving up on Mud Island and moving to a shelter that hasn't lost its primary power source?" asked Chase.

"It could come to that eventually," said the Chief. He glanced at me because he knew how much that island meant to me now. "But each shelter has its own positives and negatives. Tom said once that a shelter had to have three qualities."

Tom was distracted, but he had been listening, and he picked up where the Chief left off.

"It has to be safe from the infected, safe from the living who would want it for themselves, and safe from natural

142

disasters or the elements. You can haul supplies into a shelter until you don't have room to move, but in the end, it comes down to those three things."

I added for Tom that he and his daughter moved into the houseboat we had tied to the dock at Mud Island, and he immediately knew it was only safe from the infected, and even the infected could walk right up to the door. It was easy enough to knock them off the dock, but it wasn't safe to go outside.

"So, Chief, where to from here? Now that you've lost your plane, you're limited to the boat and walking. Walking doesn't appear to be safe anywhere," said Chase.

"Flying didn't turn out to be the safest thing in the long run," said the Chief.

He regretted it as soon as he said it, but at the same time it had to be said. In a world where people were still dying from infectious bites from other people, you couldn't always be sensitive, even if you tried to be.

Tom had been just pushing around his food with his fork, but he lifted his head and gave the Chief an understanding nod.

He said, "We need to figure out who shot you down, Chief. Whether we go back by boat or by plane, we're going to be facing some opposition on the water. Have you given any thought to how we're going to get by them?"

"No, I haven't really been able to process it, Tom. We still have to get the line laying barge up to Mud Island, and that means we have to tow it. To tow it we need a tugboat that's completely fueled. That much I think we can handle if we don't run into more trouble, but nothing seems to come too easy these days."

"It's not all on you to figure out," said Kathy.

"I know," said the Chief, "but it's in my nature."

I sensed that the conversation at the table was starting to sound like defeat even though there were two people with us who had every reason to celebrate. To them the world couldn't have gotten much worse. There wasn't a need to ask what had been done to them while in captivity. It was enough to know that they were in the hands of madmen and had suffered. Now they were sitting at a dining room table in a shelter that would defy entry and protect them from harm. There was good food in front of them, and judging by their faces, they were happy.

I stood up from my seat and asked everyone for their attention. First I raised my glass and said a toast to the Chief for getting us this far. Then I said a toast to Allison and reminded everyone that this wasn't a game we were playing, but I had a proposition to make.

Everyone was wondering where I was going with my speech, or if I had gotten myself drunk.

"If we're going to do more than survive, then let's take the fight to the infected," I said. "Let's do more than just fix the power problem on Mud Island. Let's get to work on the long term goals. Let's decide what we're going to do with the other shelters, get people living in them, and get them organized. Let's build up the defenses around them and then when we decide to just kick back and let the world go by, let someone else keep the fight going."

I sat down expecting them to all cheer my little outburst, but everyone just sat there staring at me. Maybe I was drunk, because I was suddenly sure I had just made a total fool of myself. Then they started cheering.

The Chief was the first to speak, and what he said made everyone laugh until they had tears running down their cheeks.

"My friends," he said, as he rose from his seat at the table, "I believe young Eddie Jackson has just given me the first and biggest wedgie I've ever had."

The idea of anyone giving the Chief a wedgie was right up there with believing in zombies, but the visual image was enough to make everyone stop licking their wounds.

Kathy stood up along with the Chief and raised a glass in my direction.

"To Eddie Jackson, the man who gave the Chief a wedgie and lived to tell about it."

She had downed her fair share of wine and giggled, but with her beautiful blonde hair hanging loose over one shoulder she managed to be the leader we knew she could be.

"Ed has it right," she said. "I think Doctor Bus would be able to back me up if I said the builders of these shelters had a plan in mind. They weren't supposed to just survive on their own. They were supposed to be part of a network, and someone needs to get that network up and running."

Doctor Bus was solemn when he stood. He raised his glass to everyone at the table one at a time.

"Ladies and gentlemen, I guess I should have been more thoughtful about my peers who built the shelters. I have to admit. I was so caught up in the gravity of this unprecedented world disaster that I forgot that was the original intent of the shelters. We had meetings. We talked about each type of disaster, and we planned for how we would hold on by our fingertips in our own shelters, and then how we would save our country. What none of us expected was this type of disaster. If it is now left to us to begin picking up the pieces, then let's talk about fixing the power problem on Mud Island, let's get it done, and then let's start planning how to get every one of the shelters populated with good people."

Chase said, "Wow, you folks have forgotten how to celebrate."

That earned him a round of laughter and even some applause. It wasn't like us to sit around licking our wounds, but it had been a busy day. Everyone agreed that it was time to turn in and get some rest, feeling a bit better after Bus had given his speech. He was right. We had to get started with a long range plan, even if it meant going into a city block by block until the infected were cleared, but it logically should begin with the shelters.

Kathy caught Tom by the arm as we drifted away from the table and asked if he could spare her a few minutes to talk. He was reluctant at first, but he gave in when he saw she was hurt by his hesitation. They headed for one of the exits that would take them to a room that resembled a library. It had big, overstuffed furniture in it and was something suitable for long, private talks. That was what they needed.

Bus also needed something, but more than anything he wanted to be alone. He had known Allison for a long time, and it wasn't surprising that he needed to grieve her loss privately. He said good night more quickly than usual and went to his room.

Olivia and Chase seemed a bit self-conscious about the fact that they were leaving the table with me and the Chief. All of our rooms were on one floor of the residential section, and they had been given separate rooms, but they clearly wanted to spend a little bit of time together. They were trying to find a way to get away from the rest of us without being too conspicuous. The Chief was picking up on it too.

"When's the last time you two saw a movie and had a good laugh?" he asked.

They shrugged their shoulders at each other almost as if they were checking to see if they had seen a movie together, and we were surprised to find that's what it was. They had both gone to a free movie at the student center on the college campus. Neither was with a date, and they kept trying to sneak peeks at each other. Needless to say, they kept catching each other in the act.

When they told us the movie had been a romantic comedy named The Wedding Planner, the Chief and I knew exactly which movie they would like. Every room had a big TV and an even bigger movie library, but besides the huge auditorium we had found when we had arrived at Fort Sumter, we found several smaller lounges and theaters that were meant for relaxing as a group. We took Olivia and Chase to one intimate little theater and picked out their movie. We figured Hitch would be just right for them.

The Chief and I drifted down the main corridor after getting the movie started, both feeling satisfied that we could make our new friends happy in a small way. The movie would be good therapy for them.

"This place is unbelievable," said the Chief. "It must be ten times the size of Mud Island. Did you guys have any trouble getting in?"

"No, there was a golf cart in the tunnel, so we got here faster than expected. We knew you wouldn't be back for a long time, so we went ahead and checked the place out. We didn't think you would be gone as long as you were."

I think my voice may have croaked just a bit when I remembered watching the plane crash into the harbor.

"Anyway," I continued, "we didn't even have the chance to explore the whole place yet. There's so much more here than we need."

The Chief said, "This place was obviously intended to be occupied by heads of state and a military detachment. There's no place to hide a plane or a helicopter, so I think the designer of this shelter planned on it being a little more obvious than some of the shelters. Mud Island and Green Cavern are well hidden compared to this."

"I've been meaning to ask you something, Chief. How did they design shelters that could keep salt water out so well? This shelter goes deeper than ours, and I think it's a miracle that ours keeps the water out as well as it does."

He laughed a little at the question, but not because it was a dumb question. I think he was just amused that I could find something else to think about under the circumstances. We had enjoyed many conversations like this one over the last year, and he had remarked once that he never got tired of hearing me pick apart a problem. I had explained it away as a gamer trait, but he had given me more credit than that. He said I had the mind of an engineer, and I should train it by digging into the library of textbooks we had in the shelter.

He said, "I had a ring that I lost at sea some years back. That thing is probably sitting on the bottom of the ocean without a barnacle or coral growing on it. Countless numbers of fish and bottom dwellers have been drawn to it because of the shine on the metal, but the jeweler that sold me the ring said nothing could ever scratch it. It was some kind of alloy, and as hard as I tried while I wore it, it never showed a single scratch. The walls of these shelters must be made of that alloy. Yes, you may see nice wood paneling, but behind it is something really tough."

We reached the turn that was more or less the central hub of the shelter, and I didn't really care where I went just yet, so I followed the Chief when he turned toward the control room. He had taken a quick tour of it when we came down from the surface, and he said there were a few things he had noticed that were different.

When we walked into the room, I expected him to go to the monitors to see if anything was happening on the surface. I also expected him to find a way to make radio contact with Mud Island.

"Don't bother with the radio, Chief. It doesn't even give you static to listen to."

"I figured as much," he said, "or you would have given me updates on Jean and Molly."

I wasn't as worried about Jean this time, so I had put the lack of radio contact out of my mind for the time being. I was more concerned that we were down to the one boat that the Chief had arrived in. Without it, we would be stuck on Fort Sumter. I went to the monitors while the Chief went to a different console. The lights were still on outside, and I brought up a camera view of the dock. The boat sat unmolested right where the Chief had left it.

"Ed, have you wondered at all about why this shelter is so exposed yet it has no boats or other means of escape?"

"You read my mind, Chief. I was just checking to see if that nice boat you brought back was still here."

"Is it?" he asked.

"Right where you put it. Why'd you ask if I was thinking about that?"

I walked over to the console where he was sitting and looked at a display. I couldn't believe it, but it was a real-time display showing Charleston harbor from a satellite view. It was dark for the most part, but there were small circles of light here and there. There was no way to know if they were people or just lights that were still connected to a power grid. Still, there was much more light than I had expected.

"Whoa…that's not your typical camera view, is it?"

"No," he said, "that's part of the defense system for this place." He moved the screen the same way I would have scrolled a map on Google or Apple Maps, but this time he was changing the view from a real satellite, and not from a computer app or an Internet page. Fort Sumter looked tiny and insignificant compared to the rest of the harbor, but it was blindingly bright in the middle of the surrounding water.

"How do you hide something?" asked the Chief.

I answered, "In plain sight."

He looked pleased by my quick answer, but I had a question of my own.

"You said this is just part of the defense system. Where's the rest?"

The Chief said, "I think this satellite was supposed to be the targeting system for something nasty. Too bad they didn't finish it. Check this out."

The Chief rotated the view from the satellite until it showed more of the entrance of the harbor. He zoomed out, and we were seeing the coastline going north. I was amazed as I watched him gradually bring Mud Island into the frame of the monitor, and then it began to zoom in. It was dark and remote, but something wasn't as dark as it should be. There was a lantern glowing brightly on the southern tip of the island.

"How close can you get, Chief?"

"Pretty close, and if that's what I think it is, I want to get that guy. That could be the jerk who shot me down."

"How can you tell at night, Chief?"

"I got a good view of the fifty caliber mounted on the bow. They aren't state of the art, but if you know what you're doing with one, you can target a slow moving seaplane. My problem with this guy is that he didn't have a reason to shoot my plane out of the air, but I have a reason for shooting him out of the water."

"Maybe you'll get your chance one day Chief. Right now we have an advantage, though. He won't expect you to come back after him. He thinks you're dead, and we know where he is for now. Any idea how long that satellite will transmit?"

"I don't think it has much chance of staying up there without a ground controller adjusting its altitude, but believe it or not, I don't know for sure. I have some experience with drones, but not so much with satellites. As a matter of fact, changing its view probably already had an effect on its speed and position."

"That reminds me," said the Chief. "We need to work on our plan for moving the line laying barge to Mud Island, and if our friends are still between here and there, we should find a way to arm the tugboat."

"We have more immediate problems, Chief. We only have one boat, and we need to get a tugboat running before we can arm it."

The Chief started to say something but stopped short. He placed his finger on the screen to show me what he was watching, and I saw another light next to the first one. Then there were several lights all converging on the same spot. They were all gunboats of the same style, and they all had the familiar gun mounted on the bow.

"Do you think Jean and Molly are okay?" I asked.

The Chief laughed.

"Ed, I don't think Jean is ever going to open that door for someone, and I know she isn't going to go outside on a crazy mission again. I think she learned her lesson the last time."

He pointed at the screen and said, "Check this out. They're coming back down the coast."

The gunboats had formed a straight line and were moving south at a high speed. They apparently thought their old bow mounted guns were the baddest things on the water because they were traveling with running lights on. They would be easy targets for almost any South Carolinian raised around hunting rifles, but the fact that they weren't being shot at from shore was a testament to how few people were left alive along the coast. Once they were strung out in a line, we could see there were twelve of them. If there were three or four men in each boat, we were looking at about forty armed people.

"Chief, at the speed they must be traveling, they could reach the harbor before sunrise. What if they see the boat?"

The Chief was probably already thinking the same thing because his brow was furrowed, and he didn't answer at first.

"I hate to do it, Ed, but I have to leave with the boat. If they come into the harbor and decide to stop here, we'll be stuck in this shelter for a long time. They'll either sink our boat or take it. I can't picture them just leaving it here, nor do I want to take the chance that we could be that lucky."

"You don't have to go by yourself, Chief. You could take a couple of us with you. If you have to hide somewhere for a day or two, you would at least have someone watching your back."

He thought about it for a moment then said, "First let's shut off those stadium lights over the fort. Then I'm going to get Kathy. I know Tom could use her company right now, but she knows the city better than any of us."

"You're going to the city?"

My surprise made the Chief grin. When he grinned, everyone around him got a sense of well-being. If everything wasn't all right, it would be soon. That's how he made people feel.

"That's where the tugboat is, Ed. Not to mention the armaments we need for the tug and the line laying barge."

I wasn't too happy with the idea, but we had to hide the boat, and the Chief and Kathy were the right people to send. Going back to the city would have been the last thing to have on my bucket list.

It didn't take long to find the power to the exterior lights since almost everything was labeled. As soon as I hit the switches the monitors went dark. I found the night vision mode, and they all turned bright green.

"It's a lot different now than it was before," I said. "You should have seen what it was like up there. That was a real army of crazies."

"You guys had a good idea getting the infection loose in the middle of them," said the Chief.

"It wasn't exactly a novel idea," I said. "Isn't that what happens sooner or later inside every big group like theirs?"

As soon as I said it, I had a sick feeling that I was describing an inevitable outcome for our group. It must have shown on my face because the Chief clamped a big hand down hard on my shoulder.

"Don't start thinking like that, Ed. The difference between them and us is simple. We care about each other, and we care enough not to risk the lives of anyone else in the group. Now we have two new members in our group, and we have to get them to drink the same Kool-Aid. They have to believe in the survival of the group, or they won't be able to stay with us."

"You mean they have to be willing to take care of it themselves if they ever get bitten, right? How do we get them to buy into that kind of group mentality, Chief? I think we're all wired that way. That's why we would do it. If they aren't wired the same as us, then they'll be just like that couple who tried to strand us on the road when we had to leave the plane."

"Exactly, Ed, but they didn't give us a chance to work with them. Tom gave us a chance, maybe because of Molly, but he still gave us a chance. Then he saw that if something happened to him, he would be leaving Molly in good hands. If we can get Olivia and Chase to work with us, to trust us, then maybe we can get them wired the same way as us. It's all about caring for each other, and if they feel like we care about them, then they'll become loyal to the group."

"Nice speech, Chief. Ever think about running for public office?"

The grin was a dead giveaway for the smart remark he was about to deliver.

"Wouldn't be enough people voting to worry about a recount, would there?"

******

Kathy didn't need to be asked twice. It was easy to tell that she would rather stay with Tom, but there was no doubt about who the best person was for this kind of mission. She was as fearless as she was pretty, and she was very pretty.

The rest of the group had to be told they were leaving, so we all gathered one last time in the dining area. We agreed that the Chief and Kathy were going to go to the Coast Guard base to try to find an armed boat that was small enough for them to operate on their own but also big enough to tow the line laying barge. Their main job, though, was to hide from the convoy of gunboats that we spotted along the coast. There wasn't much time, so the Chief just kept the explanation simple. We would be stranded on Fort Sumter until someone else came along with a boat, and we didn't want to just take what we needed. We needed to keep what we had.

We gathered up some gear for them to take along. A few days of rations, light weapons and ammunition were all loaded into the boat along with some foul weather gear and a folding tent.

Four of us went to the surface. Doctor Bus, Olivia, and Chase all stayed behind. Bus was at the consoles in the control room showing Olivia and Chase how to operate the cameras. The Chief had told him to turn on all of the lights on the side of the fort that faced the ocean if the gunboats arrived before they could pull away. They would at least be blinded long enough to keep them from seeing their boat as it left.

We hurried to the end of the dock and practically threw the gear onto the boat. Kathy and Tom gave each other a hug, and we couldn't tell if it was more than friends or if they were going to just keep things cool for a while. There was still Molly who would be upset to find her mother was dead,

153

and she would certainly be confused by a relationship between Kathy and Tom so soon.

Tom tossed in the stern lines while I took care of the bow. The Chief said something about us taking care of things while they were gone. Then he added that I would get my hug when he got back.

Normally I would have been stumped and unable to give him a suitable comeback, but I surprised him enough that he could only laugh and give us a salute.

"I'm going to hold you to that promise, big guy," I said.

We gave them a hard shove, and the Chief started the engine. They were just pulling away and fading into the darkness when the lights came on. Tom and I only had a second to see that they were already out of sight, then we ran up the dock. Our side was still dark, and we had to jump over the piles of bodies just inside the fort, but we made it back to the hidden door long before the convoy could make it to the fort.

When we got back to the control room, Bus told us the lights had done the trick. They not only blinded the convoy of gunboats as they passed the jetties into the harbor, they also caused them to wildly break formation. Bus excitedly described two of them cutting hard to port straight into the huge rocks of the jetties. They were smashed to pieces. Two of the remaining ten had done the same thing by turning hard to starboard and ran into shallow water. They didn't sink, but they would be stuck there until the tide came in.

The rest of the convoy fell into a loose semicircle around the leader and waited for instructions. The entire time they were bathed in the bright lights and were unable to see the Chief making good speed away from the fort.

"Okay, Bus. Let's mess with them now. Cut the lights off again."

Turning off the lights must have made them feel like they were in our crosshairs, because the lead boat immediately swung around and headed back out to sea. We knew there would come a time when they would come back, but for now they were unsure of what would happen if they approached.

I said, "They'll drop anchor just far enough out to feel safe and wait for their friends to float free with the high tide."

"In the meantime," added Tom, "the Chief and Kathy will make it to the Coast Guard base."

******

Across the harbor and around on the Ashley River side of the peninsular city, the Chief had silently drifted up to the side of a Coast Guard ship. He whispered to Kathy that they weren't going to drop anchor too close to the bigger ship because he didn't want any surprises dropping in from above. They just wanted to be hidden from view if there was anyone on shore they needed to avoid, infected or otherwise.

"We can sleep in the boat," he said. "I'll take first watch."

"If you don't mind, Chief, I'm a bit wired up. I could use some company right now."

"I can imagine so," he answered. "Of course I don't mind. It's been a long day for all of us. When I saw you guys up on the wall shooting down at the infected, I thought you had been flushed out of the shelter or something. I thought you were making a last stand. Then I found out you guys were taking the fight to them."

The Chief gestured back toward the fort, knowing that she would understand he was referring to the former occupants of Fort Sumter.

"We couldn't leave Chase in that cage, Chief. Once we knew he was there, we had to try to help him. Besides, we were partially responsible for him being surrounded by the infected."

"That was smart getting the infection to spread inside the fort, but I know it couldn't have been too easy for you to do. I don't mean logistically. I mean taking out a living person. We aren't exactly cold blooded, but we've changed."

"Yes, we have changed," said Kathy. "If you had told me a year ago that I would be killing zombies....sorry, infected

155

dead, and that I would kill a bad guy to help someone else survive, I would have thought you were nuts."

"Remember when we met?" asked the Chief?

"Of course I do."

"What did you think?" He gave her that charming smile that would have melted her if it had been on Tom's face.

"I thought you were big. What would you have expected me to think?"

The Chief said, "I would hope you thought the same thing I did. I told myself to stick with you because you were going to survive this mess."

Now it was Kathy's turn to smile. "I may not have thought those exact words, but it did make me feel good that you were big enough for me to hide behind you."

The Chief almost fell over the side of the boat as he failed miserably to control his laughter. Kathy teased him and said he was lucky to have survived because there was more of him to bite.

It was almost more than the Chief could take, but the day had so much tension that Kathy knew she had to help him let it go. She still had to know for sure, though.

"Chief, I know you told Tom it happened in the plane crash, but how did it really happen? It's okay. You can tell me, and Tom doesn't have to know. He can believe what he wants to, and that's what he wants to believe."

The Chief didn't want to relive it. He had succeeded so many times keeping people alive that he felt responsible for Allison's death. There was no hiding the truth from Kathy, though.

"We almost made it out, Kathy." The pain in his voice was almost unbearable, and Kathy didn't think she had ever heard anything like it coming from him before.

"Allison almost didn't make it through the crash. She swallowed half of the harbor, but I got her to cough it up. Then she showed a side of her we hadn't seen before. She hung in there pretty tough, and we tried to hole up for the night in the pharmacy of a grocery store. Then two of those morons from the fort showed up. They drew the infected from blocks around. One was killed, and when the other made a run for this boat, we followed him."

"Is that when it happened?" she asked.

"We made it all the way to the boat. I went down the ladder to the dock first, and there was an infected under the steps. It missed me and then bit her on the leg. She knew what it meant. We both did. I put her in the boat anyway and took her with me. I lost her somewhere between there and the fort."

"She took care of it herself?" asked Kathy. She seemed a little surprised that Allison could be that selfless.

The Chief was focused on his big hands, and Kathy saw they were shaking. Something else she had not seen him do. She realized he must be exhausted.

"I could have done it myself, but I couldn't bring myself to. She asked me to help her do it, but the best I could do was give her the chance without stopping her. I'd like to think she took care of it when I gave her that chance."

"So, you don't know for sure if she turned before she went overboard?"

"I think she jumped while my back was turned, Kathy. At least I hope she did."

"You have to make me a promise, Chief. You have to take care of it if I can't. If I get bitten, I'm going to eat a bullet, but if I don't have one to eat, you've got to do it for me. No guessing later. I want your word on it now."

The Chief tried to deflect Kathy's request by bringing it back around to Allison again.

"I wish I had been more patient. If I hadn't gotten mad at Allison and made her get back in the plane, she'd be alive right now."

"Tom doesn't blame you, Chief, and you shouldn't blame yourself. Allison might as well have worn a shirt with BITE ME written on it. She almost got us in trouble as soon as we left the shelter. Now, enough of this pity party. Promise me you'll be there for me if the time comes. I'm not going to wander around as one of those creatures trying to bite people. I need to know that you'll make sure that doesn't happen to me."

The Chief finally lifted his head. He gave her a nod and a small, sad smile.

"I wonder," he said, "what would I have done if I had cared for Allison as much as I care for you, or Ed, or Jean? Would I have listened to her when she asked me to take care of it for her?"

Kathy leaned closer and said, "You know the answer to that without even asking, Chief. In order for you to do it for someone else, you have to believe that person would love you or care about you enough to do the same for you. Allison wouldn't have done it for you, and you know it. She would have let you turn, and she would have left you here. No matter what you two went through that made you feel closer to her, Allison was always just in it for Allison, and I have no illusions that she wouldn't have helped me if I was the one asking for her help."

The Chief knew Kathy was telling it like she saw it, and her instincts were good. He also knew that right or wrong, nothing was going to change what happened. Feeling sorry about what happened to Allison wasn't going to bring her back.

"The hardest part is going to be telling Molly," said the Chief.

"Just tell her what you told Tom. He wanted to believe there was nothing that could have been done, and that's what you told him. I think if you had told him the truth, he would have doubted that she took care of it herself. He may have been in love with her once, and she was the mother of his child, but he wasn't blind to the way she was."

They both heard the faint sound from somewhere above them on the Coast Guard Cutter. It wasn't loud, but it was loud enough for them to both stop talking and just listen for a clue about what caused it. The Chief lifted the anchor as slowly as he could, and he let the current pull them along the side of the ship until they were almost to the stern. When he let the anchor slip back into the water, it made the boat swing slightly around behind the ship. They could see the name "Cormorant" above them along the side of the wheelhouse as they floated past it.

The Chief let them drift into position at the base of a ramp. Kathy had never realized that the stern bulkhead could raise up the way it did to expose a place where the crew could launch or receive a small boat. There was a ladder to the left of the ramp, and even though their boat looked like it could enter the opening, its curved hull wasn't intended for such a place. If they decided to board the ship, it would be by climbing the ladder.

"Do you think that sound came from inside the ship or on the deck?" asked Kathy.

"Inside," answered the Chief. "If you were going to hide somewhere safe, where would you go? Ships are easy to defend against the infected and the average scavengers."

"Could there be more survivors?"

"I forgot to tell you something. When Ed and I were getting the benefit of a satellite view, we saw lights here and there. They could have been random lights from odd power sources that haven't run down or been cut off yet, but some may be from survivors who are either safe enough to use light, or they turn on lights because they can't handle the darkness."

Kathy thought about what it would be like out there hiding in the city. It would be life or death every minute of every day. She wondered if she would become like those people who just had to turn on the lights, or if she would be strong enough to let the night hide her from the bad things that were wandering around. She knew the Chief would say she's the kind of person who would survive without the lights, but she wasn't so sure how long that would be true if she was alone.

"Chief, do we investigate or move on?"

"I think we should wait for morning. Whoever that was we heard, they would have all of the hatches sealed and locked from the inside. If they hole up in there at night, they've heard people crawling around on the ship before. They'd just stay quiet and wait."

"Does that remind you of someone we know?"

The Chief had to smile when he thought of the answer to Kathy's question.

"Ed's always talking about shucking the oyster. He says sooner or later, something will always pry the oyster open. He says the Mud Island shelter is like a big oyster just waiting for the right person to come along and pry it open."

"Do you think he's right?"

"Almost, but not quite," said the Chief. "Take this ship, for instance. Hatches can be blown open. Torches can cut through the metal in hundreds of places. Charges could be set that would sink it right where it sits. The worst part about it is its visibility. We don't know yet who blew up the Russian corvette, and we don't know why, but it could have been just because someone could."

"So, you think Mud Island is the perfect oyster because it would be harder to open?"

"Think about it, Kathy. If there are survivors inside this ship, they have to come out sooner or later. Their supplies won't last forever, depending on how many people are sharing them. You can stay inside Mud Island for years without coming outside."

"Why do we keep coming outside if we live in a nearly perfect oyster?" asked Kathy with a wry smile.

In the darkness Kathy could still see the Chief smile as he thought about his answer. Sometimes they talked about not being too bright and not being satisfied with what they had. Otherwise, they would just stay inside the shelter and wait until they had to do something about their power. They had a two year supply of power reserves if they cut back at all on their energy usage.

Kathy strained her eyes to see the outline of Fort Sumter, and she thought about what kind of people they had become.

"You're thinking about Tom again," said the Chief.

"Close, Chief, but I was thinking about Ed. Remember when we met him and when he told us about how he had visited the shelter the first time? There he was inside the perfect oyster, and he left to go buy video games. It wasn't perfect to him."

"Don't forget," said the Chief, "the infection started to spread after he left the shelter. If he had turned on the TV and seen news reports about people eating their families, friends, and neighbors, I doubt seriously that he would have left the shelter. He would have gone into the kitchen and made himself a big bowl of Ramen noodles, cracked open a Mountain Dew and stayed glued to the news."

"You're right, Chief, but I guess I'm saying we would look for a reason to leave even if we didn't have to. Yes, we holed up for a while after we almost lost Jean on the Russian ship, but we would have stuck our heads above ground sooner or later no matter what."

Kathy turned from the harbor to the dark hull of the Coast Guard ship. It was dark to her even though the hull was white.

"How many people usually crew this ship, Chief?"

"Only about ten. That's why there wouldn't be enough supplies on board to keep survivors fed for very long. They would have to come out and go foraging before long, but I am getting an idea. The area around here has been picked clean by now. Whoever is hiding inside will have to come out soon. If they don't, we may have to try to persuade them to come out, but this could be our ticket out of here."

"I know what you're thinking, Chief. This thing isn't very big, but will it be able to tow that barge we need?"

"It would be slow, but if we get good weather, we could do it. These things are just under ninety feet long, so they have the power. Did you see what was on the bow? There were tarps over them, but there are twin fifty caliber Browning machine guns. If the ammunition hasn't been removed, we would also be able to defend ourselves."

"Time to get some sleep, Chief. We could both use a few hours, and I don't think this oyster will open at night."

The Chief couldn't disagree with Kathy about that, and he was definitely tired. He also didn't disagree with her when she handed him a blanket and told him to go first. The last thing he heard from her was when she said she would wake him up if anything happened.

******

When Kathy squeezed his foot harder, the Chief woke up and listened. He was too well trained to wake up talking or sitting up to see what was happening around him. Instead, he listened for clues that would tell him what action to take.

What he heard was voices coming from somewhere on the dock next to the Cormorant. Kathy gripped his hand and gently pulled him in the direction she needed him to go. The current had swung their stern over toward the ladder on the left side of the stern, and they were in a good position to peek around the port side of the Cutter. There were at least two people talking in low voices on the dock.

The Chief got closer to Kathy's ear and in barely a whisper asked her if she had been able to hear what they were saying. She answered just as carefully that she heard them say they expected someone to come out of the ship at any minute. Apparently, they had been watching the ship, and whoever was holed up inside had demonstrated a pattern.

The Chief looked to the east and saw that the sun was just below the horizon, and he guessed the pattern was to come out and go foraging at sunrise. This would be their best opportunity to show someone they were the good guys. He whispered to Kathy to use the ladder, and he would use the ramp. Then he moved slowly over the rail of their boat and slipped into the water. Kathy moved away from their stern into the protection of the hull of the Cormorant and pulled herself up the ladder. She stopped just short of the top and looked down to her right. The Chief was in a prone position facing up the ramp.

There was the faintest of sounds from the metal on metal friction of the locking mechanisms inside the main door at the bottom of the wheelhouse. Kathy could see a slender figure emerge from the dark interior, and the door was locked again from inside. In that same few seconds that it took for someone to come out of the protection of the ship, the two men launched themselves onto the deck and rushed forward.

There was a female scream from the dark figure by the door, and triumphant shouts from the two men as one grabbed her arms and the other grabbed her legs. She was trying to kick and flail her way out of their grip, but she was far to small compared to them.

The flailing was cut short because none of them saw Kathy vault over the stern as the two men rushed past. The Chief emerged like a missile from the ramp. Both were trained in hand to hand combat, and their adrenaline was pumping as they hit their unsuspecting targets.

The men were too busy trying to control the struggling girl to even realize what hit them. Kathy's angle allowed her to come in low under the right arm of the scavenger who had the girl by her feet. He was laughing until Kathy punched him in the side just below his armpit. Then his laughter changed to a wheezing sound as the air left his lungs. A second punch in the same spot before he could let go of the girl produced the sound of a cracking rib that punctured the lung.

The Chief hit his target like a freight train. Since Kathy had gotten there a split second before him, the man had a chance to drop the girl's arms and reach for a weapon. That was his mistake. With the girl falling free from his grip, there was a little distance between him and his victim, and that enabled the Chief to hit him with his full weight without the girl in the way. They slammed into the metal door with the weight of the Chief on top of him. It sounded as bad as it had to have felt, and the man didn't move after the Chief backed away.

Kathy's victim was dying next to his friend. She stepped forward and put him out of his misery with a knife into the base of his skull. The Chief picked up the unconscious man he had body slammed and tossed him over the railing of the starboard side. Then he returned for the man Kathy had taken down and disposed of him the same way.

They had moved so quickly that it was over in seconds, and the girl who had come out of the ship was so sure she was next that she was curled up in a fetal position on the deck. She was a young, African American girl who had most likely been in high school when the infection started. She was sobbing softly and just waiting for her turn.

The Chief had seen the same behavior in combat, and Kathy had learned about it when she was taught about hostage reactions during active shooter events. Some victims just gave up and waited for their turn.

Kathy knew it was important to get her to just calm down and get involved with her own survival. She had to get her to become aware that she was still alive, not a victim anymore, and able to help all of them.

The Chief took up a position over at the port side along the dock. He pulled his hand gun from a holster inside his coveralls and began searching their surroundings for more danger. The girl's screams weren't awful, but they were loud enough for others to hear if there were infected or living people nearby.

Kathy had put her arms around the crying girl and was doing her best to soothe her by telling her over and over again that she was going to be okay. With the sun coming up on Kathy's face, the girl could see through partially closed and covered eyes that Kathy wasn't going to hurt her. When the full realization hit, she threw her arms around Kathy's neck and sobbed harder. Kathy let her cry it out and then gently pried the girl loose so she could be face to face with her.

"Do you have a special knock you use so someone inside will know to let you back in? You need to do it now so we can go inside where it's safe."

The girl only hesitated for a split second and then moved toward the door. The sunlight showed where they had taken care of the scavengers against the metal. She knocked on a spot that wasn't red with blood and waited. The lock began to turn after a few seconds, and a head started to poke out.

"You're back too soon. What happened?"

The boy was young, and when he saw the girl wasn't alone, he went pale. Kathy didn't think someone could get that pale. He was so petrified by the sight of someone other than his fellow survivor that he didn't react fast enough. He was going to shut the door again, but a big hand had reached out of nowhere and grabbed the top of the door. The Chief pulled it open, and the boy was literally dragged out with it. This oyster was open.

"It's okay, Sam. Let us in," said the girl.

Despite the seriousness of the situation and the feeling of being exposed in the open with the sun rising, the Chief had to smile when the girl had told the boy to "let" them in. They were pretty much past the part when he would "let" them do anything.

The girl led the way past Sam with Kathy right behind her. Sam backed inside quickly when confronted with the size of the Chief who was ducking to get through the door. The Chief turned and dogged the hatch shut behind him.

There was surprisingly more space inside the ship than they had expected, but it seemed much smaller with the Chief squeezed inside. There was a small galley made up of the kitchen and dining area, and forward of that was the berthing space.

Kathy and the Chief smiled, but that was what almost everyone did these days right before they tried to take what you had. They saw there was a third teenager, also a boy, who was frozen in place.

"I'm Kathy, and my big friend here is the Chief. I mean he's Chief Barnes, but we just call him the Chief."

"Are you going to kill us?" stammered the boy who had opened the door.

"Of course they aren't going to kill us," said the girl. "They saved me from those two mutts who jumped me when I went out the door. My name is Whitney."

She pointed at the boy who had opened the door and then fallen back into the room and said, "He's Sam, and the guy standing there like a statue is Perry."

"How have you three survived in this ship for so long?" asked Kathy.

"We haven't been on this ship the whole time," said Whitney. "We've been here about three months. We were able to stay in the Coast Guard barracks for a long time. There were lots of supplies for the first two months, so we never had to go outside. We had lots of fresh water, and we've only been using the power during the day time. We didn't want to accidentally show off some lights or something when we turned the power on, so we never do it at night. This place worked pretty good until we had to start going out to search for food."

It wasn't hard to tell Whitney was the leader of this group of survivors. The two boys seemed like they deferred decisions to her and wouldn't have made it too far without her.

"I'm sorry about my behavior out there a while ago," said Whitney. "I'm usually tougher than that, but they caught me by surprise."

"They've been watching your pattern. You've only been going out at sunrise, so they were waiting for you. Good thing we just happened to be in the neighborhood."

"I told you so," said Perry defiantly. "I told you to go out at different times."

"It didn't matter," said Kathy. "They would have just waited until you showed up. They only got the drop on you because it was still dark enough out there."

"Why were you guys there?" asked Sam. He was more composed now and had moved over to stand next to Perry.

"We were just passing through last night in a boat and decided to anchor next to the Cormorant. It kept us out of view of the docks. We heard something from inside the ship and decided to stick around," said the Chief.

The three kids had sheepish expressions, but the Chief and Kathy both caught the accusing glances Whitney and Sam both gave Perry.

Perry defensively said, "You may have heard something, but you didn't know it was someone alive."

"True," said the Chief, "but if it had been an infected banging around inside the ship, it would have kept banging around. It wouldn't have tried to keep quiet after that."

"Infected? Is that what you call the dead people?" asked Sam.

Kathy said, "That's what they called them on the news when all this started. They said an infection of some kind was spreading around, and not to let one of them bite you, so we started calling them infected, too."

"Do scavengers come around here much?" asked the Chief.

"Aren't you scavengers?" Sam asked accusingly.

"Depends on what you think we are," said the Chief. "If you think scavengers are people who can take you to a safe place, then I guess we're scavengers."

Whitney answered for the group, "We've heard them trying to get in about once a week, but sometimes it's every day and sometimes not for a few weeks. What do you mean that you can take us to a safe place?"

"First," said the Chief, "I'm going to see if I can power this thing up. If I can, it can be handled by one person if they know what they're doing. Next, we're going to make a short trip out to Fort Sumter."

All three of them stood a little straighter and looked like they were cornered.

"You are scavengers," accused Whitney.

Kathy and the Chief both saw their mistake immediately. These kids were especially aware of the people out at Fort Sumter and figured that a ticket to there was a one way trip.

"Hold on a second, kids." Kathy held both hands out showing her palms. "We're not the people you've been seeing from Fort Sumter. Those people are all either dead or gone. I know you don't know us well enough to trust us yet,

167

but do you think we would be standing here talking if we meant to harm you?"

All three of them were underweight. Sam and Perry were probably underweight and generally undersized before the infection began. They were the kind of kids who were bullied at school, and they expected to be bullied every year. They were both fair haired and could use some time in the sun, but that wasn't really an option anymore. Whitney was taller and might have been either a cheerleader or an athlete in school.

"How old are you guys?" asked Kathy.

Whitney sounded suspicious when she answered, "Why do you want to know?"

"I wanted to make sure you're old enough to learn how to shoot a gun."

That got their attention.

Sam said, "I'm thirteen, he's fourteen, and she's sixteen."

"That's old enough to shoot," said the Chief. "Any guns on this ship."

Still suspicious, they all watched each other before giving up their secrets.

"Did you just trick us?" asked Whitney.

"I have an idea," said Kathy. "Chief, cover me while I get some stuff from the boat. Whitney, I could use a hand. As a matter of fact, Sam you close the door behind us. The Chief is going to cover us while Whitney and Perry are going to help me get some food out of the boat."

The truth was that Kathy didn't need their help. She just didn't want them to lock the door as soon as she and the Chief went to get them something to eat. They might eventually get them to open the door again, but it would be a big waste of time.

"You're a better shot than me," said the Chief. "You can cover us."

Kathy grinned at the Chief as they went through the door. She could tell he had figured out what she was doing. Besides feeding the three kids, she was making them feel just a little less like victims by giving them something to do.

It took less than five minutes to get to the boat, pass their bags up to Whitney and Perry and then get back inside, but doing it as the serious business that it was made the kids feel important. They were excited when they closed the door behind us and were giving each other high fives.

"Now, let's see what we have in here that you guys can force yourselves to eat."

They all gathered around the small "mess" area next to the galley and took their seats.

Kathy made a show out of selecting from the MRE's they had hurriedly packed when they left Fort Sumter.

"You guys just raise your hands if I call out something you want. I have pepperoni pizza."

Three hands were in the air.

"Well, I guess it's a good thing the Chief likes the pepperoni pizza, because I brought plenty of it."

Kathy showed them how to heat up the MRE's. It didn't really even resemble pepperoni pizza, but the kids didn't complain. She had second helpings ready at about the same time that they finished the first ones.

"So, who wants to tell me how you three managed to get such a cool place to hide?" asked the Chief.

They kept eating, but they stared at him as if he was speaking a foreign language.

"I'm not sure they say cool anymore, Chief. I think they would say this place is either lit or live."

The Chief considered it for a minute, but he couldn't bring himself to say anything but cool.

He snapped his fingers in the air to get their attention and said, "Okay, dirtbags. That's your last free meal if someone doesn't say this is a cool place in three seconds."

All three said it was a cool place, but with full mouths it sounded like it was their turn to speak in a foreign language.

"Okay, that was close enough. Now, do I need to repeat my question?"

"We were in a school tour group," said Sam. "Me and Perry. Whitney came along later. We went to College Park Middle School, and we came down here to meet with some

Coast Guard guys for a tour of the ships. There was a much bigger ship here before, but it left. I think the Coast Guard people were trying to keep those dead things from getting on the boat because they were shooting those big guns up front." He pointed in the general direction of the bow.

"What about you, Whitney? How long have you been here?" asked Kathy.

Whitney wasn't comfortable remembering back to when it all started and everything she had been through, but she answered anyway.

"My parents brought me down here to show me where my dad used to work. He was in the Coast Guard, and he thought maybe I would like to join when I finished high school. He said it would help me build character."

Perry pointed at the Chief and said, "You look like you were in the Coast Guard, but you're too big for this ship."

The Chief was always at home on a ship. When he stood on a deck and watched the rolling swells everyone knew he belonged at sea. The comment made him smile at the boy, and all three kids visibly relaxed. He was big and dangerous until he smiled. Then everyone around him melted.

"I was in the Navy, Perry. After that I was working for a cruise ship company. That's how I met Kathy."

"Are you two married?" asked Sam.

Kathy shook her head and told them that the Chief was married to the sea, that is until things went bad.

"Back to you guys," said Kathy. "So, you were on a field trip, and Whitney, you were here with your folks. You've been here since? That's a long time."

Whitney spoke for the group, "We've seen what happens when one of those sick people bites you. We didn't have any choice. Those Coast Guard guys, Coasties, they took really good care of us, but at the end they had to lock themselves outside because they were bitten. My mom stayed outside with them and helped fight them off at the beginning. My dad tried to get her to stay inside with us, but she said she wanted to be with him."

She told us about that first day when it seemed that you didn't know who was okay and who wasn't. Police came and tried to help. There were firemen, ambulances, and people who just wanted to do whatever they could, but gradually there was no one left that wasn't trying to bite someone else. She saw Sam and Perry's teachers attacking children in their classes, and then the kids were attacking each other.

She said they seemed like they were going to stop the infected people at the gates of the Coast Guard base, but someone inside had been bitten already, and they started biting other people who were inside. Then they had to back up to the ships. One of the ships left with a lot of people on it, but there wasn't room for everyone. They tried to get people onto this ship, but the same thing happened as before. People didn't tell anyone when they got bitten because they didn't want to get left behind, they wound up with a lot of infected people on board.

Whitney told it as if she was talking about someone else. After months of being resigned to this way of life, she had plenty of time to grieve. There was very little emotion in her voice when she talked about those last days when the Coast Guard base had been overrun by the infected. She understood her parents had stayed outside so she could live.

She explained when the food started running low, they started going out for supplies and stocked up ahead of time. She said they talked about it after the first time scavengers tried to get in. They agreed they needed plenty of food for those times when they couldn't go out for more. One time the scavengers had camped on top of the Cormorant and tried to wait until the kids came out. They almost ran out of water that time, so they had made sure since then that there was always an emergency supply.

"Have you seen many of the infected in this area?" asked the Chief.

"Not for a long time," said Perry. "Even though Sam and I are just kids, we didn't want Whitney to be the only one who had to go out, and two of us could hunt for stuff faster."

"We've checked the houses for blocks. There were infected in some of them," said Whitney. "We took care of them."

Kathy and the Chief couldn't picture these three kids killing the infected, and their expressions didn't hide their thoughts too well.

Whitney didn't get angry. Being a teenager she always felt like someone was patronizing her, so it almost gave her a feeling of comfort and familiarity.

"We didn't try to stab them in the head, if that's what you're thinking," she said.

Sam said, "No, I'm too short to get most of them in the head, but it's really easy to make them follow you. We just let them out of the houses and then led them down here. When we got them to the dock we just hopped into this rubber boat tied up behind the ship and paddled away from the dock. The dummies would just walk right off the edge and sink."

"I didn't see a rubber boat," said the Chief.

"Scavengers took it," said Sam. "We weren't using it anymore anyway. We went back to the houses after we let everyone out and carried everything back here that we might need."

"Well, we won't be needing anything from the houses around here," said Kathy. "If this ship has enough ammunition left, it has everything we need. What do you say, Chief? Can this thing take on those gunboats we saw?"

The Chief had been thinking the same thing since he saw the Cormorant, but he wasn't so sure. The odds were bad. The Cormorant had size and three fifty caliber guns, but there were twelve of those gunboats. If they could reduce the number a bit and catch them by surprise, then maybe they had a chance. Of course this wasn't the first time he was outnumbered and outgunned in his life.

11 CHIEF JOSHUA BARNES

Perry was a typical young teenager, and to young teenagers, there were very few topics that were off limits, including age.

"How old are you?" Perry asked around a mouthful of pizza and gestured toward the Chief.

Kathy grinned. She hadn't even asked the Chief that. She knew he was around her father's age, but he carried himself like he was much younger.

The Chief's brow furrowed as if he was having to add up the years.

He said, "I asked my dad that same question once. You know what he said?"

"That he wasn't going to tell you?" said Perry.

"No, but close. He said that was for him to know, and for me to find out. So I said back to him that I was trying to find out."

Perry said, "You just took away my answer. Does that mean I'm not going to find out?"

"That means I'm not going to tell. If you find out, it's going to have to be some other way than by asking me."

Perry was persistent, though, and fairly smart for a kid his age. Kathy was enjoying the exchange, and was privately rooting for the kid. The Chief was as physically fit as any man her age, but she had respected the Chief as her senior since the moment she had met him. Even then she had deferred to his wisdom because his age meant experience. She may have been given a blank check by the cruise ship to organize a way to stop the infection from spreading, but when she was introduced to him, he didn't seem in the least bit offended that a young woman had been given the responsibility. The only person who had been offended was the ships's doctor, and he was just an ego with legs.

The next question seemed to surprise the Chief, because his eyes found Perry's as soon as the words left his mouth.

"So, if you won't tell me how old you are, will you at least tell me when you went to Kodiak for your cold weather training?" he asked.

"Someone's been paying attention in class," said the Chief. "Okay, I'll give you that much. I went to Kodiak in 1988."

"I knew it," said Perry triumphantly. "You're between fifty and fifty-five years old, but man you're ripped like you're twenty-five. You must've been hell on wheels in training."

"Wait a minute," said Kathy. She was digging up a memory from somewhere about 1988 and Kodiak, Alaska.

Perry, Sam, and Whitney were all focused on Kathy. It was her turn to furrow her brow, and her eyes had found the ceiling as if the memory was up above her. When she lowered her eyes down to the Chief, her mouth was half open, and the Chief felt uncomfortable.

Always modest when people talked about his abilities, the Chief turned away from Kathy. His achievements were likely to make it even more uncomfortable for him than his abilities, and Kodiak had been on the news for weeks. Everywhere he turned, someone was calling him the hero from Kodiak.

Kathy was only a few months old when it happened, but she remembered from a History class in school that there had been a weak attempt made by foreign troops to establish a foothold on American soil.

Her teacher had been talking about the War of 1812 and about how the United States was one of the few countries in the world that would be difficult to invade. For one thing, the Bill of Rights had ensured there would be armed resistance, but the US military was second to none.

Kathy's mouth was still open when the Chief finally asked, "Do we have to talk about it?"

"I think the kids would like to know what you did in Kodiak, Chief. I mean, hell. I've always felt safe with you along for the ride, but I would've felt even safer if I had known that was you."

"What happened in Kodiak?" asked Perry.

The Chief still didn't say anything, so Kathy gave the conversation a little nudge.

"You're sitting with the man who led a group of Navy SEALS in the successful defense of American soil. In 1988 a small force of North Korean soldiers managed to reach Alaska with the idea that they could set up a forward base and bring in more troops. The news said they probably had help from the Russians."

The Chief cleared his throat and said, "Maybe you should let me tell it, Kathy."

"We're all ears, Chief." Kathy was more than glad to sit back and let the Chief take over. He so seldom talked about himself that there was plenty she didn't know about him even after all they had been through.

"The training center is named Naval Special Warfare Cold Weather Detachment Kodiak," the Chief began. "It's where they sent Navy SEALS after the initial twenty-six weeks of SEAL qualification training."

Sam said with awe, "You mean it was training for people who already finished SEAL training?"

"Something like that," said the Chief. "The base was built as a cold weather training center to get SEALS ready for covert operations in North Korea. At least that was the original idea. The funny thing was that the North Koreans who tried to take the base from us didn't know two things. They didn't know the base was a Navy SEAL training center, and they didn't know we didn't have any guns."

"Their intelligence was so bad, that they didn't know anything was even located on the island except a state park, but the woods were so thick it was easy to get lost."

"Did you say you didn't have any guns?" asked Whitney. "Why wouldn't SEALS have guns?"

"It was only training for survival in cold weather, not fighting," said the Chief. "We only carried rubber rifles. They were as heavy as regular weapons with ammo, but they wouldn't get messed up by being in freezing cold water, and they made sure we spent plenty of our time in freezing cold water."

The Chief examined the faces of the three young people in front of him, and he could see he had their attention. He also saw out of the corner of his eye that Kathy was watching him with a kind of sparkle in her eyes. She was proud of him.

The Chief went on, "They dumped us out in the woods with a compass, very little clothing to keep us warm or dry, and expected us to find our way back to the base. There were forty of us, and when we stumbled into the North Koreans, we thought it was part of the training at first. After all, we were training to fight those guys, and they showed up on our island."

"What happened?" asked Perry.

"They opened fire on us, and we scattered. Half of our training class was captured and taken back to the base, and all we had for weapons were rubber rifles."

"Chief," said Kathy, "did you ever find out how the North Koreans even got to Kodiak? I mean, our defense systems must be watching for the Russians all the time, so how did they even get there?"

"As strange as it seems, Kathy, and in our case ironic, they used a cruise ship. Everyone monitoring the ship thought it was just an Alaskan cruise."

"I'll bet that doesn't happen again," said Perry.

That got a good laugh out of everyone, especially when the Chief said he didn't think the North Koreans would make that mistake again, either. It might have worked if they hadn't tried to take on the Navy's best.

"Anyway, we were outnumbered and they had real guns, so we did what we were trained to do. We made weapons from trees and rocks and began taking them out. As we did, we took their weapons until we had as many as they did, and then we really took the fight to them. Every time one of their patrols would spot us, they would try to follow. We just led them deeper and deeper into the woods until they were lost."

"Did you kill them?" asked Sam.

The Chief thought it over for a moment, and he knew there really wasn't much sense in saying they didn't kill the North Koreans. They didn't know how many troops were in the invasion force, so they had to reduce the number of hostile combatants. They also didn't have the ability to take prisoners. There would be no place to keep them, and you only took prisoners if you intended to also take care of them.

"We didn't have much choice, Sam. They were holding half of our squad back at our main camp, and we learned they were torturing them to try to get enough information to figure out who we were and why we were on the island."

"When we were ready, we went into the water at night and began to swim down the coast on the mainland side of the island. It was deeper water, and we could go a greater distance without being detected."

"That had to be cold," said Whitney.

"That's why we were there," said the Chief. "We learned you could go into freezing cold water for a lot longer than we thought we could. Anyway, when we were far enough down the coast to come out of the water, the sentries weren't expecting us. They had their rifles slung across their backs, and they were messing up their own night vision by lighting cigarettes."

"We caught most of their force asleep, and to get them to talk about why they were on Kodiak, we just took their clothes away from them and tossed them into the water."

"What he's leaving out," said Kathy, "is that he was the leader of the squad that took out the invasion force. They called him the Kodiak Bear because of his size. The North Koreans they captured told interrogators that they had been afraid of the big bear that walked on two feet like a man."

The kids laughed again, and for once the Chief was appreciating the attention. For a fleeting moment, Kathy thought it would be nice if he was twenty-five years younger.

"Did you get to do anymore real fighting after that?" asked Sam.

Whitney smacked him in the back of the head. Sam must've seen it coming because he dodged most of the impact.

"Are you a fool or something? The man led a bunch of SEALS with rubber guns against thousands of North Koreans."

This time it was the Chief's turn to laugh.

"It wasn't thousands, Whitney, but every time I hear someone else tell the story something gets added to it. I've heard that we made bows and arrows, and I've even heard that we ate the ones we killed because we didn't have enough food when we had to hide in the woods."

That was meant to be funny, but it reminded them all of where they were and what was happening all around the world.

"Do you think you can stop the infected from biting more people?" asked Sam.

We all noticed Sam's voice crack just a little. He was sitting in the presence of a huge man who had done some huge things, and Sam was hoping the Chief could do some more.

"Sam, I may not be able to save the world, but I can promise to take good care of you three."

Kathy saw the hint of sadness in the way the Chief's eyes were partially closed, and she could tell he was thinking about Allison. It would be a long time before he would forgive himself for her death, even if it hadn't been his fault.

Perry brought the conversation back to the Chief's history by asking if he was also a hero in Desert Storm. He said they had learned about Desert Storm in school, and he learned that Navy SEALS had been some of the first to go into Iraq by SCUBA diving.

"I was in Desert Storm, Perry, and there were a lot of heroes there. I was just one of the guys who did his job. There have been thousands of heroes since then, especially the ones who have given their lives over there in the Middle East."

"I'll bet the men who went into combat with you would say otherwise, Chief," said Kathy. "Just knowing you were there with them had to make them feel better."

Kathy reached over and squeezed his hand, and she could feel the bond between them. The kids, not wanting to be left out of the moment, all reached across the table and stacked their hands on top of Kathy's.

A scraping sound from above broke the mood, and they all snatched their hands back to get ready to defend themselves. There was a knock on the big watertight door that was unmistakably from a live person. There was nothing for a few moments, and then the knock was repeated.

A man's voice, muted by the thick steel door, called out to the kids.

"You have to come out sooner or later, you know. Why not get it over with? We'll even let you live."

"They don't know about me and you, Chief?"

"It would seem that way," said the Chief. "Just like the North Koreans. We need to find a way to use that to our advantage."

The Chief drew Whitney over to him and whispered, "Do you know who this guy is?"

She nodded and said, "We've seen him around. He's like a vulture. He let us do all of the clearing before he tried to move in."

"Would he believe you if you offered to let him in if he came alone?"

"I think so. He doesn't seem too bright," she whispered.

"It's the best we can hope for," said the Chief. "We need to pilot the ship from above, and the only reason he hasn't done it yet himself is because he doesn't know how to.

Kathy, get in position as high as you can. Sam and Perry, you two can hide. I'll be up there by the galley. Whitney, back away from the hatch as soon as you unlock it."

Everyone got into their positions, and Whitney moved closer to the door.

"Mister, how do we know you won't hurt us?" she asked through the door.

"We have to stick together, little lady. It's the only way any of us are going to survive."

He tried to put on his sweetest, most charming show, but even through a steel door they could tell he was smirking.

"What if I just let you in? Maybe we can talk and work out a deal?"

There was an even longer pause than before. They couldn't see outside to tell what was happening, but the vulture was overconfident and had signaled for the three men he had with him to go ahead and climb from the boat back onto the dock. He felt like he could handle the three kids on his own. When he and his gang had arrived, they didn't even pay attention to the area down past the stern. If they had, they would have seen the boat tied at the opening of the raft retrieval bay.

"Okay, little lady. I'm all by myself. You can open the door now."

Whitney kept her eyes on the Chief to be sure, and he was counting down with one hand. He wanted her to delay for just a few seconds, or the guy might think it was a trap. When he was done counting, Whitney stepped forward and removed the steel pin from the lock. She spun the locking wheel and stepped back quickly. As soon as it was unlocked, the jerk outside yanked it open and came through. He made it about two feet when he heard the unmistakable sound of a hammer being pulled back and felt cold metal touch the side of his head above his left ear.

"The safety is off in case you were wondering," said Kathy.

He started to turn her way, but the Chief said from his right, "Keep your eyes straight ahead. Act like you're just standing there talking with someone, or I'll tell her to blow your brains out. Nod if you understand."

He nodded, and even though he wasn't told what to do with his hands, he had kept one on the door and the other still held his gun aimed at the floor.

"If you drop your gun, she will definitely pull the trigger. Carefully tuck it into your waistband and then step one more step inside so your friends won't be able to see you clearly. The little lady will then step forward and remove the gun from your waistband."

The leader of the scavengers tried only once to convince the Chief he was alone, and he barely had the words out of his mouth when he forgot what he was saying. When the Chief stepped into view the guy gasped and took one involuntary step backward. To his friends outside he was just having a chat with someone and sizing up the opposition.

The Chief was doing exactly that inside. The man's hair was long, and he was wearing an ankle length leather coat despite the comfortable weather. That meant more hidden weapons. The man cocked his head to one side and was likely to be figuring the odds of grabbing Whitney when she stepped forward to get the gun from his waistband.

"Did you forget about me?" asked Kathy. She pressed the gun just a little harder against his head.

The size of the Chief really did make him forget he had a gun against his head. When he remembered she was still there, he wondered if she was the same size as the big guy who was moving slowly toward him. He started to gradually turn his head in Kathy's direction when a massive hand grabbed him by the front of his shirt and yanked him forward.

The scavengers outside had been watching their leader's back the whole time, and when they saw him pulled inside like a rag doll, they had that split second of indecision anyone would have, and then they started to react.

That split second, though, was all the time the infected dead would need. The men had been so intent on the door of the ship that they hadn't checked behind themselves for too long. Their screams pierced the air with such agony that they startled everyone inside the Coast Guard ship.

The Chief was just about to make an example of the leader when the screaming started, and he knew without needing proof what must have happened. He kept his hold on the man while he reached past him and pulled the door shut.

As soon as the door was shut, the screaming sounded like it was far away, and then it stopped. Shots were fired by the three scavengers on the dock, at this point with only revenge in mind. When the shooting stopped, the Chief and Kathy knew what to expect next.

Bullets began bouncing off of the steel door as the three enraged men shouted insults at the kids inside. They still didn't know what had happened to their leader, but to them the kids were the reason they were all going to die. In between the bullets, there were curses and threats, but the Chief didn't plan on opening the door until he knew it was all over.

The leader was still in the Chief's grip, but he tried to twist free. The Chief only had to tighten his grip to stop the struggling. He pulled the much smaller man up to his face.

"Try to get away again, and I'll toss you out there with your friends. We all know what they'll be in a few minutes if they were bitten."

Kathy climbed down from her perch above the door and searched the surprised man for weapons. She started by pulling off the ankle length coat. There was another pistol in the small of his back, and he had a couple of knives. He had expected a woman built like a linebacker, not a gorgeous blond.

"What's your name?" asked the Chief. "And don't make me ask you twice."

"Frank Tupperman, but my friends call me Tupp," said the man. He held out his right hand like he thought the Chief would shake it.

"We're not your friends Mr. Tupperman," growled the Chief. "What would you have done to these kids if we hadn't been here?"

Whitney, Sam, and Perry all stepped into the light where he could see them.

"Nothing, I promise. We just wanted them to share this ship with us, that's all." His voice started to take on a pleading tone.

"He's the one we saw giving tied up women to those guys out at Fort Sumter." said Whitney.

"She doesn't know what she's talking about," said Tupperman, but he could tell they weren't buying his protests.

"Okay, okay, I was only trying to survive like everybody else. You can't blame me for that."

"Yes, as a matter of fact we can," said Kathy. "We just rescued one of those women and a young man, and we killed all of the parasites who were living in Fort Sumter."

Tupperman was afraid before, but if these two had anything to do with wiping out the gang that was holding Fort Sumter, they must be even worse than he thought.

"What are you going to do with me?" he pleaded.

Kathy thought he sounded so pitiful that he was going to ask for a lawyer.

The Chief said, "When your friends have had enough time to die, then turn into infected dead, and then either fall overboard or down into the boat retrieval ramp, we're going to toss you out there with them. We don't take prisoners, and I don't want you to survive at someone else's loss any longer than you need to."

The Chief tied and gagged Tupperman to keep him quiet. They were surprised to see he was crying at one point, but he was the kind of person who would go right back to what he had been doing before if they let him go. The crying was just an act, and they had seen acts before. He was still crying when the Chief threw him out the door.

Whitney caught them off guard when she asked, "What are you going to do with us?"

Kathy and the Chief both understood at the same time that they had built up hope in the three young children, but they hadn't come right out and said they were going to help them.

"Whitney, if you guys would like to go with us, we have more than enough room for you, and you would be very safe," said Kathy.

All three of them beamed. They had been on their own for the better part of a year, and they were a lot tougher than kids their ages should have to be, but they were using the backs of their hands to catch the tears that were leaking from the corners of their eyes.

Kathy suddenly felt that she was seeing them as real kids for the first time. They had rags for clothes, they needed long, hot showers, but more than anything they needed grown ups to make them feel like everything would be normal again. She stepped forward toward them and held her arms wide, and they didn't hesitate to accept her hug.

The Chief was shifting from one foot to the other, and Kathy used one arm to pull him into the group. If the kids didn't feel completely good before, they did now.

"Okay, kids. Let's get organized," said Kathy. "We have some work to do. The Chief can pilot just about any kind of ship, and this one is going to be a cinch, but he's going to need a crew."

Whitney said, "We've been talking about using this ship to escape since the day we had to lock the door. My parents said to stay inside no matter what happened, but they also said to try to use the ship to get away if we could. The machine guns were loud, and they were shooting for a long time. When they stopped and no one came back, we started trying to figure out how to start the boat, but we didn't know how."

"The wheelhouse is up above," said the Chief. "The scavengers like Tupperman must not have been able to figure it out, either. They would have gladly used it to at least be safe out on the water, but they weren't sailors."

"We need to check on our friends outside," said Kathy, "then we'll get going. We can make a quick stop at Fort Sumter if there's no one else around, and then we can make a run for that barge we need."

"I want to check our fuel and ammunition first," said the Chief. "If I'm correct, there's an ammo locker forward of crew's berthing. That way ammunition could be loaded easily to the guns topside."

Kathy went to the door and listened, but she couldn't hear anything. That could mean anything since the infected tended to just stand around when they had nothing drawing their attention.

The door lock spun as smooth as silk, and the door was easy to push open on its well-greased hinges, but the infected was facing her way when she tried to see outside. One of the former scavengers came for her at a stumbling fall as it tripped over debris and gear left on the deck. Kathy jumped backward, and the infected slammed against the door, pushing it completely shut. Kathy spun the wheel to lock the door again. They were going to be stuck inside for a while unless the infected lost interest.

"There's another hatch up front, but we've always kept it shut," said Sam. "We used it once, but it was heavy and hard to get closed again."

"Show me where," said Kathy.

The Chief started forward too, but Kathy stopped him.

"No offense, Chief, but I wouldn't want you to get stuck going through a hatch."

The Chief was indignant and just about to give her a piece of his mind, but Kathy stopped him again. She laughed and gave him a hug.

"There are at least three of the infected out there, Chief. I can shoot them if they're in the wrong places, but you need to get up to the wheelhouse fast if we have more company. I'll relay word to you when it's clear."

The Chief had to admit he needed to stand by and let Kathy run things so he could do his job, and he was pretty sure it was because he had relived the rescue at the Kodiak base that he was having a hard time handing over control. He didn't brag about being a hero, but he did like taking charge when things got bad.

Kathy went forward to where Whitney had unlocked the forward hatch.

"There shouldn't be anything up on the front of the ship," said Whitney. "We blocked the little walkways on both sides of the ship when we had the chance. That way nothing could surprise us if we had to use the front hatch to escape."

Kathy pushed the hatch up and cautiously poked her head out into the sunshine. She turned in a circle and was relieved to see that the wheelhouse totally blocked the view of the aft area. She climbed out the rest of the way and peeked around the corner of the wheelhouse. She could see one of the infected wandering around near the stern, but the narrow walkway along the side of the wheelhouse had assorted pieces of gear piled up in a haphazard pattern.

Kathy had to admit the kids were bright. There was only a low rope railing along the edge of the walkway. The Coasties who had sailed the Cormorant knew how to navigate that narrow path when the ship was at sea, but the infected dead couldn't navigate it when the ship was sitting still.

She let out a whistle, and the infected immediately turned in her direction and started for the path. When it reached the pile of debris, it tried to go around it and did a perfect head first dive into the water.

The commotion the first infected caused was all it took to draw the other two from wherever they had been standing around to her side of the wheelhouse. It was like watching the Three Stooges go through the door at the same time as they pushed against each other to be the first to reach Kathy. It wasn't long before one caused the other to flip over the rope railing to join its former friend in the water.

"Two down and one to go," said Kathy.

This one she didn't wait for. She calmly walked toward it as the infected eagerly stumbled toward the debris from its side. When it reached over the debris and tried to grab her, she caught it by the back of its forearm, rotated it toward the water and gave it a shove.

There was one thing about the infected dead when they fell that always fascinated Kathy. They didn't have a fear of falling, so they didn't put their hands out to catch themselves. Instead, they just face-planted into whatever was there. In this case, it had been nose first into the water that was gently lapping at the side of the Cormorant.

Kathy climbed a small ladder up the side of the wheelhouse and could see there were no more infected dead on the ship, but she could also see there were more on their way. The earlier gunshots had drawn them from outside the base. There was a green and white sign at the corner that said Tradd Street, and there were at least a dozen infected walking past the sign and through the front gate of the Coast Guard base.

She stuck her head down the hatch and yelled, "The deck is clear, but we have lots of company heading our way. We need to move fast."

The Chief didn't need a second warning. He and the kids went out through the cabin door onto the stern as quickly as they could. He only stopped long enough to tell Whitney to get their boat secured by a tow rope and to tell the boys to cast off the lines.

Whitney said, "I can do better than a tow rope."

The Chief didn't ask her what she meant. He was too busy getting up into the wheelhouse of the Cormorant. He rotated fore and aft on the eighty-seven foot craft to locate the sound of an engine and couldn't believe it when Whitney pulled up along side the Coast Guard ship and waved up at him.

"My dad was a Coastie," she yelled. "I can drive any kind of boat because he taught me."

The Chief gave her a broad smile and waved back. He had to admit. Having someone steering their boat was better than towing it. He watched as she idled close to his starboard side and handled a slight chop in the water without bumping against the bigger boat.

On the port side he saw the boys had already brought in the fore and aft lines and were helping Kathy push the bow away from the dock. It was much more comfortable knowing the infected weren't going to be able to come aboard.

The distance between the dock and the ship slowly widened as a result of being pushed away, but the Chief hadn't started the engine yet. She held her arms out wide with her palms up, hoping he would understand she was asking why they weren't powered up and pulling away yet.

He responded by showing his palms to her and then facing them toward the ground. It was a signal they had used many times to say, "Wait."

When the infected reached the edge of the dock the crowd had swollen to about thirty. There were more passing the Tradd Street sign, and there was no end in sight. More and more came around the corner.

Down on the deck Sam and Perry both wanted the Chief to get them out of there, but Kathy told them not to worry. The Chief had his reasons, and the gap between the dock and ship was over six feet wide and getting wider. That was more than enough. They tried not to worry, but this was by far the biggest crowd of the infected they had seen in a long time.

"Aren't you going to shoot them?" asked Sam.

"No reason to waste the ammunition," said Kathy.

As the crowd grew bigger, it eventually filled the paved and concrete sections of the dock, and from the birds eye view of the wheelhouse, it didn't appear there was room for more.

From the deck level view of Kathy and the boys, it was like they were watching a slow parade coming straight toward them. Whitney had coasted to a spot just forward of the bow, and to her it was like a solid wall of injured people in various stages of decay.

Kathy knew what the Chief was waiting for and told the boys again not to worry. They understood why when the wall of infected began marching over the edge, and once it began, it seemed like it would never end.

She jumped just a little, but then she started laughing when the Chief's voice came through a large speaker above the wheelhouse.

"That's it, you ugly, groaning jerks. Walk right out here and go for a swim."

The loudspeaker agitated the infected, and the groaning did increase for a few minutes, but as more and more fell over the edge of the dock into the water, the noise began to subside.

Perry held a thumb up in the air in the Chief's direction. He understood that the Chief had a golden opportunity to reduce the infected dead population, and there was no reason not to take advantage of that opportunity.

The Chief returned the gesture and then tried the ignition. The well tended engine turned over and the vibration rumbled through the ship, but the Chief didn't pull away from the dock. He figured as long as the dead kept coming, it was worth it to see them go where they wouldn't be any harm to living people.

Kathy got his attention and pointed at the starboard side. The Chief walked across the deceptively large wheelhouse to get a better view down at the water. There were infected dead popping to the surface on the other side of the Cormorant, but they weren't staying afloat. After sliding over the surface for a few feet, they went back under for a second time. The Chief saw bodies doing the same thing behind the ship, but instead of just popping to the surface, some were virtually launched into the air. Most were coming up in pieces. With more than a little amusement, he realized the twin screws were swirling the infected around under the ship and ejecting them.

Whitney saw the water was getting crowded and proved she had good sense by moving their boat to a safer distance. She also moved forward since most of the bodies were going aft.

They watched for close to thirty minutes as hundreds of infected dead walked over the side and fell into the water. Perry and Sam were worried that they could climb aboard at first, but they accepted Kathy's explanation that they wouldn't climb a ladder if you threw it to them. She also told them the bad news, and that was the infected dead were still dangerous in the water. She explained that they would sink, the current would carry them away, fish and crabs would eat them, but they could still bite you if you fell into the water with them.

"The crabs?" asked Sam in a higher than normal voice. "I love to go crabbing with my friends."

"Well," said Kathy, "I wouldn't recommend eating blue crabs anymore."

Sam was a little sick, and that reminded Kathy of Jean. If there was ever anyone who got sick when she thought about the blue crabs eating the infected dead, it was Jean, and she was that way before she got pregnant. After getting pregnant, you could get her to turn pale just by mentioning blue crabs.

As the parking lot and ship loading areas emptied of the horde of infected that had swarmed into the base, the Chief continued to coax them forward over the loudspeaker. In the meantime, Kathy inspected the fifty caliber machine guns mounted on the bow. She was surprised to find there was no protection for the person firing the guns until she discovered they were remote controlled. That meant they weren't aimed manually and were deadly accurate. She was also pleased that a third gun was mounted ahead of the other two on the bow. It was under a tarp, and had ammunition being fed to it from below.

Kathy found an interior communications microphone on a forward mount and keyed the switch.

"Chief, the hatches forward of the wheelhouse aren't for passing ammunition to the machine gun operators. The fifty calibers are remote controlled."

The Chief keyed the microphone to the loudspeaker and said, "Surprise."

Kathy inspected all three weapons and thought about the Coasties and the parents who had gone topside to protect their children. They had told the kids they were going to fight to save them, and they should stay below. Maybe they had used the fifty caliber machine guns from the wheelhouse, but it was becoming more and more obvious they had taken the fight to the infected dead out on the decks of the Cormorant. What they didn't know, and what they could not have known was the extent of the crisis. They hadn't known it was a worldwide apocalypse.

If they had known there was no way to win the fight, they could have sailed the Cormorant to safety. Then again, they would also have carried as many wounded as possible with them, so it was fortunate for the three survivors after all. If they had sailed out of Charleston harbor seeking the safety of the open sea, they would have been no different from the cruise liner that Kathy had escaped on. They would all have died from within.

The gap between the Cormorant and the docks had grown to yards instead of feet, and the last of the infected were falling into the water. There were a few stragglers, but they were still walking toward the sound of the ship as it was drifting away. The Chief called out on the loudspeaker to Whitney that he was coming to starboard, and she increased her distance ahead of the bow. Eighty-seven feet wasn't a big ship, but it could do twenty-five knots and had some lethal firepower on its deck. The Chief found himself excited about running into the Cuban gunboats that had shot him down.

Kathy came through the door of the wheelhouse and was impressed by the spacious bridge and sophisticated electronics.

"Do you know how to operate all of this stuff?" she asked the Chief.

"Most of it is basic. I'll show you where the remote controls are for the guns in a minute. As I recall from a ship this size out in Alaska, they could single target or they could all be aimed at one target. If you've ever played a video game, it's not much different."

"Eddie should really enjoy that part," said Kathy.

"That's what I was thinking a minute ago," said the Chief. "Eddie's going to get to play his video games after all."

After they shared a laugh, Kathy asked the Chief why the Cormorant had three of the remote controlled fifty-caliber machine guns. She said she had seen plenty of the Coast Guard ships when she was a police officer in Charleston, and that they usually only had two guns.

The Chief, being a wealth of information when it came to ships told her the Cormorant must have been assigned to patrol near one of the Navy submarine bases at some point, maybe Kings Bay, Georgia. He explained that they typically were equipped with three guns to make them just a bit more deadly, and he wasn't going to complain.

As the Cormorant turned to starboard and pulled away from the dock, Whitney powered up their boat and moved to the port side. She matched their speed and waved at her two friends who were still out on the bow. Kathy and the Chief could see all three kids were happy to be free of what had been little more than a prison for almost a year.

After everything the Chief and Kathy had seen so far, the sight of Whitney cruising between the Cormorant and the homes along Charleston's historic section was beautiful and somewhat surreal. The Chief almost let the beauty of the city make him forget just how dangerous it could be, and he used the loudspeaker to get Whitney's attention.

"Cruise to my starboard side, Whitney."

Over the drone of her engines Whitney heard the rather curt message and guessed the meaning immediately. She increased her speed and passed the Cormorant, taking up a position on the starboard side where she was protected by the larger ship.

Kathy said, "Did you know this type ship is known as the Marine Protector Class, Chief?"

"That's appropriate for what we have in mind. I want to meet those guys who shot me down. I think the reason I'm still so mad about it is because they didn't have to shoot me down. They just did it because they could. I don't have to sink them now. I just want to."

12 SIEGE

After the Chief and Kathy had gotten far enough away, and the lights had been turned off over the fort, the rest of the group began to feel the stress of the day taking its toll. There wasn't anything we could do about the gunboats, and there wasn't anything we needed to do yet. We would have to decide after the Chief and Kathy returned.

Chase took Olivia's hand and led her out of the control room leaving me, Tom, and Bus. Of the three of us, Bus appeared to be the most down.

"Are you okay, Bus?" I asked.

I didn't have to spell it out for him. There had been enough distraction for all of us to avoid thinking about Allison, but now that the day was over, and there wasn't anything left to do about the threats outside, there was only time to think.

"I'll manage," he said. "I was just thinking about Molly."

It was easy to see the effect that had on Tom. He was holding his head up as best as he could, but telling Molly was going to be hard.

"I think it's time to get drunk," said Tom.

Tom put his arm over his old friend's shoulders and walked him out of the control room. I was left to watch over the dead world outside, but I couldn't forget about the fleet of small gunboats that were floating not far from the jetties. I could see their shapes in the wide angle view from the satellite, but for some reason I couldn't get the satellite to rotate for the view that would allow me to see far enough up the coast. It had been nice to see Mud Island, but maybe the satellite could only do so much before it ran out of fuel.

I knew enough about satellites to know this one was geosynchronous, meaning that it stayed in one spot, orbiting at a speed that matched the Earth's rotation. Changing its view the way the Chief had done would require fuel for small rockets, and maybe it had already been low on fuel when the Chief had turned it.

Whatever was wrong, it was nothing but a small disappointment, and I had been learning how to deal with disappointments in the last year. At least the Chief had come back from the dead...not as an infected but as the living, breathing leader of our group. I smiled despite the loss of the satellite angle.

My eyes drifted over the monitors, and I saw there was nothing moving in the fort above us, and the gunboats had apparently dropped anchors. The tide was coming in, and the two that were trapped in shallow water were beginning to make some progress pulling themselves free of the muddy bottom.

I must have dozed off because the next time I opened my eyes, the two boats were almost gone from sight. They had undoubtedly gone out to deeper water than the rest of the boats, not wanting to be embarrassed by getting stuck in the mud for a second time.

The sun was coming up behind the fleet of intruders, so the lights weren't going to be a deterrent until it got dark again. I zoomed in with the satellite camera, and I could see people in several of the boats had binoculars aimed toward Fort Sumter. They had to be trying to decide how to approach the fort, and they had no way to gather more intelligence. They could see bodies on the rocks, so they could tell there had been a recent battle. What they couldn't tell was whether or not the battle was over. As far as they knew, Fort Sumter was deserted, but there could easily be a trap.

Putting myself in their shoes, I figured their best bet was to pass on this target, but they must have been hoping to find something of value, or maybe they just didn't like losing two of their boats because someone had turned on the lights. I also considered which boat was the leader of the others, guessing that the others would be less organized if they lost their commander.

I watched for a sign and saw similar behavior from the crews on all of the boats until I saw the man with the binoculars in the closest boat signal with hand gestures for the second boat to come closer. When it pulled alongside the lead boat, the man pointed in the general direction of the harbor, but I was certain he was telling them to circle around to the other side of the fort.

The boat immediately increased its power and sped across the harbor until it was near Castle Pinckney. It was a relatively small island, and the remains of the fort were nothing more than a single wall and some sand, but it afforded cover for the boat from a possible attack from the rear.

It was in position for only a moment when the second boat followed it, and as soon as it arrived the first boat left. It circled from the small island all the way to where the Ashley River marshes came up behind Fort Sumter. I was thinking about how much fun it would be to see the first boat get stuck in the mud. It was deceptively shallow in some spots, and I could see by the channel markers that he was very close to making that mistake.

A third boat followed the pattern and then a fourth, but after one went to join the first boat, two stayed by Castle Pinckney. I wondered if these morons had read any American history, because Fort Sumter was surrounded during the Civil War and easily captured. In this case there wasn't really anything to capture. There were still weapons scattered among the dead, but it wasn't like we really cared if they found them. There wasn't anything sophisticated, and since they wouldn't suspect a hidden bunker to be under the surface of the fort, there wouldn't be any strategic value for them to occupy it. They were more of a problem to us as long as they were in their boats, and if they were inside the fort, we could always consider doing the same thing to them that we had done to the last occupants.

I watched for almost an hour as the boats on the Ashley River side of the fort slowly inched their way forward. It certainly appeared they were aiming for the dock. Zooming in with the camera I could see that one of the crewmen was using a pole to test the depth of the water, and my best guess was that they were only clearing the bottom by about a foot. It would get deeper as they got closer, but they were trying to skim along the marsh much closer inland than the dock. I wondered how they would feel if they knew all they had to do was just drive straight up to it. Since tour boats had docked there before the infection, it had to be deeper water.

When the first two boats were about halfway to their goal, the two boats by Castle Pinckney both raced toward the marsh and stopped at the starting point of the lead boats. Two more boats rushed to the spot vacated by the second pair. Six boats were upriver to the left of the fort, and four were to the right by the jetties.

The sun had risen well above the horizon, and I had all the camera angles I needed. The harbor was probably more beautiful than it had ever been. The morning air was so clear that I could make out details in the shallow water, and because there hadn't been any big container ships stirring up the mud on the bottom I could see deeper than ever. I saw shadows moving that were larger than sharks or alligators. From above it looked like dark clouds under the surface of the water. I aimed a camera toward the sky just to be sure it wasn't a cloud blocking the sun, but there was nothing but blue sky.

When I brought the camera back down, I saw that the first boat was directly in the middle of the shadow, and the shadow appeared to be growing. The crew of the second boat was slow to realize that the first boat had stopped moving forward, and the man with the pole was pulling on it like it had become stuck in the mud.

The second boat moved over the growing shadow to join the first boat, and the second pair coming down the Ashley River behind them was starting along the same path as the first four.

I suddenly remembered that I could record the events from the console where I was seated, and I hit the red button. I had a feeling that I was seeing something that could be important later, and I also had a feeling that we had been seriously lucky that what I was going to see hadn't happened to us already.

There had been so many times in the last year that we had been out on the water, and sometimes it had been shallow water. I wondered how many of those times we had moved away just before disaster was about to strike. It was like we had walked through the alligator pits at the zoo, but we weren't attacked because we didn't make enough noise.

The two boats were practically touching each other at the bow and stern when they started to rotate in unison. They both began to turn clockwise as if they were synchronized. The shadow under the boats had also turned darker, and it took on the shape of an oil slick. There were four men in each boat, and they were all scrambling to find something to hang onto. One man on the lead boat jumped onto the bow and grabbed the fifty caliber machine gun. He pulled back on the handle on the side of the weapon and aimed as low as he could at the water. The silent weapon sprayed the huge bullets into the water at the shadow as the boat began to turn faster and rock from side to side as it rotated.

The scenario on the second boat was strikingly similar, with the exception of the man with the pole. I watched as he struggled with something trying to pull it from his hands, and he didn't know when to let go. He lost his footing in the rocking, rotating boat and was pulled overboard.

I remembered when we had docked our seaplane at a marina near Guntersville, Alabama, and we found that the bottom of the lake near the shore was crowded with the infected dead. There had been no current to push them away from the place where they had entered the water, so they had just been standing there on the lake floor just waiting for unsuspecting prey to pass too close to them. The difference there had been that the lake bottom had been about ten feet below, so they were unable to reach high enough to grab us. There had been some close calls, but the depth of the water had kept us relatively safe.

Here in the harbor along the marsh that lined the Ashley River, there was a treacherous bottom of mud that could suck your feet under and never let you go. The depth that you would get stuck depended on what was under the mud. If there was an old oyster bed hidden below, you would get sucked down and left standing knee deep in the mud. When the tide would go out, your head might rise above the water, but you would never leave that spot.

The shadow I had seen growing under the boats was simply more and more infected dead joining their unfortunate brothers and sisters as they became stuck in the mud. Unable to move and unable to pull themselves from where they were held in place, all they could do was reach up and touch the bottoms of the two boats. I could see arms from the elbows to the fingers reaching, trying to find something to grasp. They couldn't reach into the boats, but hundreds of wet hands slapped against the hulls.

Now the rotation began to slow, but both boats were pointed straight toward the shoreline and the marsh grass. The second boat had also opened fire on the infected dead that were holding the boats in place. The flat surfaces of the stern on each boat presented more area for the slapping hands, and the boats began to be pushed toward the shallower water.

Someone on boat number two decided the engine propellor would be a good idea, and they increased the throttle. Their mistake was only that the propellor was in the water, so they succeeded in driving the boat straight into the mud flats only inches below the surface. They were safe from the infected because they couldn't follow the boat through the sucking mud, but they weren't going anywhere for a long time.

The crew of the second boat apparently decided that stuck was better than dead, so they engaged their engine and drove up alongside the second boat. The shadow stayed just out of reach for the time being, but then I saw something I wouldn't have believed if I hadn't seen it with my own eyes.

With growing horror, the crews of the two boats saw the same thing I was seeing. There were more and more infected dead coming in from upriver, being carried along by the current. Hundreds of infected that were not stuck in the mud began piling up on the infected that were stuck below them. They made slow progress, but using the dark mass of infected below them, they were crawling from body to body in the direction of the two boats.

Less than fifty yards upriver from them, the second pair of boats were watching helplessly as their friends had become mired in the bodies. The crews felt something bumping against the hulls of their boats but were too late coming to the conclusion that the bumps were more infected dead coming from somewhere upriver.

I figured the huge shadow in the water had been the dead that had fallen from the dock on the previous night, but I couldn't imagine where all of the new infected were coming from. The last time I had seen the Chief and Kathy was when they had gone up the Ashley River to the Coast Guard base, and I wondered if they had anything to do with it. If anyone could be responsible for hundreds of the infected being washed out of Charleston in the rivers it would be those two.

The crews of the second pair of boats could have turned toward deeper water and raced away, but they were too slow to react, and they were pushed by the growing tide of bodies moving with the current. Their hulls were being slapped hard from the port sides, and they were quickly forced into the shallow water of the marsh grass just like the first boats. Their fate was determined more quickly than the first two boats because the mud wasn't as deep. The boats were stuck, but the infected dead were pushing themselves into standing positions and beginning a slow walk toward them.

The gunners on the two boats began firing at the infected, but they were panicked. The bullets were wasted on bodies and even thin air with very few heads being hit. They succeeded in knocking down the growing army that was closing in on them, but it wasn't long before they ran out of ammunition, and the infected were pulling themselves onto the stern. All eight crewmen went over the bow and were trying to cross the marshy mudflats between the river and the mainland. It wouldn't be long before they found themselves in the deeper pockets of mud that dotted the flooded marshes. There was nothing predictable about where the mud was solid and where it was a deathtrap, and one by one there were eight living people immobilized to the knees by the mud.

The infected dead that followed them were moving at a much slower pace, and many of them became stuck in the mud just as the living had done, but whenever they became stuck, it forced those that were coming from behind them to take a different path. Gradually the mud pockets were filled, and the infected were almost walking unimpeded to their prey over more solid ground. They bumped into their fellow infected. They fell and were sometimes knocked over again before they could even get back up. They even got stuck when others fell on top of them, but they kept coming.

The eight crewmen were spread out across the mudflats standing between patches of green grass, but the wall of slowly advancing infected dead had grown to dozens. I could see the crewmen twisting and turning, trying to pull themselves free. One of them broke free from the suction of the mud and found himself on a patch of solid ground. For once, I saw that one show some common sense. He began moving carefully in the direction of one of the other men until he could grip the other man's outstretched hand. They were far enough from the others to take their time, so they worked together to get the trapped man free.

For a moment they moved toward a third man who was facing them. Even though I couldn't hear them, I knew the trapped man was begging for their help. I also knew from experience that the slowly advancing horde was increasing the pitch of the groaning they did when they advanced on a victim. Then I could tell that the two free men were telling the others how sorry they were that they couldn't help. One of them did the sign of the cross as he turned from the others. Even as they turned and began cautiously finding solid ground between the patches of mud, the first of the infected dead reached the first of the living men. He seemed to be sucked up in the swarm of bodies just as he had been sucked in by the mud.

The two escapees were holding onto each other and making steady progress toward the mainland. If they didn't panic, they would make it.

I shifted my view a little and zoomed in on the first two boats. It was like seeing a logjam of bodies, and it reminded me of when we saw the mass of bodies pop to the surface behind Mud Island after the Russian ship had blown up. The difference was that these bodies weren't swollen and bloated from being in the water for months. They weren't covered by blue crabs and unable to move because of the extra water weight. These infected were able to grab at the growing mass of bodies and begin crawling forward.

Crewmen who jumped from the bows of the first two boats became stuck immediately. There were fewer patches of solid ground available to them once they were closer to the dock. Those that stayed in the boats had a choice between trying to fight off the infected dead or joining their living friends. Then there was the third choice. I saw one crewman put a gun in his mouth and pull the trigger. Yet another crewman went up on the bow of the first boat, took aim, and mercifully shot a crewmen who had become stuck in the mud. I saw him put the barrel of the gun to his own head, and then he pulled the gun down and studied it for a moment. He didn't have a bullet left for himself.

On the monitor view that faced the mudflats I saw the two crewmen exiting the marsh grass and disappearing into the woods. For now they were safe, but I had no idea what it would be like for them where they had found safety.

The six crewmen who had been with them were all vague shapes in a sea of swarming bodies. I hadn't seen if any of them had taken the fast way out by eating a bullet, but it didn't matter anymore.

The man who had run out of bullets was standing on the bow doing a good job of clubbing infected dead with the empty pistol. If he couldn't shoot himself, he was at least going to take as many of the infected with him as he could.

During the massacre, the two boats that remained by Castle Pinckney had problems of their own. They had watched as the other four boats were gradually doomed by the floating horde of infected. When they finally decided to attempt a rescue, they found their propellors were so fouled by bodies that had drifted down their side of the river that they wouldn't turn. They were busily pushing at the bodies with anything they could find when one of the crewmen screamed in pain. I couldn't hear him, but I knew what had happened by watching his shipmates. They rushed to him as he pulled back a badly bitten arm.

They had entered the harbor with twelve boats and lost two in the first minutes. Now they had lost four more and had an injured crewman on one more. They had six boats, but two were still trying to get themselves free as they tended to the wounded man. Their commanding officer had watched with growing anger and a fair amount of confusion. They had mocked the dead when they were examining a camera on a small island to the north, but now they were being beaten by the infected in the water.

He ordered his remaining four boats to move in at high speed to try to at least free the two boats by Castle Pinckney. If he had known the officers on those boats were too cowardly to assist the other boats sooner, he would have had them shot. Now he was having to rescue them.

I wished for about the tenth time that the others were awake to be watching this, but at least it was being recorded. I had no sooner made the wish when they all arrived, laughing and joking after a long night of safe sleep. Olivia and Chance had dropped all pretense of simple friendship. They had their arms interlocked and leaned into each other as they walked.

I was frantically waving at them to hurry up, and the laughing stopped as they ran over to my console to see what was happening. Tom and Bus got to me first with Olivia and Chance close on their heels.

The shock on their faces was obvious. Swarms of infected dead were out on the marshy mudflats behind Fort Sumter. Four boats full of infected dead were only a short distance from the dock, and there was a man standing on the bow of one boat swinging a pistol like a hammer. The main view was a monitor that showed four boats racing at high speed toward Castle Pinckney where two other boats seemed to be just sitting in the shadow of the old castle wall. Even as we watched, a group of the infected dead appeared at the top of the wall and began falling onto the boats below.

"Where are they all coming from?" asked Tom. The note of disbelief in his voice could not have been disguised.

"Beats me," I said, "but they seem to be coming from upriver somewhere. There's been a steady flow of them. I got it all on film, but trust me, I'll never try to get away from them by driving a boat into the marsh."

Chance said, "Hey, everyone, check this out."

He pointed at a screen I hadn't been watching, and when we turned to it, we got the surprise of our lives. A Coast Guard ship was charging toward the four boats at high speed, and it was all business with three fifty caliber machine guns mounted on the bow. Even before it seemed to be in range of the four speeding Cuban gunboats, the machine guns opened fire.

Remote controlled guns had the advantage of not placing men in harm's way, but their biggest advantage was accuracy. They could compensate in a split second for waves or swells, and they began targeting sooner because the computer told the gunners when to open fire.

The fifty caliber rounds ripped through the gunboats as if someone had reached out and torn them in half down the middle. The lead boat that carried the commanding officer disintegrated first, and the others were shredded as they tried to turn away and run.

The crewmen of the remaining two gunboats thought better than to open fire on the bigger ship as it began a sweeping turn toward them. They had managed to toss the infected overboard and still had only one wounded crewman, and they wanted to keep it that way. They all climbed quickly onto the bows of their boats and got down on their knees with their hands behind their heads.

As the Coast Guard ship came across their bows, they watched the fifty caliber guns rotate together as one. We were sure they were going to be cut apart the way the other four boats were, but the ship cruised past as if it was slicing through the water and began another sweeping turn back toward Fort Sumter.

"That has to be the Chief," I said.

"And Kathy," added Tom. I noticed he had a trace of a smile on his lips.

"There's another boat coming from upriver," said Bus. "It's the boat the Chief and Kathy left with, but I can't tell who's driving it."

The Coast Guard ship completed its turn and came up broadside to the dock at the deepest spot. The name on the side of the wheelhouse said it was the Cormorant. We watched through our cameras as Kathy and the Chief emerged from the wheelhouse along with two teenaged boys. The other boat was being driven by a teenaged girl, and she disappeared somewhere on the other side of the eighty-seven foot ship. We saw Kathy help her climb aboard over the port side railing.

"Smart," said Bus. "They're keeping the boat out away from the dock in deeper water."

It wasn't that we thought it could be anybody but the Chief and Kathy coming back with guns blazing, but this time we were all amazed. The Chief was always coming up with a way to beat the odds. He just didn't believe in losing. No wonder he was so hard on himself when he came back without Allison.

They knew someone would be watching through the cameras, so Kathy and the Chief got the two boys and the girl to line up with them on the deck of the Cormorant facing the fort. On a signal we couldn't hear, all five of them held hands and then did a deep bow for us. We started laughing and applauding at the monitors as if they could hear us.

I turned in time to see Tom disappearing through the door of the control room. At first I thought he was just doing what I would have done if it was Jean down there on the deck of that ship, but then the urge hit me too. That was a real Coast Guard ship down there, and it had the potential to have me back with Jean much sooner than I had expected. I jumped out of my chair and caught up with Tom before he reached the tunnel to the surface.

We each hit the ladders at full speed, and if not for the fact that I almost beat him to the top, I wouldn't have even paid attention to the fact that I was physically more fit than I had been in years.

Tom opened the door and was running as fast as he could. The sunshine felt good, but the place really reeked because of all the killing in the last couple of days. Since I had to stop to close the door, Tom put some distance between us. We were like two kids trying to win some sort of prize. At least we were until Tom stepped on something that made his feet fly out from under him.

He had gone through the tunnel and was making the turn on the dock when it happened, and it looked like he was airborne forever. He sailed out over the mud and landed not far from the first gunboat that had been stranded near the dock.

No one could have been more surprised than Tom, but all of us felt equally helpless. Tom was closer to the boat than to the dock, and all we could do was yell at him to climb. We were all so focused on Tom and the infected dead that were trying to reach him that we hardly noticed the obvious. One of the hands that was reaching for him was the crewman on the boat who had been fighting the infected with an empty gun. Tom reached up and grasped the man's hand in his, and made it to the bow of the boat just ahead of the snapping jaws of an infected dead.

The bow of the gunboat was separated from the main section by a windshield that had managed to stay intact despite infected that kept trying to climb over it. The man that had pulled Tom up with him was leaning over the windshield and cracking heads as fast as he could, but Tom didn't have a weapon. All he could do was watch.

The sound of the bullhorn on the side of the Cormorant was much louder than the Chief had expected, but the results were what he had hoped for. The infected dead in the back of the gunboat turned toward the sound and also made themselves easier targets for Kathy. The Chief yelled into his microphone for Tom to get down on the deck and to take the other guy with him.

At first the Cuban sailor misunderstood what Tom was trying to do, and he resisted, but when Kathy began firing the fifty caliber machine guns in their direction, he didn't need more explanation. Kathy kept the shots as high as she could and shredded the infected that she could target. There were still a few left standing, but the Chief was already in a position on the dock where he could shoot effectively.

When it was all over, Tom helped the rather uncertain sailor to his feet. Even though he had rescued Tom, he wasn't sure how they would treat him. What he didn't know was that the Chief already admired him for putting up such a good fight. He still had a grudge against the Cubans, but he might not have had anything to do with shooting him down.

Getting them from the bow of the gunboat to the dock was a bit tricky because there was still a dark shadow under the Cormorant that was growing. More infected dead emerged from the water and crawled over the bodies that accumulated there. Kathy and the Chief took turns shooting them as the infected crawled closer and closer, but they were never in danger of losing control of the horde. It occurred to the Chief that the number of infected was much larger than normal, but then he started to laugh. Kathy thought he had lost his mind.

"Care to let me in on the joke, Chief?"

As he sighted in on another infected he said, "I just figured out where all of the infected dead went after we walked them off of the dock back at the Coast Guard base."

"You have to be kidding me," said Kathy. "We did this?"

"I guess so. We must have emptied out the city. If there are any survivors left in Charleston, they're going to have a quieter night than usual."

I threw ropes over to both men so they could be pulled loose if they got stuck, then I lowered a rope ladder from the dock. Tom came up first, and the Cuban sailor followed. When they reached the dock, Kathy was there to hug Tom. The Cuban stood off to one side and wasn't sure what he should do next.

When the Chief walked up and glared down at the man, I thought he was going to jump back over the side. The Chief had a mean frown on his face, probably remembering what it felt like when his plane was crippled by one of the gunboats, but he held out his right hand to the frightened man. The Cuban studied the size of the hand compared to his own then tentatively shook the Chief's hand.

The Chief said thank you to the Cuban in Spanish then said something I totally didn't understand. The man answered and gestured toward the harbor. The Chief explained to us that the Cuban said his commander had bragged about shooting down a seaplane. The Chief asked him a series of new questions and then told us we had one last chore to take care of. He said we were going to do the right thing and take the Cuban sailor back to his remaining friends who were still stranded at Castle Pinckney.

Tom and Kathy walked back down the dock still holding hands, and that's when I remembered the kids. The three of them were still standing on the deck of the ship not sure what to do.

Kathy introduced them to Tom and then to everyone else. One at a time they shook hands with the adults that were beaming at them like they had never seen a kid before. Tom sized up the boys and figured they were in their early teens.

He was big when he stood next to them and he said in a fatherly way, "I have a daughter who's just a little younger than you guys. You know what that means?"

They weren't sure what he was getting at, so they both said in unison, "No, Sir."

"That means she's too young to date. You follow me?"

"Yes, Sir."

Kathy stepped in front of Tom and said, "Don't pay any attention to him. You'll get to meet Molly when we get back to our shelter."

Up to now the kids hadn't been told everything. It had been enough to feed them and protect them from the scavengers at the Coast Guard base. It might have been difficult for them to be told they were going to be leaving home behind, so Kathy and the Chief hadn't mentioned the shelter.

"Are we going to live here now?" asked Whitney.

Kathy said, "Let's go, guys. We can explain everything when we're all safe inside."

The Chief signaled for Tom and me to come with him and our Cuban friend. He explained that we were going to drop off the sailor with his shipmates, but we were also going to be faced with making them understand they couldn't keep anyone alive who might have been bitten. The way the infected were dropping in from the top of the wall, it was possible someone had been a victim.

Kathy started for the fort as we pulled away. I was hoping to see the reactions of the three kids when they went down the rabbit hole. I was sure they would be as surprised as we were, but I would just have to wait to see their faces when we reached Mud Island.

Kathy told us later that the big difference for the kids was when they entered the tunnel into Fort Sumter. We had no reason to clean up the mess we had made when we had first killed the scavengers and then disposed of the infected dead that were left behind. Bodies were everywhere, and the smell was beginning to be overpowering. Kathy hurried them along as quickly as she could to get them away from the stench. She said they were more than grateful when she pushed them through the hidden door that led to the shelter below.

The Chief asked me to drive the smaller boat over to Castle Pinckney. Tom shook the Cuban sailor's hand one more time before he climbed into the boat with me. I powered up and started across the harbor and was really surprised how quickly the Chief pulled alongside in the Coast Guard ship.

The Cuban sailors were still being rocked by the infected dead under their boats, but at least they had stopped raining from above. I saw one of the sailors had a towel or something wrapped around his right arm, and it was soaked with blood. They didn't know why we were coming back, so they got on their knees again. Then they saw their shipmate with me and started waving like we were old friends. The Chief turned the Cormorant broadside to the two boats, and Tom kept the machine guns aimed at them as a safety precaution.

I pointed at the coiled ropes on the bow, and my Cuban passenger understood what I wanted him to do. He climbed onto the bow and scooped the line up. Without getting myself in the same mess the others were in, I got in close enough for him to throw the rope to the first boat. We backed away until the line was taut, then repeated the maneuver with the second boat. There was cheering on the two Cuban boats even though they were most likely thinking they were going to be prisoners.

With the boats free to move again, I let mine drift in close enough for the Cuban sailor to jump over to his friends. He gave me a sharp salute, turned to the Cormorant and gave a salute in the direction of the wheelhouse, then jumped over. I could see I was right about one man being bitten, and the Cubans couldn't have survived this long without understanding the consequences. Either way, I didn't feel like hanging around to see how they dealt with it.

I turned my boat just ahead of the Cormorant and began racing back to the dock at Fort Sumter. We were doing much better than we had hoped by getting the Coast Guard ship. I imagined it could tow the barge back to Mud Island with no problems.

The only thing that could have made it a better evening for me would have been Jean being with me. I had tried more than once to establish radio contact with Mud Island, and I imagined Jean had Molly trying from their end. Sometimes I felt like it was better that we couldn't talk with each other. If we had been able to, we would have worried Jean needlessly about seeing the Chief and Allison crash the plane into the harbor. We also would have been forced to tell Molly that the Chief had come back, but Allison hadn't.

Our group had grown in size in a short time. Besides myself, the Chief, Kathy, Tom, and Bus, we now had Olivia, Chase, Whitney, Sam, and Perry. I wasn't sure how we would manage with twelve people at Mud Island, but at least we had a large cache of supplies below Fort Sumter.

We talked about the possibility of splitting into two groups and having someone stay behind at Fort Sumter. It would be useful to us as a well hidden advance warning station, but the inability to establish radio communications from the fort only made it good for extra living space and storage. Kathy joked that we could use it as a vacation home. We all felt like we at least had some hope. With three shelters at our disposal, it would be possible to give safe haven to a few people.

Supper was a celebration again. This time we had overcome some major obstacles just as big as some we faced in the past, but the addition of the Cormorant was awesome. Of course it would only be a temporary addition because we didn't want to advertise our presence on Mud

Island, but it would at least help us get home with the barge we needed.

13 PROMISES

Jean was experimenting with baking bread when Molly started yelling for her to come into the living room. Molly had been alternating between the radio and the cameras, and either one or the other had produced results. Jean couldn't tell if the results were good or bad.

When she got to the living room, Jean saw it was the camera monitor that had caused Molly to yell. Molly was pointing at it and saying something about men, so Jean didn't expect to see anyone she knew. Her first thought was that the Cubans had returned. When Jean was in position to see the monitor, she saw that the houseboat was occupied once again. By her count this was the fourth time.

A man was just inside the door of the houseboat with his back to the camera, and another was on the dock. The one on the dock was in a low shooter position and was rotating back and forth toward the dense brush of Mud Island. Both were wearing military combat uniforms, but the shooter had his arms in a position that kept her from making out the patterns on his sleeves where insignia would be worn.

Jean switched on the camera inside the houseboat just as the man inside stepped into the area that the camera didn't cover. A moment later he passed by it again as he walked out onto the deck of the houseboat. She thought she saw something like an American flag on one arm, but she still wasn't sure.

"Are they bad guys, Aunt Jean?"

Molly still sounded so young and innocent to Jean, and it made her just a little sad that Molly had sorted people out as good guys and bad guys. Still, it would keep her alive longer to think that way.

"I don't know yet, Honey. I can't make out the sleeve patches, can you?"

She had no sooner asked when the man in the houseboat stepped back out onto the dock. He turned left and right assessing his surroundings as if he expected to find more than he was seeing. Jean felt a lump in her throat when she saw the American flag was one of the patches, and she was fairly sure the bars on the collars of the uniform made the man a Captain.

"Aunt Jean, that's an American flag. Those are the good guys, right? We can let them in?"

Jean almost said yes just out of reflex. When the infected dead began attacking people, it was the United States military that everyone had turned to, and she had continued to hope for rescue by the military long after. When she and the others had tried to seek the protection of the US Navy at the Naval Weapons Station in Goose Creek, they had blindly pinned their hopes on joining up with them. They had been turned away by the Navy because the infection had gotten to them from all directions, and to this day, they didn't know if anyone had survived.

"Molly, we don't know them. If your daddy was here right now, he and the Chief could decide if we should talk with the men outside, but since they're not here, I have to keep the door closed."

The Captain was standing on the dock next to the houseboat. Another soldier had approached him from the beach side of the dock, so Jean switched the monitor to display several cameras. She saw at least twenty men and women in US Army uniforms on the beach. They appeared to be setting up a camp on the beach. Several were carrying branches they had cut from trees and building a crude fence. With as much firepower as they had, the trees were only intended to slow down anything that came out of the water. As Jean knew all too well, the infected dead washed up on the beach in unpredictable waves. You could go weeks without seeing any, but then you would see plenty of them every day.

Jean realized the soldiers were cutting some big trees, and the big trees were close to their main entrance. It wasn't visible from the beach, but if they ventured far enough into the island for trees, they would eventually find the door.

When she brought the camera view of the front door up on the screen, there were two young soldiers standing directly in front of it. One of them was talking into a satellite phone. Jean glanced at the view of the dock and saw that the officer standing in front of the houseboat had a satellite phone to his ear, and it didn't take a genius to guess who he was talking to.

He brought the phone down from his ear and became interested in the end of the dock where the camera was well hidden, and Jean had the distinct impression that he was able to see her.

"That man is looking at us," said Molly.

"Not yet, Molly, but he knows we're here. He just doesn't know where we are."

The Army Captain said something to the other soldier and started walking toward the end of the dock. He walked right by the hidden camera, but it was no secret that he had found the path toward the center of the island. He only had to walk a mile to join the two soldiers out front by the door, so Jean switched to the beach view and the front door.

The soldiers at the front door weren't doing anything in particular to try to open the door, so Jean assumed they were just standing guard for the time being. On the beach the sun was in the east, and it was still mid-morning. It was a fairly clear day, and the weather was warm enough for the soldiers to be comfortable. She saw tents being set up, and it was obvious that they planned to stay. The sides of the tents were rolled up on the inside perimeter of the camp, and since the camp was roughly a horseshoe shape, she was able to see their progress.

"What are they doing, Aunt Jean?"

"They're setting up camp. See that tent with the table? That would be the command tent. There's a guy getting ready to use a radio. Why don't you get ready in case he talks with us?"

Molly was surprised, but she wasn't afraid. Although Jean was wary of everyone, she had a lot of hope that the US Army was going to be helpful. Her biggest fear was that they would take away their shelter in the name of national defense. She had seen enough movies and read enough books to believe that was possible. The country was in a state of emergency, and that could mean the military was as rogue as gangs they had seen.

Jean saw something like a mess tent being erected, and she got nervous. She hoped they weren't eating seafood. After this much time since the end of civilization, the ocean may have become the only food source. The idea almost made her turn green again. The sight of the bloated bodies coming to the surface after the Russian ship had blown up, and the crabs roaming from body to body had caused her to have a bad day.

They had never seen evidence that eating the seafood after the crabs and fish had eaten the infected dead would be dangerous, but they didn't want to find out the hard way. They had seen an entire community of about five hundred people who had cut themselves off from the mainland by severing an entire marina from land access. They were using the bodies of the infected dead as bait for blue crabs. They would never have a shortage of food, but the crabs were eating poisoned flesh. Jean couldn't help believing the crabs were poisonous to eat.

Their group had never been back to that marina, so they didn't know if those people had survived, but in her mind, Jean expected they were dead by now. She also didn't see how those people could have lost their humanity by using the once living people as bait, and she saw it as only a short leap between that and cannibalism. If they ever ran short of crabs or maybe just got tired of such a narrow diet, they may have started eating the bait.

Now she found herself watching very closely to see what went into the pots that were being set on cookers in the mess tent, and she wondered what was in the crates that had been stacked by the cookers. Fresh water was poured into the pots, and flame cookers were being turned on.

Jean saw from the front door camera view that the soldiers were still alone, so she turned to the other camera views around the island. She saw on the mainland side that there were still bodies on the surface, but not as many. The current had been gradually tugging at the twisted mass of bloated, floating bodies, and some were being carried away to the south where they would exit out to sea. She couldn't watch that view very long because they were still crab food.

The camera on the southern end of the island was the camera they had placed on the other side of the moat that separated Mud Island from the mainland. The camera discovered by the Cubans in the gunboats was long gone.

She saw several of the infected dead emerging from the thick trees headed for the general direction of the moat. They were walking past the camera as they stumbled toward the water. She didn't know if they could hear the activity of the Army camp in the distance, or if they were just doing what they do, which was just wandering around. Sometimes one would groan, and others would flock to that spot. More of them would groan, for whatever reason, and the next thing you knew you had ten or twelve more join in on the groaning. Any given place could become a horde gathering in a matter of minutes.

The view of Mud Island wasn't great news. There were several soldiers examining the area around the hidden boat. When they had built the hiding place for the boat, they knew it would pass inspection from the casual observer, but the soldiers had been sent out to see what they could find, and it wasn't long before they determined the deadfall covering their hiding place wasn't natural.

It occurred to Jean that the inspections she saw happening at the ends of the island could only mean one thing. Someone knew the shelter was there. The two soldiers standing at the shelter entrance had been part of the team that had been sent to the middle of the island.

One of the soldiers inspecting the deadfall of branches had just gone down to the place where the sand met with the slight rise toward the trees. He found the edge of the big door they had made and lifted it upward as a fellow soldier covered him. From Jean's angle, she could see their Boston Whaler on its trailer. She was slightly confused when the soldier lowered the door again, and everyone took a minute to carefully restore the hiding place.

Molly said, "Aunt Jean, the man on the radio is talking about something, but I don't know what he means."

"What did he say, Molly?"

"He said a lot of funny words in a row like bravo, echo, and tango." The last word she said with a giggle.

Jean giggled too. It had to sound funny to a kid. "That's the way they speak so you know what the first letter is. Try to remember the exact words and then spell a word from the first letters."

Molly got out a pad of paper. She waited until the broadcast began again, started writing. When she stopped, she handed the pad to Jean. In clear writing for a child Molly's age, it said, "Charlie, Hotel, India, Echo, Foxtrot, Bravo, Alpha, Romeo, November, Echo, Sierra,"

Jean stared at the pad. She didn't bother to ask Molly if she was sure she had gotten it right. It was too obvious they were broadcasting a message to the Chief. Jean felt her heart racing at the implications.

"You did good, Molly. Please keep listening to see if they keep repeating the same message or if they change to something else. Don't worry if you miss the start. They'll repeat it."

"Yes, Ma'am," said Molly, "but foxtrot and Romeo are funny." Molly was smiling from ear to ear.

Jean smiled too. She still didn't know if she should let the Army know their message was being received, but she was hopeful. One thing was for sure. Now that they knew about the hidden boat, the door, and the dock, they were also sure that Chief Barnes was somewhere within radio range.

The officer arrived in the view of the camera over the front door. He said a few words to the soldiers who were standing guard, and then he smiled at the camera. Jean expected him to say something, wave, or give some indication that he knew he was being watched, but all he did was walk away. A few minutes later she saw him reappear at the tent where the radioman was broadcasting. He handed a sheet of paper to the radioman who turned back to the microphone.

Jean saw Molly begin to write again, and then she handed the pad to Jean.

It said, "Callsign Chief, callsign Miller. Respond when you are ready. Will wait."

Jean had no doubt that the message was asking for the Chief, and she wished she could answer for him. She still hadn't been able to reach the Chief or anybody else in her group, and she wasn't sure if she should answer, but she was sure of one other thing. The officer had to be Captain Miller, and if he was, he was a man who said he owed a debt to the Chief.

14 THE MISSION

Everyone got a good night of sleep at Fort Sumter, even though we rotated standing watch on the bridge of the Cormorant. The harbor had been dark with no surprises. If everything went well we would be heading home to Mud Island by the end of the day. The Chief told us he felt like he could tow the line laying barge with the Cormorant at night if the weather was good, so we might be able to complete our plan once we got started.

The kids had all discovered they really didn't mind bathtubs as much as they remembered, with the exception of Whitney who had always appreciated soaking in the tub. After they had eaten the night before they were all tired, but they were given a big surprise. Kathy and the Chief sat down with them and explained they would have a big job to do the next day while the adults were away.

The kids panicked at first when they heard the adults were leaving, but calmed down when they were told what it was they were expected to do. Kathy told them there were over two hundred rooms in the shelter, and as soon as they were done with breakfast, they were going to inventory the rooms.

The Chief added, "We need to know what's in this shelter before we leave. If we ever come back here again, it will be good to know that this shelter has something we need. We may also come back here after we're done getting the barge just to get something that you find that we didn't know was here, so you guys will need to work fast. It shouldn't take more than a few hours for some of us to come back. If you don't finish, that's okay."

"Can't we just take pictures with the digital cameras we found in that one storeroom?" asked Whitney.

"That's smart thinking, Whitney. As a matter of fact, we can make the lists from the pictures. Go get some breakfast and get started."

The kids were excited. Exploring was something any kid would want to do, and discovering hidden treasure in the rooms was like being set loose at Disney World. They didn't need to be asked twice, and they charged off in the direction of the dining room.

Kathy and the Chief followed the kids, and over breakfast the Chief laid out the plan. We would take the Cormorant and the other boat. The Coast Guard ship was for protection and towing, and the smaller boat was for mobility if we were in any tight spaces. The Chief also filled us in on another part of the plan that he hadn't yet disclosed. We were going to find another seaplane.

None of us felt like we would disagree with the idea, but we didn't know of any seaplane friendly docks in the area. There were pictures in the Fort Sumter shelter just as there had been at Mud Island and Green Cavern in Guntersville. The pictures we had at Mud Island had clearly shown us where the Tennessee Valley Authority seaplanes would be parked by the country club docks in Guntersville, but there wasn't anything in Charleston harbor that showed the same.

It was doubtful that we would have gone near the seaplane docks if they were by the Patriots Point marina. That area was the most likely place to find pockets of survivors with guns. So far we had given that side of the harbor a wide berth. If someone had managed to secure the World War II aircraft carrier Yorktown that was parked at Patriots Point, it would be easily defended. As a matter of fact, we had considered an attempt to contact people who may have seen Fort Sumter light up when we had scared the Cubans out of the harbor. Whoever was alive over there, they were also curious about the Cormorant parked at the dock, and they were also aware of the heavy gunfight the night we rescued Chase.

After discussion, we had decided to let people come to us. If they were friendly, they would approach cautiously. If they weren't friendly, we didn't want to find out by crossing into their territory. We all agreed that there might come a time when we should visit the Yorktown, but this wasn't the right time.

The Chief said between bites of food that he had been studying some of the high resolution pictures he had brought along from Mud Island, and one of them showed seaplanes parked at a small marina up the Ashley River. There was no guarantee that there would be one parked there now, but the pictures showed the pilings of the dock at the marina were the same type they had at their dock on Mud Island. If there was going to be a seaplane in the area, it would be parked at that dock.

"Okay, Chief. What's plan A?" I asked.

"It's a simple plan," said the Chief, "but it could take over twelve hours because of the tides. Low tide will be around 1:45 this afternoon, and we have to go under the Ashley River drawbridge then. Since it won't be open, we have to hope the Cormorant will fit under it at low tide."

"How close will it be?" asked Kathy.

The Chief ran a big hand across the stubble on his chin and said, "Probably just a few feet."

We all stared at him. The mental picture of the Cormorant passing under the bridge with a few feet to spare wasn't too attractive.

"What's the rule for drawbridges?" asked Kathy. "How did they decide before when it had to open?"

The Chief knew the rule, or he wouldn't have even considered going under the bridge only at low tide. He knew it was going to be close even at low tide.

"If a ship has fourteen feet of clearance or less, the bridge had to be open for them to pass," he said.

"Why do we need twelve hours?" I asked. "You don't think we could make the trip to that boat landing and be back before the tide gets too high?"

"We might, but it'll be close. I think we could try coasting up to the bridge before the tide is completely low. If it's low enough, we can go through and make a fast run up river. Bus can get the plane in the air, and the rest of us can pour on the speed getting back."

"Why do we need the Cormorant?" asked Kathy. "Do you really think we're going to run into that much trouble?"

"There are at least six places where we could run into trouble, depending on what has happened since the first day. If it was as bad as Tom described on the Waccamaw River bridge, then the Ashley River bridges are like auto salvage yards. The infected dead may not be able to move around freely, but I expect there will be some that decide to drop in. The Cormorant might not be able to get close enough to the marina, so we need to take both boats."

"Did I hear my name?"

Tom sat down with a big plate of food next to Kathy. The others were right behind him.

"You guys got an early start," said Olivia.

Chase was walking behind Olivia with a heaping plate of food, and the kids were returning with theirs. Bus had appeared out of nowhere, and he was all ears when we told him we were going to try for another plane.

"I never thought I would say I liked powdered eggs," said Bus, "but this stuff grows on you. I won't even ask what this stuff is that tastes like bacon."

Once everybody was situated at table, the Chief began laying out the plan. He explained that there were likely to be infected dead falling from the bridge onto the deck of the Cormorant, so some of us had to be standing by to pitch them overboard. The smaller boat would be tagging along astern of the Cormorant, and it would have to time its passing under the bridge so it wouldn't catch any of the falling infected dead. Bus would be on that boat, and once they were clear of the bridge they would make a mad dash upriver to the marina where the planes might be.

The Chief explained that there was a minor league baseball park on the starboard side not long after they passed the bridge. He said he had studied the construction of the park in the pictures, and it would be a good place to defend. He said he wouldn't be surprised to find someone had moved into the park and secured it.

Tom said, "You're right, Chief. I played in a lot of minor league parks. They have high walls, security gates, and good visibility from the highest places, such as the press boxes. They could have someone up there with a good sniper rifle ready to pick us apart."

"I don't know why the survivors of this mess have to be shooting at each other," said Olivia. "If they would all pull together, they might be able to stop this thing from killing the rest of the people in the world."

"I can't argue with that," said the Chief. "The people who shot down my plane didn't have a good reason for doing it."

"After the bridge, we're going to increase speed for a couple of miles and make a run for the marina. We'll drop Bus off at the planes, give him some time to get one in the air, and then make a run back the other way. Except for when we're passing under the bridges, we'll keep the smaller boat on the port side of the Coast Guard vessel. If someone takes a shot at us, the Cormorant can act as a shield. Any questions?"

No one had any questions, so we finished our breakfasts and got down to the business planned for the day. Whitney, Sam, and Perry got their digital cameras and started with the storerooms we had already been plundering. Taking pictures was a good idea right from the start. With over two hundred rooms to photograph, they wouldn't be able to get done if they had to list everything now. Perry had the bonus idea of the day when he suggested that they make a sign for each room and take a picture of the sign with the supplies. A simple piece of paper with something written on it saying what level the room was on would save time if they had to come back for something.

The adults all packed their gear and weapons. All hands would be needed today for various jobs. I got the job of driving the smaller boat, and of course the Chief had the helm of the Cormorant. Kathy was manning the remote controlled fifty caliber guns from the bridge. Bus was with me so he could be dropped off quicker. Tom and Chase were on the deck of the Coast Guard ship ready to deal with any of the infected that fell from the bridge. Olivia wanted to go along, but she drew the short straw and got the job of monitoring the security cameras in case someone tried to occupy Fort Sumter while we were gone.

We still hadn't been able to figure out why communications weren't working at the fort. Something had gone wrong somewhere, but there would be time to deal with that later, so we worked out a series of signals Olivia could use. The lights installed around the surface of the fort could be individually controlled instead of all being on or all being off. If one was on, someone was in the fort. If two were on, it wasn't safe to return, and we would come back for the kids and Olivia after delivering the barge to Mud Island. If everything went as planned, we would fly back and get them by landing down by the tunnel entrance hidden at the end of Morris Island.

Once we were all set, I saw the Chief holding a thumb in the air, so lines were cast off from both boats, and we pulled away from the dock. We coasted out about one hundred feet and then watched the lights on the fort. They flashed on and off three times at a slow pace.

The Chief had figured someone would be watching as we left the fort, and he wanted them to have no doubt that the fort was still occupied by a force powerful enough to remain in control. The boats and number of people observers would be watching should be enough to make people think we were at least an organized group. Whether the observers were friendly or hostile, it had to be convincing. If not, the fort would be occupied as soon as we were out of visual contact.

I pulled away to the port side of the Cormorant as the Coast Guard ship picked up speed. Within minutes we were passing White Point Garden again. This time it was beautiful in the noon sun of a clear April day. Everything was green and blooming, and it would have been the Garden of Eden if not for the shambling infected dead that were walking along the railing of the seawall. They could hear our engines, and they were being drawn out of the trees, across Murray Blvd., and up onto the wide concrete sidewalk.

We passed the large L shaped dock at the Coast Guard base, and it was eerily still now. The hundreds of infected dead that had walked off the dock and were caught in the current of the Ashley River as it rushed toward the ocean had served one last purpose on Earth by washing in among the Cuban boats.

The James Island Expressway was coming up next, but it was so high above the water that we weren't worried about it. We had passed under it not far from this same spot on our first trip down to Charleston, and it hadn't posed a problem. If something fell from that bridge, we would have time to move out from under it before it reached the water. We all kept our eyes on the city marina to our starboard side and a smaller marina to our left.

Both marinas had their fair share of boats that were sunk right where they were berthed, and some were charred black from the fires that had spread from boat to boat. In among them were those rare boats that didn't have a scratch on them. The Chief told us to watch for those because they were the ones that had arrived after those insane nights when everyone was trying to escape the spread of the infection.

Tom had told us how he had passed boat landings and marinas on that night when he and Molly had escaped first to Conway and then south on the Waccamaw River. His descriptions were so graphically clear that we could picture what had happened at these marinas. There would have been people running to their boats, and people running from the infected. There would have been screaming, and there would have been gunshots. Now the marinas were graveyards, and hiding in among the tombs were frightened people who were watching us go by, unsure of whether or not it was safe to hail us.

It seemed almost too soon that the moment of truth was on us, and we were approaching the twin Ashley River drawbridges. There were so many cars on both bridges that we couldn't tell at first if there were any infected dead walking around between them, but as we got closer the engines began to draw them to the railings. First there were only a few, then they were lining the railings like people at a sporting event. They weren't coming to watch us go by, though. They wanted to get over the railing that was blocking their way.

The Chief was coasting toward the bridge at a very low speed, but because the tide was going out, he was having to maintain his speed against a strong current. I was having to increase my power to drive against the current too, and the engine noise was whipping the crowd up above into a frenzy. There must have been more of them than we expected because we could hear them above the sound of our engines.

We were arriving over an hour before low tide, and the slow approach into the current was giving the Chief a good opportunity to measure the height of the masts atop the Cormorant. From our angle in the boat, we were sure the Chief was going to rip the masts off, but he had a much better view. Kathy was probably giving him advice, as well. They kept approaching slowly, and we watched as the masts cleared the underside of the bridge by less than a foot.

Bus and I heard Tom yelling at Chase to watch out above, and we saw the first body falling toward them. This one landed on the port side rail down on the main deck by the stern. It couldn't have been planned, but it was a perfect head first dive...straight into the metal railing. Since head trauma was the way to permanently kill them, this one wasn't going to be a problem. The body crumpled outward and fell

226

overboard on its own. We started through with the Chief and watched nervously for anything falling in our direction.

The second one hit in a flat landing down inside the boat retrieval well. It wasn't going to be able to climb up onto the deck from down there, so we were able to watch for the next one. Number three missed the boat completely, and by then the Cormorant was past the first bridge into the space between the two drawbridges. We didn't see more flying bodies from the first bridge because they had all crossed to the side of the bridge when we approached. They didn't have the reasoning power to know we had gone under them.

The crowd on the second bridge was falling over the rails before we got there. We could see that it was going to be much worse than the first bridge because they were raining down the way they had at Green Cavern when we had watched the bodies shower from above.

Our momentum had us moving closer even though it was into the current. To turn left or right between the bridges could cause either boat to catch the concrete supports of the bridge and rip a hole in the hull. We were going to have to go through whether we wanted to or not.

We were only a matter of a few yards from the bridge when I saw the three bow mounted fifty caliber machine guns point skyward in unison. They only blasted a short burst of rounds as they rotated slightly to the left and the right, but it was enough. The wall of bullets may not have killed the infected, but the force knocked them backward into each other, and there was a brief pause in the shower of bodies. The Chief increased his speed, and I did the same as soon as I heard his engines increase their output.

A body landed in the back of our boat right in front of the bench seats. It was still moving, but when we increased our speed, the bow rose, and the stern dropped. Bus took care of the rest. The infected was facing directly away from us when it stood up, and Bus kicked it squarely in the middle of the back. It tumbled over the stern and disappeared in our wake.

Several bodies missed or grazed the railings of the Coast Guard ship, but we were through the first hurdle of our trip upriver. The second hurdle was the baseball park, and it was coming up fast. Bus took over driving the boat so I could watch the shore with binoculars, He brought us up along the side of the Chief so we would be sheltered if there was a sniper on the starboard side at the ballpark.

Tom came around the port side of the wheelhouse and grabbed the railing. Chase joined him only a second later. He yelled down at us that there was someone watching us from the press box level. We didn't know if they were friends or enemies, but it made sense not to give them a target.

After the ballpark passed from view, we had a long stretch of river ahead of us with no real threats except small docks. There could be people at them waiting for boats traveling on the river, but the weapons on the Cormorant would make anyone think twice. Tom and Chase moved from the side of the wheelhouse to deal with the infected dead that had fallen into the boat well. When they got there, they were surprised to see it walking out through the stern of the boat straight into the churning wake. The stern bulkhead could be raised and lowered to open the well when the Coast Guard needed to launch or retrieve a boat, and the Chief had simply raised it when he increased speed. The infected dead took the open door as an invitation.

15 VERY IMPORTANT PEOPLE

Two hundred rooms at least, and what seemed to be going so fast at first was taking way too long. The three kids started out together at first, but they eventually decided they were just photographing the same things from different angles. They discovered that Sam was taking pictures of things that Perry had already done.

"There's only one way to get this done faster," said Whitney. "We need to do different floors, and we need to put an X on the door of each room we do."

"I think we should put an X on the door of each floor, too," said Perry. "We should put the mark on the door as we go in. That way, the other two can pass right by the floor to the next level."

"Let's use the central stairwell. It has a door at each floor," said Whitney.

When they entered the central stairwell, they each went to the railing and looked down. It seemed to go on forever, and even though there was a light on every level, they couldn't see the bottom. They went down one flight. Whitney put a big W on the door.

"I like that better than an X," she said.

Sam and Perry halfheartedly smiled at Whitney and then went down to the next level.

"Who gets this one?" asked Sam.

"I'll take it," said Perry. "Go on chicken. There's nothing down there you haven't seen before."

Before Sam could put an S on the door, Perry marked it with a big letter P. Sam reluctantly went down the stairs. He could feel the fine hairs on the back of his neck moving on their own. He reached for the door, put an S on it with his marker, and pulled it open.

******

Before the virus began to spread, before the government began to scatter, Harold J. Thornton III was an important man. Over thirty years in the Senate had made him powerful and influential. As the President pro tempore of the United States Senate, he was third in line to the Presidency, and that meant he was so influential he had been given a first class ticket to safety.

Officially the government had called it an extinction level contagion, but since they had a way of saying things in reverse order like Yoda, it was called, "Contagion: Extinction Level," or CEL for short. In the remaining few days of the government evacuation, they had called it CEL Day, then CEL Day + 1.

On CEL Day, Senator Thornton was at the White House when the first reports started coming in. There were attacks within a block of the place where he and the President were watching TV. A Marine helicopter had landed on the White House lawn for the President and his family within minutes of those reports.

The Secret Service wasn't going to mess around. They had already shot one infected dead that had walked right up to the east entrance. When they ordered her to stop, she just kept coming toward them. The Agents were trained to shoot for the heart, and they did repeatedly. The shots punched her backwards, and she fell down once, but she got back up and started toward them again. It was a single shot to the head that stopped her, and after that the Agents didn't bother with the center mass training.

There were also the people who were trying to get away from the infected that were following them through the streets of Washington. When they reached the fence around the White House, it was the symbol of safety. Scores of people jumped over the fence, not running toward the White House, but away from the infected. Training is training, and the agents trained to protect the White House had received training for all out frontal assaults as well as lone gunmen. To them this was just another scenario for which they had trained.

Their shots to the chest were effective. One by one the people who were running across the White House lawn were eliminated until there were only a few late arrivals to deal with. As they were reloading and showing a bit more nerves than they would have expected, one of them noticed the first of them getting up again. They sat dumbfounded and watched as more and more rose to their feet.

Late arrivals jumping over the fence thought they were jumping to safety, and before they could be shot, crowds of previously eliminated threats turned on them. The snipers on the roof of the White House had to shoot the same people all over again, and just as their fellow agents at the east entrance had learned, it took a single shot to the head.

Harold Thornton had watched the shooting through a window as he waited for his ride away from Washington. His normal bearing with his full head of silver hair made him appear fit for his years. His height added to the illusion. He had been given word that the Vice President and his family had also been taken to a secure location at a bunker somewhere in upstate New York. He was also told that someone was locating his family, and they would meet him at their secure location.

When Senator Thornton boarded the Marine helicopter he was given the message that his family had been successfully retrieved, and that the President had arrived at his secure location. It was confidential, but he knew it was somewhere near Columbus, Ohio. He figured the President had that arranged from the start since he graduated from "The Ohio State," as he liked to call it.

Senator Thornton was told his helicopter was heading to Charleston, South Carolina. He didn't know what the shelters were like, but he liked the restaurants in Charleston better than Columbus. It was a Sikorsky UH-60 helicopter, and the flight would be about three hours, so he made himself comfortable.

The helicopter was smaller and less accommodating than one of the big Sea Kings the President and Vice President were traveling in, but it was getting him away from the CEL. An intern had brought him updates until he was ready to leave the White House, and the Senator had secured passage on the military flight for the attractive young lady. She sat across from him in the helicopter, and the Senator thought things could be worse.

The pilot gave them updates from time to time about the spread of CEL. It seemed the entire world was in chaos, and no one even knew where it had started. He wondered if someone had been experimenting with a viral agent, and it had escaped. They weren't even half way to his secure location when they received a message that every major city in the country had evacuated their mayors. Where they were evacuating to was a good question.

The pilot brought his last message back just minutes before they would arrive. He said they would be landing in a small, secure landing pad, but there had been an accident when another helicopter had landed. The pilot gave him a long list of important people who would be arriving at the same secure site. Senator Thornton was surprised at how many people would be there, and who they were.

When the Sikorsky UH-60 dropped toward the landing area, the door opened facing a dark wall that was only a few yards past the range of the spinning rotors of the helicopter. Someone pulled open a door that seemed to be hidden in the wall, and the white light from inside was almost blinding. He climbed out of the helicopter ahead of the young intern and ran for the door, but as he crossed the darkened area between his helicopter and the door, he saw another helicopter laying on its side, and his wife was standing next to it. He could recognize her long red hair anywhere.

The Senator ran to his wife and didn't make the connection between the still smoking helicopter and his wife until it was too late. As soon as he reached for her, she reached for him, and the bite on his face felt like fire.

Somehow he found himself inside the white light. He had pushed past the attractive intern and the man who had held open the door for him. Once inside he grabbed the door and pulled it shut behind him. When he locked the door, it sealed so tightly that he couldn't even hear the helicopter...or the screams. There was a long ladder behind him, and somehow he climbed down to the bottom. Elevators in an area that was a lot like a hotel lobby stood in a row, and when he blindly stumbled into one, he selected the bottom floor. It just seemed like the right thing to do.

He was dead when he walked out of the elevator. It didn't matter anymore where he was. Senator Harold J. Thornton III was alone in a shelter where no one else could enter because he had locked the door, and the pilots were never informed of the emergency entrance at the end of Morris Island. The next arrivals didn't have a clear place to land, so they eventually diverted with their important passengers to secondary locations.

16 ASHLEY RIVER

The Ashley River bridge connecting North Charleston to West Ashley had been built high enough to be no concern to river traffic. As we approached, we could see the logjam of vehicles sitting where they had been left on the bridge, and the occasional infected wandering among them as if searching for their own cars. The scene was like so many we had witnessed since the first day, but there were fewer of the infected. That could be explained by the fact that there were fewer people living near the area after those who died in the snarl of traffic had wandered away.

On the night that followed the beginning of the attacks, the cars had backed up on this bridge only because I-26, the main interstate highway through the area, had become a parking lot. Some people went toward the interstate from West Ashley, and some went toward it from North Charleston. Combined with the traffic from downtown Charleston and traffic from Mt. Pleasant, gridlock was inevitable.

We had out of necessity become experts on the local roads and had studied the maps many times. Ironically, no matter which direction you chose, on that night you would have been going toward death, but the best routes out of the area would have been away from the interstate. Even when the State Department of Transportation opened the east bound lanes to west bound traffic to relieve the pressure on the main artery out of Charleston, there were still too many people trying to leave. If not for the shelter at Mud Island, I could have been one of the thousands of people who died on bridges and overpasses.

As we approached the bridge, the usual body drop began, but this one was spread out and random. It wasn't like the infected knew enough to go to the center span of the bridge and time their jumps with our passing. The only reason there were more on the drawbridges we had already gone under was the metal surface on each bridge. The Chief had speculated that the vibrations from our engines would be stronger there, and the infected would already be congregating on that part of the bridge. Since this bridge was all concrete, it was only the sound of our engines that drew them over the railings, so they were landing far from their targets. Some were landing in the mud flats up to one hundred yards away.

Of course there had to be that one in a million, random chance of catching one of them, and the Cormorant had one impaled on one of its side railings. Tom was forced to put a bullet in its head because it was still snapping its jaws and reaching for him and Chase when they tried to get rid of it.

Once we were clear of the bridge, it was smooth sailing to the marina where it sat in the shadow of I-526, the Mark Clark Expressway. The marina wasn't large by most standards, but it was large enough for the three seaplanes that were tied up at the last three slips. I knew the Chief had to be excited when he saw them because Bus practically cheered.

"See anything you like?" I asked Bus.

"Take your pick, Ed. Those are three beautiful planes. I'd still pick the de Havilland DHC-3 Otter over them all, but any one of those things would be fun to fly. The one on the right is the older brother of the Otter, and I'll make you a bet that the Chief would pick that one. It's a de Havilland Beaver. Bush pilots and people like the Chief have been known to stand at attention and salute when one passes over."

"What about the other two?"

"The red, white, and blue one is a Cessna 180, and the one in the middle is a Super Cub. That one is on floats, but most of them have a big fat pair of wheels on them, and they can land in some pretty weird places. I've seen pilots put them down on the side of a mountain where there's no airstrip and then take off almost like they're falling off of the mountain."

"You said they would be fun to fly, but which one would you pick for our needs?"

"No doubt about it, Ed. I'm with the Chief. The Beaver needs a little more room to take off than its younger brother, but it has a big cargo area. It can seat eight people or carry a lot of gear. The main thing is they last. If this one has been relocated from the bush all the way to South Carolina, someone really loved it, and they would have put some money into furnishing it. Our Otter was comfortable, but I'll be surprised if this one isn't a real show piece inside."

I said, "Someone tried to reach that plane to get away from the infected and didn't make it, which means the marina crew would have fueled it up to get it ready if the owner called ahead."

"Good thinking," said Bus. "Don't be surprised if the Chief asks to let him fly it back and asks me to pilot the Cormorant. Let's get me onboard that thing before he has a chance to try."

I laughed as I cut across the bow of the Coast Guard ship. As we did, Bus went to the stern and climbed up on the bench seats. He got his feet spread as wide as he could and made sure the Chief could see him from the bridge. Then he very ceremoniously raised his right hand with his palm and fingers as straight and rigid as a board. His elbow was perfectly straight out to the right. I thought he was going to give the Chief a salute, but instead of his hand pointing at the right side of his forehead, the thumb came away from his hand and touched the tip of his nose, the fingers pointed straight upward, and then they began to wiggle at the Chief.

Tom and Chase were on the side rails next to the wheelhouse and could see the gesture. Both were laughing their butts off. I couldn't make out for sure if the Chief was smiling, but I knew he would want the last laugh.

The three machine guns on the bow of the Cormorant had been pointing skyward, but as Bus wiggled his fingers, the guns rotated forward and slowly began to lower toward us. I chose that moment to bring our forward momentum to a rapid stop, and Bus fell backward onto his rear end.

I thought Bus would have a few choice words for me when he got up, but he was laughing too hard. I could also see the Chief better, and he was fully appreciating the moment. Kathy was hanging onto him and was aiming a digital camera at us.

I knew we all needed the release of tension by the time we reached the seaplanes. It was a gamble to come upriver because there were so many pockets of survivors, good and bad. In some ways, we ran as much risk from good people who needed our help as we did from those who would outright kill us to take what they needed.

The saving grace for us was ironically what also damned the people we could have helped. There were larger pockets of the infected dead, and we had the capability to deal with them.

The dock sat straight as an arrow out from the land, and there was a standard boat ramp next to it. The tangle of boats, some burned and on their sides, was a silent testament to the chaos we had seen on boat ramps throughout the Lowcountry, as South Carolinians called it.

Halfway out from land the dock had split into two docks. One came straight out to the planes, and the other went to a second dock that ran parallel to it. There were about two dozen slips for boats. Some were empty, some had sunken boats in them that were still tied to the dock, and only a few had boats still afloat. None were as good as the boat we were using, but they were worth checking for a working radio, the one thing our boat lacked.

Thousands of people had flocked to their marinas in an attempt to escape the infected dead, but too many of the boat ramps were near major highways, and the lucky few who reached their boats were not only attacked by the infected, but by the desperate families who had abandoned their cars on the Mark Clark Expressway. In this case it had been an all out riot, and the boats had been taken, but the planes had survived untouched. There weren't that many people who could fly them, and those who could were somewhere in the mass of victims.

As I docked by the planes, we could see we already had company. Up in the parking area beyond the boat ramp was a large storage facility where people could rent space to keep their boats without having them in the water. On the day of the mass evacuations, it was useless to try to retrieve a boat from storage and then get it to the congested boat ramp, but that didn't mean people weren't going to try. There had been huge crowds inside the storage areas, all of them demanding their boats to be brought out. The owners of the facility were doing their best to accommodate their customers amid threats of lawsuits and lost business, but the reality was that the infection was on its way.

When it arrived, it spread through the screaming crowds who ran for the water. Fuel that was being pumped into the empty tanks of the boats that were brought out of storage was spilling down the parking lot to the boat ramp and the dock. When it ignited, it exploded in a fury that spread even to boats that were pulling away to safety. The blaze traveled out the straight dock all the way to where it split to the right but had stopped there.

Our company was coming from the storage area. Some of the infected were charred remains that could walk and still had dangerous teeth. The test of the damage from the fire came when the infected reached the burned section of the dock. We could only hope for once there were a lot of the infected dead, so the damaged dock wouldn't hold up under their weight.

I decided there was only one thing to do, and it was a tactic we had learned way back at the beginning when we had been forced to leave our plane at a private dock after it had been damaged by a bullet.

"Tie off the boat, Bus. I have something to do."

As I said it to Bus, I grabbed my rifle and jumped onto the dock. I ran as fast as I could to get to the place where the burnt portion of the dock began. It crossed my mind that I had really changed in the last year. I had gone from being a video game playing procrastinator, who didn't take life seriously, to being a survivor, and I wasn't going to let these non-survivors stop us from getting what we needed.

I dropped to a knee and took careful aim at the first of the infected dead that was stumbling out onto the dock. I waited until it was on a span roughly midway between pilings before pulling the trigger. The infected fell backward onto the blackened wood exactly where I wanted him to. The second and third infected tripped on the first one and fell over the side. That was fine with me, but I wanted more of them to stay on the dock.

I got my wish on the next three in a row and had a pile of four bodies all stacked on top of each other. The infected trying to get to me from behind them kept falling over into the river and disappearing with the current, but eventually one crawled to the top of the stack. When I shot that one, its weight slumped forward, and I saw the stress on the damaged wood begin to spread.

The section of dock attached at the set of pilings behind the pile up began to crack and separate from the stronger wood. More and more of the infected dead crowded onto that section, pushing each other into the pile and over the side, but eventually there was an ear splitting crack, and the entire section fell into the water. There would be no more company reaching us by walking out on the dock.

I went back to where Bus had been working on the lines of the de Havilland Beaver, trying to pull it away from the dock if he needed to do a preflight check away from infected that would have been climbing onto the floats.

"Nice work, Ace." He flashed a pleased smile in my direction. "I guess I can do my preflight without rushing now."

"My thoughts exactly," I said. "And while you do that, I'm going to check for a radio in these boats over here. I shouldn't be long."

Bus gave me a thumbs up, and I started for the boats. As I did, I glanced up in the direction of the Cormorant and waved at the Chief. He used the bullhorn on the outside of the wheelhouse to respond.

"Are you okay with us heading back? You guys should be able to handle it from here, and we can probably reach the Ashley River bridges before the tide gets too high."

I gave him a wave and a salute, and the Coast Guard vessel began a wide turn away from us. I only watched for a moment after exchanging waves with Tom and Chase, then I went in search of that radio.

The dock felt naked and exposed when I started with the first boat that was still floating. They were all fairly small, but someone was bound to have a working radio. In fact it was uncommon that our boat didn't. It was most likely stripped by the pirates who the Chief had liberated it from when he escaped from Charleston after he was shot down. I found what I needed in the third boat and went to work retrieving it as Bus checked out the plane. The boat was moored in its slip facing the three planes.

There were three big splashes in the water between the boat I was in and the bridge behind me. I turned around in time to see two more bodies hit the water. It must have been the same at every bridge in the country, and I couldn't help wondering if that would be how we could defeat the disease that had caused the end of the world. If we could get every infected dead in the world to fall into the water, sooner or later they would all be fish food. No one would ever eat seafood again, but no one would ever get eaten by a relative, friend, or neighbor again.

I heard the engine of the plane begin to turn over, so I watched Bus as he got it started. It took a few revolutions of the big propellor, but it burst into life and let out a loud roar. It certainly was louder than its younger brother, but I wasn't going to complain.

I hurried back over to our boat and jumped in. I didn't want to keep Bus waiting once he was ready to go. Hooking the radio up wasn't difficult because the Chief had shown me often enough how to make the wires under the dash of our boat appear to be normal after he had disabled the ignition wires.

The Super Cub and the Cessna 180 were between me and the de Havilland Beaver, so I couldn't see Bus anymore, but the engine of the Beaver began to sound better and better. I knew from flying with him and the Chief in his beloved Otter that it was a good idea to burn off the fuel in the lines before taking off. That way you would learn whether or not the fuel pump was working. Sitting still at the end of the dock for so many months could have caused sediment in the fuel to settle in the tanks and then foul the pump. When the engine began running smoothly, it was obviously getting fresh fuel.

I keyed the microphone and said, "Testing, 1-2-3. Testing, 1-2-3."

"I read you loud and clear," said Bus.

"How's the seaplane coming?" I asked.

"Just for the record," said Bus, "you should get used to calling it a float plane. And those big, yellow things you've been calling pontoons are floats. It's ready to go. How's everything on your end?"

"I'm ready here. Let's see if we can catch up with the Chief," I said.

I jumped back onto the dock and untied the mooring lines to the Beaver. Bus cut the engine off so I could help him turn the plane away from the dock without bumping a wing against the Cessna 180 next to him. It was because we were watching the distance between the two planes that we saw the door on the Cessna open. When it was wide enough, the infected dead that fell from the opening landed flat on the starboard side float, and it immediately tried to crawl over to the port side float of the Beaver.

That's the problem with crawling on water. It's just so hard to do. As soon as it put its weight on its outstretched hand, it went head first into the river. Unlike the infected dead who were in the Guntersville lake under the planes, the current would keep this one from walking up the boat ramp and trying again.

I looked at Bus. He and I had apparently both watched the door of the Cessna open, and I imagined he was glad that thing had been inside the Cessna 180 instead of the Beaver. To add insult to injury, the otherwise professional Doctor Bus, gave the infected dead the same wiggling finger salute that he had given the Chief. I resumed rotating the plane by pushing its wing, and Bus restarted the engine. He throttled up and turned away from the dock at the same time and began his run to the center of the river.

The roar of the engine was attracting a larger than normal crowd on the bridge, and as Bus began his takeoff run downriver, the infected dead were pouring over the side.

It was a longer takeoff than I was used to seeing, but it was smooth. I could imagine Bus in the cockpit cheering like a school kid as he went to full power. The radio crackled, and his voice came through the speaker.

"How was that, Ed? Over."

"Picture perfect from here, Bus. Did the Chief give you orders to fly back to Mud Island or meet at our current residence? Over."

We had all agreed the radio contact shouldn't give out information that could be intercepted. No one would know where Mud Island was, but everyone would know where Fort Sumter was.

"Rendezvous at the current residence for now. I'll provide overwatch on the Mud Island run, over."

"Copy that, Bus, over."

I cast off my own lines and pushed off from the dock. I was amazed to see there were still infected dead walking down the boat ramp and still falling off the bridge as I turned the boat to go down river.

17 SUB-LEVEL EIGHTEEN

Whitney finished her floor and went out into the stairwell. She looked over the edge of the railing first but didn't see or hear any activity below her. She went down one floor and saw a big P on the door, so she went down another floor and saw an S. She quickly took the steps two at a time to her next floor, determined to reach the bottom floor first.

Sam was bogged down and frustrated. He was sure he had gotten the short straw by getting the floor he had because it had been storage for all kinds of dry goods. He felt like he had to be taking pictures of a Walmart warehouse because there was something of everything. If it could be stored in a cardboard box, it was on this floor. He even searched for something that would tell him what the inventory was, because it didn't make sense that they would have this much stuff and not know where to find it. He gave up after a while and started taking the rest of the pictures.

Perry came out of his floor sure he had finished before Whitney or Sam. He went down one floor and saw the S on the door, so he took the stairs three at a time hoping to be ahead of Whitney. When he saw the W on the door he didn't bother to slow down. He sped past to the next floor, quickly put his letter P on the door and dove inside. The thrill of competition was cool, and he didn't want to lose to a girl. They were also finding some neat stuff.

By the time Sam finished his first floor and walked out into the stairwell, Perry and Whitney had each finished two whole floors and came out into the stairwell somewhere below him. When he leaned over the edge of the railing, he saw them dashing down another level. They were laughing, and he figured it had to be about him. As the youngest in their group, they were always telling him what to do. Just before Perry went through another door he hear him yell at Whitney.

"I'll get to the bottom floor before you do."

"No, you won't," she yelled back. Then she laughed again.

Sam wasn't even in the race as far as they were concerned, and he wanted to show them both what it felt like to get beaten. He started down the steps as fast as he could go, passing their P's and W's on the doors. When he got to an unmarked door he only paused for a split second, then he started for the bottom again. He would show them, and the mental picture he got of them arriving at the bottom floor and finding a big S on it was so satisfying.

*****

The Chief could almost hear the longest mast on the Cormorant scraping against the bottom of the bridge as he passed through. If he could complain to someone about the first span being at least two feet higher than the second one, he would.

When he pulled up to the first span, he watched the tide markings on the supports and did some mental calculations. From everything he had read about the height of the bridge, the height of the tide, the height of the masts, and the depth of the Cormorant's keel, he should have no problem passing through. He poured on the speed and was pleased to see his mental math had been accurate.

When he got to the second bridge, he did the same calculations while checking the markings on the support, and each time it came up as a big maybe. The height he needed to have was within six inches instead of several feet, and he knew it wasn't because the tide had risen that much more. It could only be because the navigation charts needed to be updated to account for seventy or eighty years of the bridge settling under its own weight.

At the last second he decided he wasn't going to sit between the two bridges for twelve hours and wait for the next low tide. He went ahead and rushed toward the center span and tried to will the ship to draft a few feet deeper.

Sometimes the Chief felt like gambling was the only way to beat the odds, and this was one of those times. He remembered a scene from a movie back in the 70's when a guy was playing blackjack. He had eighteen but was sure the dealer was sitting on twenty because he had a face card showing. He told the dealer to give him a hit, and when the dealer gave him a card, it was a three. The gambler just said to the dealer, "I'm blessed."

The Chief wouldn't go so far as to say he was blessed, but he would go so far as to say he thought he would make it. He just wished he was drafting a bit deeper. As the bow got within a few feet of the bridge, the horde of infected dead up above had grown because he had delayed for a few seconds to make his calculations.

The numbers swelled against the already damaged concrete and steel railing, and a mass of bodies tumbled over the edge of the bridge together. Tom and Chase had hung back toward the stern when they saw how many infected were threatening to fall, and it was a good thing they did. Forget being bitten...they would have been crushed.

What the Chief needed was exactly what he got. A pile of bodies, even though they were lighter due to decay, they were enough to force the bow down deeper into the water just long enough for the ship to make it through. It popped back up like a cork bobber, but the masts had cleared the steel deck of the bridge by that time.

The ship was rocking so much from the burst of forward speed and the bodies landing on the bow that it was hard for them to untangle themselves from each other. Tom and Chase had no trouble pushing them overboard as they stood up and tried to walk, and by the time the Chief was halfway to the Fort Sumter dock, the bow was clear again.

They had no sooner gotten the bow clear when a deep throated roar came up on them from behind and passed almost even with the wheelhouse. The yellow fuselage with red stripes was so much bigger than the Otter, but the Beaver was built like a workhorse. Bus was obviously enjoying being behind the stick of the plane, and the Chief obviously couldn't wait for his turn.

It was turning into the kind of day they were all hoping for. All they needed to do was go get the line laying barge, and they would be able to start for home.

*****

Sam didn't like the bottom floor. There was something wrong with it. From the moment he put his S on the door and went inside, it didn't feel right. All of the other floors had a different feel to them. He was too young and inexperienced to recognize what his senses were telling him. The upper levels felt sterile. They felt clean, and above all, they smelled clean.

The bottom floor didn't feel or smell clean. There was a rotten odor that he couldn't identify because he had lived with that odor for so long that it had dulled his sense of smell. He was well inside the maze of rooms on the bottom floor before he recognized that smell, and he didn't know if he was recognizing it too late. Worse yet, he was lost. He had been so distracted by that eerie feeling you get when you know you aren't alone that he didn't pay attention to where he was going.

He had passed the elevators when he had first reached the bottom floor, and he considered just getting in one and riding it back to the top, but he didn't want to hear Perry and Whitney saying he was a chicken. To make matters worse, one of the doors opened while he was standing in front of it giving it some serious consideration. When it opened, a bell went, "Ding".

Sam gave the empty elevator as much room as he could and was totally creeped out by the idea that the elevator car was even on the bottom floor. Something in the back of his mind told him that elevator cars stayed on the last floor they went to unless someone else summoned them to a different floor.

It was also a little darker on this floor, and up ahead there were several open doors that had no lights on in their rooms. So far, Sam hadn't seen anything like that in the shelter. Every room had lights on like the electric bill didn't matter. The storerooms and stairwells all had lights, but some of these rooms were darker than midnight.

If Sam had paid any attention at all to where he had already been, he decided he would go back to the elevators, but he had already lost track of them by making a couple of turns to avoid the dark rooms. By the time he decided he was scared and should take the easy way out, he didn't know if he should go left, right, straight, or backwards.

He decided going backwards was most likely the right choice, but when he went that way, he found himself standing directly outside one of the open doors of a pitch black room...and he was sure something moved in there.

Sam backed away from the open door wanting desperately to close it, but to do so he would have to reach inside and grab the handle of the door. He couldn't see a thing inside the room, but whatever was in there had to be able to see him, and he wasn't about to go in there with it.

He kept backing away, keeping both eyes on the door, hoping to put some distance between himself and that dark rectangle before something came out of the room. His main hope, though, was to find the elevators again. He would even be happy with the stairs at this point. Sam didn't realize that he had begun talking to himself out loud, and that the sound was able to carry as far as it did.

The thing that Senator Harold Thornton III had become didn't know anything about what was happening in the world, and it didn't really know the difference between a room with the lights on or off. What it did know was that there was something alive nearby. There was something that made noise when it walked, and sometimes it made other noises that drew it in that direction. Above all, there was this deep urge to bite into the flesh of the thing moving outside of the room.

Sam's eyes widened as he saw what was coming out of the dark room. He didn't know if it was one infected dead or twenty. He just knew it was coming out of the dark room he had backed away from moments ago. Sam suddenly recognized that smell, and knew he just hadn't expected to find it here.

The thing he feared the most stepped into the hallway, and Sam didn't know if it could see him, smell him, or was just aware of him being a living person, but it started in his direction just as he had seen them do for almost a year. All Sam knew to do was run.

*****

Olivia became bored watching the monitors. When the Chief had explained her role to her, she had accepted quickly. If she didn't have to go outside, it was all fine with her. The first couple of hours were sadly interesting to her because she was able to sit and study the inside of the fort. It was an ugly sight. Flocks of seagulls were landing on the bodies, and some much bigger black birds. She had seen her share of vultures, both human and birds, and she didn't care for either.

As the day passed, there was no other activity out in the harbor, and she could only sit and watch the birds feeding on the bodies for so long. She didn't want to think about what those men had done to her, nor what they would have done if her new friends hadn't come along.

Olivia thought about the group of people who had saved her and Chase. Up until the moment they appeared out of the darkness, she wouldn't have believed there was any chance she was going to live.

She rotated one of the cameras a few degrees to see if there was anything on the harbor that was moving. Nothing was there, so she went back to thinking about her rescuers. Her feeling was that it was all too good to be true, but she couldn't help the fact that she was already starting to trust them completely. She wondered how long it would be before she quit waiting for the other shoe to drop.

If she was wrong about them, she knew it would be an awful surprise, and a worse price to pay, but she was starting to think she would make all the same choices again. After all, they had not only rescued her and Chase, they had rescued the kids, and then they had kept her safe by giving her this job instead of dragging her along.

They had explained everything to her about Mud Island, but she still didn't see why they couldn't just stay where they were at Fort Sumter. There were enough supplies to last for years, and there was so much room she didn't think they would even have to bump into each other if they didn't want to. She wondered for a moment how they would feel if she asked to stay behind when they went home. Of course, she wouldn't mind if Chase wanted to stay too. That brought a smile to her lips. The thought of the two of them being all alone in a perfectly safe underground hotel was inviting.

The boredom started to set in again, and Olivia wondered why the kids hadn't checked in. The Chief had told them it would be a good idea if they at least just dropped in on Olivia from time to time. He had explained to all of them that time was the maker and breaker of all deals. If something was going wrong with them, checking in periodically was one way to make sure that it didn't go wrong for too long.

Kathy showed Olivia that there were cameras inside as well as outside, but from what they could tell, they weren't on inside the lower level storage areas. Kathy had said that was an issue they planned to explore when they had the chance, but it was a back-burner issue for now. When they were done with connecting new power to Mud Island, they would fully explore the Fort Sumter shelter which had clearly dwarfed their own shelter in size.

Olivia switched on the interior cameras and started scanning each floor to spot the kids. She was sure they were just enjoying their new responsibilities, and she had never known a kid in their age group who wouldn't have wanted to explore the rooms and floors below.

She found one camera that showed the stairwell the kids had used, and the angle showed a door with a big W on it. Well, she didn't know where they were yet, but she knew where at least one of them had been.

The button for that camera was in a row that had numbers on them, and when she pressed the next one, she saw a big letter P. So, Whitney had been on the fifth floor down, and Perry had been on the sixth floor down. She hit the next button, and there was another W. She thought it would have been an S, but maybe Sam had teamed up with Perry, boys against the girl.

She just happened to still have her eyes on that monitor when both of the doors flew open almost at the same moment. Whitney came flying down from above while Perry ran right under the camera. There was no sign of Sam, and Olivia quickly punched the button for the next floor in time to see it closing behind Perry, and there was a big P on it. Whitney sped by it as it closed, and Olivia brought up her view as she was marking the door.

Whitney and Perry were both fine, but she couldn't help thinking something was wrong. Just as she was having a hard time believing she had been rescued, she had a hard time believing the nightmare was over.

Olivia started pressing the buttons one at a time going lower and lower down the stairwell. She wasn't sure what she thought she was going to find because all she was seeing was blank doors. She froze when she reached the last door. Kathy had been wrong about the lower level cameras. They were at least working in the stairwell if not inside the rooms of each level, and the last door, the door to sub-level eighteen had a big S on it.

Olivia didn't know why that could be bad. She just knew it was. She watched the unmoving door for a moment, unsure of what she should do. She checked the view of the harbor and didn't see anyone returning yet. She couldn't see far enough to tell if they were on their way back, but judging by the time, they should be. She knew the Chief had a time limit before he would be stuck on the other side of the bridges, but she wouldn't know if he beat that time limit or not until he showed up at the dock.

The elevators were right down the hall from the control room. All she had to do was ride down to the bottom floor, find Sam, and then give him a piece of her mind. Olivia didn't know she was that nervous and that afraid of what she might find, but the thought of going down there made her feel ill.

Olivia forced herself to get out of her chair and walk. Her feet felt like they weighed a ton, and by the time she reached the elevators, her heart was pounding.

"Oh my God," she thought. "If I'm this scared just walking to the elevators, what good am I going to be if there's something down there?"

The elevator doors were just like any she had seen in any lobby in the world. Stainless steel, up and down buttons, and numbers over the doors. The first two had the number one illuminated. The third door had the number eighteen illuminated. She tried to remember if it had always been like that, but she had to admit, she was only impressed by the fact that the shelter had elevators. Then when she saw the rooms they would be staying in, she forgot all about the elevators. When it became obvious that Chase was going to be staying in her room, she forgot there were other levels. She knew all she needed to know.

She didn't really know what she hoped to accomplish by pressing for the elevator button. It was just something you did when you wanted the elevator to come up. And she had expected that eighteen to change to seventeen. She almost jumped out of her skin when the other two doors opened, and each elevator sounded its own little "ding".

Determined to make a difference, she pressed the down button again. This time the eighteen went out, and the number seventeen lit up. Before it made it past three floors, the other two elevator doors closed, and they started descending. She wondered at first, but then it dawned her that someone had summoned an elevator just seconds after she had.

"What's going on?" she asked herself out loud.

*****

Eighteen floors below, Sam circled through one corridor after the next. All he wanted to do was find the stairs or the elevators, he didn't care which. The problem was they were right near each other, and he didn't have a clue where either was.

There was a "ding" up ahead, and the nearly silent smooth sound of the elevator door shutting. Then he heard the hum of machinery. Disregarding what else might have heard the same sound, he ran in that direction.

When Sam rounded the corner and saw the elevator doors, he also saw the infected dead that had been stalking him. It had gone in search of him and had gone by the elevator doors and then the stairwell. It had almost made it to the end of the long corridor when the elevator dinged. The good news was that it was the same one he had seen earlier and not a new one. The bad news was that it was already coming in his direction. Sam made a dash for the elevators and saw that the door to the stairs was not an option. The infected dead was only a few feet from the stairwell door as it stumbled toward him.

He practically slid past the elevator buttons, but started jabbing the up button as hard as he could. He was too scared to even think that there was no down button on the bottom floor, but he wasn't too scared to notice what floors the elevators were on. Two were on their way, but they were only passing two, three, four...too far away. The other was going up past ten, nine, eight...

Sam couldn't wait for the elevator, so he turned around and ran again. This time he was paying desperately close attention to every detail of every corridor. When he came to the dark rooms again, he eased past the open doors, not knowing if there were more infected inside, but feeling the hair standing up on his neck again was enough to make him believe the dark room was full of the infected.

Once past those doors, he started trying to figure out if there was a way to reach the stairwell from the other side. If the infected followed him, then he would have to find a way to loop around behind it. Sam figured his reasoning had to be good because the infected had somehow gotten around on the other side of him.

He mentally kicked himself when he realized he could have been marking walls to know where he had already been, but then he calmed down and accepted that he had only been afraid. Being scared can make you do exactly what he had been doing, and that was running around like an idiot. He had spent a long time dodging the infected in Charleston before being rescued, and they were everywhere. So far he had only seen one in this place, so he had the upper hand.

Sam drew an arrow on the wall to show which direction he was going at this given spot. If he came to this same spot again, he would try a different direction. He kept going for about ten more minutes, finding corridor after corridor and room after room. Some of the doors were open and some were shut. Too many were dark. He kept expecting to find one of his arrows written on a wall, but to his surprise he found the door to the stairs.

He put his hand on the panic bar of the door and started to push, but his curiosity got the best of him, and he had to check. Sam went over and stood in front of the three elevator doors, and they were all on the bottom floor. All three eighteen buttons were illuminated. He didn't know why they were all on the bottom floor, but he would get back to the safety of the top floor a lot faster by riding up, so he pressed the button.

The bell dinged on each door as they slid open. He jumped into one and pressed the button for the first floor and pressed the button that said Close Door just for good measure. Those buttons never seemed to speed things up, but just as the door slid shut he caught a glimpse of the infected dead moving toward the elevator. He preferred to think that this time the Close Door button had worked.

*****

Olivia rode the elevator all the way to the bottom floor. Somewhere around the tenth or eleventh floor it occurred to her that she could have at least brought a steak knife or something with her, but she could have done even better because there were guns in the shelter. She asked herself what could she be thinking by rushing off with nothing but her fists. She suddenly felt naked standing inside the well lit box with nothing in her hands. Part of her was saying it was just nerves, but another part of her was becoming more and more scared.

When Olivia had been six years old, she had gotten mad at her parents and run away from home. Just like all kids that age, they only make it so far before they turn around and go home. They usually think they have been gone long enough for the parents to be worried sick, but in reality the parents don't even know they're gone yet.

Olivia went far enough to not recognize the neighborhood anymore, and before she knew it, the sun was going down. She was brought home by a policeman after an elderly couple saw her standing on a curb with tears streaming down her face. Standing in the elevator, she felt like that six year old again. She was afraid, and there wasn't going to be an elderly couple or a policeman this time.

The numbers arrived at eighteen sooner than she wanted, and she wished she had hit the big red STOP button. Until she figured out a way to go back up from wherever it stopped, she would have been content not the reach the bottom floor. When the bell dinged her arrival, and the door slid open, the shape that stood there didn't rush in, but she screamed anyway. The shape wasn't really there because it was just the way the light came down the hall. Not all of the lights were on, so there were some odd shadows here and there.

After she screamed, Olivia felt really embarrassed because she had let out a good one. She hoped the kids were far enough away that they didn't hear that scream.

"Wait a minute," she said out loud. "I hope they heard me loud and clear."

Olivia peeked around the corner into the corridor and didn't see anything, but she did smell it. Something was definitely overripe. She couldn't tell if the smell was coming from the left or the right, but she could see she wasn't far from the stairwell door. Just to be sure she was in the right place, she went and checked to see if there would be a big letter S on the door. There was.

She let the door swing shut as she stepped back inside. "Sam?"

As soon as she called his name she felt stupid. She didn't know why, but she didn't think that was the thing to do.

"Is it because there's something down here, and you don't want it to know you're here too?" she asked herself. "Better yet, if there's something down here, then why am I down here?"

Olivia decided if she was going to be part of this group, she had to do her job. If Sam was down here, then he could use her help taking the pictures of the supplies. If he wasn't down here, she had to at least make sure he was okay. On the other hand, if he wasn't down here, she needed to be back up top watching the outside of the fort through the monitors.

She decided she would just take a look around before going back up. There was a corridor up ahead that she thought might be a main area of some kind. There were rooms with the lights turned off, but she told herself Sam might have turned them off himself. Then she told herself kids don't turn the lights off.

Eighteen floors above her, Whitney and Perry had arrived together only moments before in one of the other elevators. Worried because they had not seen Sam or doors marked with an S, they had decided to go up and check to see if Olivia had seen him. They checked the control room and saw that Olivia was gone, and there was no sign of Sam. Whitney glanced at the monitors and saw that one of them was on in the stairwell. It showed the door to the bottom floor, and there was a big letter S on it.

"Hey, Perry. Check it out. That little weasel, Sam, went all the way to the bottom floor so we couldn't claim it."

Perry walked up beside her just as the door with the big S on it opened. It was so unexpected that Perry and Whitney grabbed each other. Both of them let out a scream before they saw it was just Olivia.

"I won't tell anyone if you don't," said Perry.

"What scream? I didn't hear anybody scream."

Before they could even get around to asking each other why Olivia was on the bottom floor, the elevator outside the control room dinged again, and Sam practically fell out onto the floor. He really was screaming.

Besides scaring the hell out of both of them, it did at least scare them into motion. After almost a year of dodging the infected and staying alive on that ship, they weren't going to let Sam make them run and hide, despite the fact that was exactly what he was yelling at them to do.

Sam bolted from his prone position on the floor and ran for the control room, and he was screaming something about the infected being inside. He ran right by the two of them and shouted.

"Where's Olivia?"

Whitney checked the stairwell monitor again and said, "She was right there a moment ago."

Sam turned completely white, as if he wasn't already the whitest boy Whitney had ever met. He started babbling and crying at the same time. There was something about being chased around by the infected dead, and then something about the bottom floor and the lights being off in some of the rooms. Three minutes later Perry and Whitney were loading hand guns, and three minutes after that they were back at the elevator doors.

They were tempted to take the stairs, but eighteen floors was a long way. They made a promise to each other that they would hold their fire when the door opened at the bottom floor just in case Olivia was outside the door. Perry told Sam to watch the monitors in case the adults came back. They couldn't tell from Sam how many infected he had seen, but it sounded like it had been an army of them.

Olivia eased past the same dark rooms Sam had. She found a better lit corridor and followed it past a dozen closed doors before coming to a turn that felt like it was taking her back to her starting point. She was surprised that it did no such thing. The hallway she turned into had a dozen doors along each side of the hallway, and they were all open. There was also that familiar smell.

She tried to backtrack, but the corridor ended in some kind of service room, and it wasn't hard to figure out it was like a hotel laundry. There were huge washing machines, dryers, and folding tables. There was an odd smear across one of the otherwise sparkling steel tables. This room had never been used, so that smear shouldn't be there.

The fine hairs on the back of Olivia's neck had a life of their own. For the tenth time she cursed herself for being too stupid to bring a gun. There was a change in the air, and even though it couldn't have been something she really felt, she could have sworn it felt like warm air. She swung around in time to see the infected dead moving out from behind some stainless steel equipment. It was watching itself move in the reflection, but Olivia gasped before she could cover her own mouth.

The infected dead groaned and started for her, and all she could do was run. Olivia was close to another door, and she didn't care where it went, so she went through. It was another hallway with too many doors, but something was familiar. The soft light coming from around the corner ahead was like the light where the elevators were, but the stairwell door was even closer. She bolted through the door and started the long climb upward.

Before the door to the hallway had swung completely shut, the elevator door opened. Whitney and Perry were both in a shooter's stance ready to blow away anything that came through the door. Perry held out a hand and cocked his head to one side to listen. He couldn't have known the sound he had heard was Olivia making her way to freedom as the door to the stairwell clicked shut.

"Cover me," said Whitney as she stepped out into the corridor.

Perry didn't know exactly what she meant by that, but he stepped out of the elevator facing in the opposite direction as Whitney. They kept their backs together as they moved down the corridor in the direction of the dark rooms. When they got to the first one, Whitney whispered to Perry.

"We need to know what's in there. Olivia could be hiding."

"I know," he said, "and we can't exactly yell her name."

"On three," said Whitney. "I'll step in the room and hit the lights. One, two, three."

She stepped inside and hit the spot where the switch should be, and the room lit up so bright it blinded them.

"Jeez," said Perry, "what were they planning to use this room for. The lights are so bright they could grow crops."

"She's not in here," said Whitney.

She turned slowly in a circle to see all of the room. Everything was so bright and sterile that the hallway behind Perry was much darker than it had been when they came into the room, and it almost seemed like it was growing darker.

The bright lights inside the room had blinded her and robbed her of the opportunity to see what was about to happen in time to help Perry. The sound of the much taller infected dead biting Perry on the back right where the shoulder touched the neck didn't sound real, and then she couldn't hear anything except his screaming. His eyes were panicked and he'd shut them at first, but then they were wide open with pain as the fire in his skin spread.

Whitney had seen too much in the time they had been together. She and Perry had hidden under porches, in closets, and behind doors. They had climbed out of second story windows and jumped to the ground. They had outrun more infected dead than she could count, but in the quiet times, they had talked and made solemn promises to each other that if the time ever came that one of them needed the other one to end it for them, they would make it fast. There could be no hesitation, because if they hesitated, then they might not go through with it.

Even through the pain, Perry screamed at Whitney.

"You promised me, Whitney. You promised me."

She could see there were tears on his cheeks, but he was being more brave than she thought she ever would be. Without thinking, she raised her gun and fired two shots, one for Harold Thornton III and one for her good friend Perry.

Olivia made it up six flights before she started to slow down. She made it two more floors before she sat down on the stairs and started to cry. The two gunshots came from somewhere below, but they were muffled. She pushed herself up from the stairs and went through the door of the tenth floor. There was a W on it.

The elevators were nearby so she ran over to them and pressed the button to go up. When the door opened to the middle elevator, she expected to find the thing inside that had been chasing her. As she got in she noticed the numbers on the left elevator were steadily coming up from eighteen. She didn't think the infected dead could push an elevator button, but she didn't want to find out. She stabbed at the button for the first floor repeatedly, hoping she would get to there before the other elevator.

It seemed like it took forever for the door to close, and then it seemed like it took even longer for the elevator to go from the tenth floor to the first floor. When it finally opened, Olivia ran out just as the first door opened. She screamed when she saw Whitney standing there with a gun pointed limply at the floor. Whitney was wracked by sobbing and shook from head to toe.

Sam ran out of the control room to see what was happening and found Olivia helping Whitney walk from the elevator. She couldn't talk, and she was shaking her head from side to side.

"Where's Perry?" asked Sam. "He was with you when you went down there."

Sam sounded frantic and kept trying to see if anyone was behind Whitney and Olivia in the empty elevator.

"He's not coming," said Whitney. "He's gone."

Now it was Sam's turn to cry. He knew what must've happened, and even though Perry had picked on him from time to time, he had still been like a brother.

"Maybe he's okay," he choked out at Whitney. "Maybe we could go down and bring him back up here."

Whitney just slowly shook her head at Sam. She knew Sam had probably been the cause of this, but she felt more sorry for him than mad. She knew he would blame himself no matter how long he lived from this day forward.

Olivia was piecing it all together. She didn't know about the promise between Whitney and Perry, and she didn't know that Whitney had ended it for Perry, but she understood that Perry was dead, and Whitney had a gun in her hand. She also saw something unspoken between Whitney and Sam that said it wasn't their fault, whatever it was that had happened.

"Whitney?" asked Olivia. "Can you tell me if there's still an infected in the bottom floor?"

"Not anymore," she answered barely above a whisper.

"Was there just that one?"

Whitney thought it over for a moment then shook her head.

"I only saw one, but I didn't go in every room."

Sam was crying, but he managed to add that he only saw one old guy, and he went in a lot of rooms trying to get away from it.

Olivia helped Whitney and Sam to the control room and scanned the monitors that showed the harbor. The Coast Guard ship was tied to the end of the dock, and she could see the men helping to steer a plane into position at the long side of the dock.

The adults were all excited and ready to move on from Fort Sumter when they came down the ladders into the shelter. They expected to find Olivia and the kids just as excited, but when they saw the tear streaked faces and that Perry wasn't with the others, they didn't need a crystal ball to know something bad had happened.

The Chief, Tom, and I took and elevator and headed for the bottom floor without hesitation. Kathy took Whitney and Sam to another room to see what she could do to get them calm. Bus went along because the obvious had to be done. They would need to check the three of them for bite marks. Olivia was content to let Chase check her, but Bus and Kathy both said she had to come with them. There was no guarantee that Chase would tell them if Olivia had been bitten.

On the bottom floor, it didn't take long to find where it had happened. We saw that Whitney had done Perry the ultimate favor, and she hadn't missed. We searched through the rooms and found the massive laundry area. There were sheets still in their packages, so we took two we could use to wrap the bodies in and carried them to an elevator. Bus told us there was a morgue on the third floor near the main surgical suites, and we decided that was a better place for Perry than trying to take him outside.

As we rode in silence up to the third floor, the Chief checked the pockets of the infected dead and found a wallet. When he flipped it open, he was surprised by the name on the Washington, DC license.

"This explains the crashed helicopter topside," said the Chief, "but how the hell did he wind up as an infected all the way down on the bottom floor?"

He showed the license to us, and we were just as surprised.

"Wasn't he like number three in line for the Presidency, Chief?" I asked.

"As far as I know, yes. I hope the President and Vice President did better than him."

When the elevator doors opened, we carried the bodies to the morgue and found they had sealed drawers. There wasn't much we could say after closing the drawers so we just went back to the elevators and rode to the first floor without talking.

Kathy and Bus met us at the control room and reported that no one had any bite marks. The common opinion was that there had only been one infected dead on the bottom floor, and we were all being tough on ourselves because we had not taken the time to check all of the floors below.

The Chief said, "We sent the kids down there to inventory stock, and it never occurred to us that there could have been an infected dead down there. Hell, there could have been one on every floor for all we knew."

"Don't blame yourself, Chief. We all agreed the rest of this place was safe," said Kathy.

"Maybe we did get a little careless," he argued. "We made an assumption, and that got one of us killed. We have to be smarter. Ed's uncle wouldn't be saying we've been thinking like survivors."

"Speaking of surviving, Chief. We don't have time to worry about what's happened," I said. "We have most of the day left. What do you say about getting this job done?"

18 OLD FRIENDS

Jean had to make a decision. The longer she left Captain Miller and his soldiers out there, the greater the danger for them. They gave every indication that they were here to stay, and they were setting up a fine perimeter against the infected dead, but someone had blown up the Russian ship sitting in their moat, and whoever they were, they were still out there, too. There were also those men in the gunboats, and she didn't want to see them kill any US soldiers.

Captain Miller had periodically rebroadcast his message asking for Chief Barnes, and Jean was tempted to answer, but something kept her from just pushing that microphone button.

"Aunt Jean, there's a man outside the front door."

Molly had been watching the camera feeds from all around the island. If the rest of their group came back, they would see the large encampment on the beach and might try to enter through one of the emergency hatches. Jean wished over and over again that she could make radio contact with Eddie so she could tell him about the Army being outside.

"Aunt Jean?"

Jean had heard Molly, but she didn't react because she was so deep in thought.

"I'm sorry, Molly. I didn't mean to ignore you. What's the man doing?"

"He wants to talk to the Chief, and if the Chief isn't here, he wants to talk with someone who can tell him where the Chief is."

Jean was confused about how Molly knew so much about what the man wanted, so she joined her at the monitor. Captain Miller was holding up a sign in front of the camera that said exactly what Molly had told her.

Before Jean could change her mind, she keyed the microphone button and said, "Miller, this is Barnes."

They could see the Captain react outside, and it was the smile that convinced her she had done the right thing. Captain Miller was ecstatic.

Before he could answer, she keyed again and said, "Unsecured transmission."

The Captain stopped short of pressing his radio button then said, "Roger, awaiting instructions."

Jean thought about her choice of words. She saw that Molly was watching her intently. Above all, she had to be sure Molly stayed safe.

"Molly, I need for you to do something for me. I'm going to have him come inside alone. On my signal, I want you to push this button."

Jean showed her the button, and Molly said she understood. Being a bright girl, Jean had explained all of the controls to her. She knew that button would lock the door from the inside, and the only way out would be if you knew the combination.

Jean keyed the microphone and said, "Door will open in five if all clear except Miller."

She was pleased to see he didn't hesitate. It was a good sign when the men standing guard by the door hurried down to join the rest of the soldiers. Captain Miller checked his watch then went to stand by the big vault door that kept Mud Island secure.

At five minutes, the big wheel lock rotated, and the door swung silently open on its massive hinges. Captain Miller stepped wide eyed into the outer room. Jean enjoyed his expression. Everyone who saw the inside of Mud Island was impressed by the outer rooms, then they got a real shock when they saw the main rooms.

The Captain had barely gotten inside the door when it began to close. He got out of the way and watched the lock spin until there was an audible sound from the metal pins that slid into their slots. He turned and was surprised that there was a cute little pregnant woman standing in the next doorway watching him.

Jean already knew about the promise Captain Miller had made about owing Chief Joshua Barnes a favor at Fort Jackson, but Captain Miller wouldn't know who she was.

"Hello, Captain Miller. I'm Jean. Forgive me, but we have some rules about letting people come inside Mud Island. I need for you to get naked, please."

Captain Miller was the kind of man the men and women in his unit respected. That was in part due to the fact that he led by example. He was genuinely shy around forward women, and despite the fact they were in the middle of an apocalypse, he reacted as if Jean was being personal. He blushed and couldn't even speak.

"Don't worry, Captain. I wasn't making a pass at you. I need to check you for bite marks. I'm a nurse, and I'm pregnant, so I'm not just using that as an excuse to check out the package."

Jean smiled, but inside she was laughing. She was trying not to let it out and was losing the battle. She had never referred to it as the "package" before, and she had said it to sound tough, but it had come across funnier sounding than she thought it would.

Captain Miller was a deep shade of red as he took off his uniform.

"Just out of curiosity," he said, "what would you have done if I had refused?"

"You wouldn't ever be able to get back outside to your men and women," she said, "and if I know anything about officers, their people are family. Besides, I think you understand."

He did understand, and she was right about his people. He wanted them to be safe and he wouldn't sacrifice them for permanent safety for himself. He felt really exposed, but he finished undressing and then rotated in a circle with his arms spread.

"Satisfied?" he asked.

"Don't misinterpret yes as being enthusiasm," she said. "Just take it as appreciation for easing my mind."

Despite being caught off guard, Captain Miller liked this little pixie brunette with the courage to make him follow the rules. As he put his uniform back on he told her they had a similar procedure in place for his troops.

That was good news to Jean. So far, she and her friends had seen enough examples of people hiding their bites and then infecting others. Families protecting family members, friends protecting friends, shipmates protecting shipmates, and most likely soldiers protecting soldiers. They may be even worse about it because of their rule never to leave a fellow soldier behind.

"When we make camp, all soldiers, myself included, have to report in at the medical tent once per hour for examination. After we have contact with the dead, everyone gets inspected at the same time. This may be the longest we've gone without having someone else check my package. When we're on the move, we try to stop every two or three hours for an examination. From what we've seen, there have been more units killed and ships sunk by ignoring that rule. People just don't want to admit when they've been bitten."

"That has been our experience, as well, Captain. Thank you for understanding," said Jean.

Jean motioned for her guest to follow her, and he couldn't wait. When he stepped through the door, the first thing he saw was the decontamination room, and he had the decency to say he was impressed, but when he stepped through the hatch and walked into the main living room, he couldn't speak.

Molly came up to stand close to Jean, and Captain Miller introduced himself. Molly was polite but suspicious, and he sensed it.

Before he could reassure her that they weren't the bad guys, Jean took the lead again.

"Captain Miller, we realize you could take what we have, but we hope you aren't that kind of person. We'll be more than happy to give you some supplies, let your people get some hot showers, and even wash your clothes for you, but you made a promise to Chief Barnes, and we hope you keep it."

Captain Miller gave Jean his best smile and said, "Jean, when I told that group out there we found Chief Barnes, all they wanted to do was shake his hand."

He took in the monitors, the furniture, and the overall living conditions. All he could do was shake his head. He could see into the kitchen and dining area and knew someone had put everything they had into this place.

"I didn't see the plane out there. The Chief's not here?"

"No, but I'm hoping they'll be back soon. We lost our main power cable when someone blew up a ship that was sitting in the waterway between the island and the mainland."

Jean led Captain Miller into the kitchen and got him a cup of coffee, which he breathed in as if he hadn't enjoyed the experience in a long time. After she got him situated at the table with the coffee and a slice of pie, he fidgeted like he wasn't sure of what to do or say next.

"Is there something wrong?" asked Jean.

Molly sat down next to the Captain with a piece of pie for herself and a glass of chocolate milk. Jean could see that he was choked up with emotion and most likely couldn't swallow. He had tears in his eyes that were just starting to reach the point of rolling out.

"I'm so sorry," he said, "but it almost feels normal here. How did you do all this, I mean this is incredible?"

Jean sat down with her own coffee and told Captain Miller about Uncle Titus, the cruise ship, how they met

Eddie, and everything since. When she got to the part about how they took Molly and her father to Alabama and brought back Molly's mother, Captain Miller explained how Chief Barnes had saved hundreds of soldiers by pulling one of the craziest stunts he had ever seen. She told him that was just the way the Chief does everything.

She went on with her story and told him about the Russian ship that had arrived out of nowhere. She explained that they captured her and she almost died on the ship. When she told him about her fever after being scratched, he told her that answered one question. They didn't know if a scratch was as fatal as a bite, and now they knew. His best theory was that the virus became active if it transferred in bodily fluids like saliva or blood.

Jean said, "As I told you, I'm an RN, and I didn't want to test the theory first hand, but since the body is mostly water, I would worry about sweat, blood, and saliva. I don't know why they still have saliva, but I don't plan to do an autopsy on one to find out."

The Captain ate some of his pie and took a swallow of coffee. From the satisfaction on his face, she could tell he appreciated both.

"The last thing the Chief said about you guys was that you were probably on a ship north of here at a place called the Norfolk Canyon?"

Captain Miller kept chewing, but there was a pause. He took another swallow of coffee, and Jean refilled his cup.

"I still can't believe you have coffee," he said.

"We have enough for all of your people, Captain. I'll get it for you if you want."

"That'd be great, Jean, but I'll answer your question first."

"We were trying to put together a counter strike from a carrier group over the Norfolk Canyon. It was close enough to the mainland for us to put together a good effort, but we kept running into problems. The Chief and the rest of your group came along during one of our attempts to establish a forward base. That's why we were at Fort Jackson. The problem was that you just can't underestimate what those things can do. The sheer numbers of them, the fact that they aren't afraid to die, and the fact that only head shots can kill them are all things that make them hard to beat."

"You tried again?" asked Jean.

"Repeatedly," said Captain Miller, "and getting the brass to understand the logistics was a nightmare. They kept insisting that we bring back any civilians we found alive, especially VIP's. They sent us into DC to search for the President even though everyone knew he had to be in hiding somewhere. We finally found someone from the Vice President's security detail, and even though he had a bad bite mark, the brass insisted on bringing him back. The next thing we knew, we were fighting for our lives on our own ships. The last time we saw the carrier we were staying on, there were people jumping overboard to get away from the infected. We escaped in several helicopters, but none were completely fueled, and we had to abandon them up the coast."

"How long have you been on the move, Captain?"

"A couple of months. We've just been trying to find a place that would be secure so we can rebuild to fighting strength."

"Maybe we can help with that," said Jean. "The beach isn't as secure as being inside the shelter, but you have everything under control out there. You can use the houseboat as a command center."

"We'll take you up on that offer for now, Jean, but food is becoming a big problem. The mess officer wants to catch seafood, but so far enough of us are worried about the fact that the fish and crabs have been eating the infected dead. If we don't find another food supply soon, we may have to try the seafood."

Jean must have turned pale or maybe a shade of green, because Captain Miller got a bit worried. She told him she used to eat a lot of blue crab, but since blue crab really seemed to enjoy feeding on the infected, she had lost her taste for them. She told him about the people at the marina and how they were using the infected as bait to catch more crabs.

"Captain, how many people did you say you have out there?"

"Just over a hundred," he said.

"Well, we can't feed all of them for a long time, but if you set up a base of operations here, maybe we can find a food supply and bring it here to the island. One of our group, Molly's father, says the only perfect shelter protects you from the infected, protects you from people who will take what you have, and protects you from the elements. With your people here, Mud Island can be the perfect shelter."

"I thought you said you lost your main power supply," said the Captain.

"We did. That's where everyone went. They're supposed to be bringing back a cable laying barge so we can connect a spare cable across the moat. I'm starting to get worried, though. They've been gone for days."

"Maybe I can send a squad down the coast to find them."

Before he could even finish the suggestion, Jean stopped him.

"Captain, no disrespect intended, but your people could use some rest and maybe some good food. I'm worried, sure, but they're a good bunch when they go out. There must be something just slowing them down. Why don't we take care of your troops first?"

The Captain couldn't disagree with Jean about his people. They had been through a lot, and they could use some decent food.

Jean said, "Let's start there. Maybe you could send in a few people to carry out some cases of MRE's. They aren't the best things in the world, as you know, but they're nourishing."

"Sounds like a plan. How much can you spare?"

Jean started to laugh but stopped herself. In the first place, this world turned upside down had produced different societies. Some people would take what you have, yet he wasn't assuming she would have enough to give. Secondly, they not only had plenty of rations, they had a whole shelter full in Guntersville they could tap if they started to run low. They could fly there a few times a year and replenish their stocks any time they wanted to.

"We can spare more than you're going to believe, Captain."

Molly finished her pie and chocolate milk and asked to be excused. Captain Miller was impressed that even during the end of civilization as they knew it, a child could still use manners.

"Is she your daughter," he asked?

"No, but she could be my little sister. Her parents are on the trip with my fiancé and the Chief. We also have a doctor and a Charleston police officer. Some of them were with the Chief when he helped you guys at Fort Jackson."

Jean pushed back from the table and put their dishes in the sink.

"Let's go, Captain. Your people could start getting those hot showers. You probably noticed there were several stalls in the decontamination room. We can run them through in groups for the showers, but we can feed everyone at the same time since you have your mess tents set up already."

It was nice to walk outside for a change without worrying about being blindsided by a stray infected dead that had gotten tangled up in the bushes. Jean explained about the infected being drawn literally up onto the beach side of the island by the tremendous explosion of the Russian ship. Captain Miller didn't know if the US military had anything to do with it, but he had a theory.

It never really occurred to Jean or her group that Mud Island was putting out enough energy that its heat signature would be detectable by a satellite. Captain Miller explained that they had been using the heat signatures to know where survivors were holed up, and they had sent out patrols to try to make contact. Some of the patrols were welcomed, and some met with open hostility. It had become somewhat of a given that the US government had been playing around with biological agents, and that one had escaped. Other people were smart enough to know that it was worldwide, so any government could have been the guilty party.

Jean let Molly come with them when they walked out of the shelter, and the sight of the cute little eleven year old was almost more than some of the soldiers could handle. They had all lost families, girlfriends, boyfriends, or just people they had cared about, and it picked up their spirits to see a happy child smiling back at them. Jean had carried a sidearm just out of habit, but she saw that this group had secured the entire northern end of the island as well as a large stretch of beach. Molly had one case of MRE's in her arms that she started to pass out.

The Captain called together his NCO's and told them to organize a detail to help bring out the food. It wasn't long before everyone who wasn't on watch was getting a hot meal, and the overall mood of the troops was sky high.

"Captain," said Jean, "you never finished what happened to the rest of the military. You were on ships somewhere off the coast. What went wrong?"

It was clear that the Captain found the question painful. He faced the water as if he could see something on the horizon. It was a clear day, and the water was flat as far as the eye could see.

"It was supposed to be safe out there," he began. "There weren't supposed to be any mistakes. We all knew that a bite was fatal, and before each mission, we ended the briefing with a reminder that no man left behind had taken on a new meaning. If you were bitten, you had to think of your comrades in arms. You couldn't bring the infection back to a ship."

"So, what went wrong?" asked Jean.

"Someone changed the plan. The plan always was to establish land bases and then expand outward. If we could control territory, we could gradually repopulate safe zones. We were keeping an eye on Mud Island because your group was showing us how it should be done. There are other heat signatures that are bigger, but they never change. That usually means no one is drawing energy. Through the winter,

272

for instance, your energy bloomed just enough for us to know someone was consuming energy."

"When the Russian ship blew up, I'll bet you saw a bloom, didn't you?"

"Actually, it must have blown up after we lost control at sea, so we didn't see it happen, but it may not have been an aggressive strike."

Jean was confused. "What does that mean?"

"It may have blown up on its own," he answered. "We were picking up a heat signature inside the Russian ship from the time it arrived in your front yard until it parked in your moat, as you called it."

"You mean you were watching it the whole time?"

"Sure, but it wasn't really a threat, and they ignored our radio hails. We figured they were suspicious of our motives, and they didn't believe in safety in numbers. They were right, as it turned out, but there isn't much safety in keeping to yourself, either. In any case, their heat signature appeared to be increasing after they parked in your moat, and no one was doing anything to reduce or consume the energy. They may have blown themselves up by neglecting to control their own systems."

"Well, they would have needed to have someone alive to do that I guess," said Jean.

Captain Miller's eyebrows were raised.

"The crew was dead? Everyone? How?"

"They made that fatal mistake everyone seems to make. It's a long story, Captain, but let it be enough to say for now that the moat wasn't a great place to drop anchor. They got hung up on something, and when they sent divers down to find out why their anchor wouldn't come back up, they found out the infected dead are just as dangerous in the water as they are on land. The Russians pulled at least six bitten crewmen aboard their ship and tried to treat their wounds."

Captain Miller groaned openly. He could imagine what happened next.

"That was when they captured you, so you were actually onboard when the infection started doing what it does," he said.

"I was in a cell. I had to escape from the cell and then escape from a ship full of those things. That was when I got scratched by one of them, and it caused a really nasty infection. If my fiancé and the rest of them hadn't gotten there when they did, I wouldn't be here right now, but even though it was just a scratch, they treated it as if it was a bite. We didn't know if it was the same as a bite, either. Doctor Bus treated me, but I was kept in quarantine and strapped to a bed."

"Were you pregnant at the time?"

"I know what you're thinking," she answered. "There's no way to be sure if it had an effect on the baby, but Bus does prenatal checks, and so far the baby seems to be quite healthy. Back to your story, Captain. You didn't finish telling me what happened."

"Oh, yeah," he said. "Someone in the upper ranks changed the plan, as I said. When our attempt to establish a forward base at Fort Jackson failed, they started talking about trying to find a cure. To find a cure, they needed test subjects."

The thought gave Jean a chill because she could see the only direction that decision could take.

"Let me guess," she said. "If someone was bitten while on a mission, they weren't going to be left behind anymore. They would be brought back to be studied."

"It gets worse," said Captain Miller. "If no one was bitten, we were supposed to make contact with survivors and bring them back to be used as test subjects."

"That's terrible. Did you do as ordered?"

"No, Jean. None of my people were bitten, and the other squads felt the same way we did about killing innocent people, but it was inevitable that someone would be bitten, and when they were, they were brought back. The Vice President's security detail was one of them. One thing led to another, and before we knew what happened, crewmen on the Navy ships were bitten by their test subjects. We escaped to the mainland with limited supplies. I told my men and women to carry ammunition, weapons, and water. Most of them carried far more gear than normal. We managed to make it ashore with helicopters, but as I mentioned before, they were all low on fuel, so we landed on the coast and started working our way south. We figured we would try for the heat signature at Mud Island, and then we would check out a massive heat signature at Fort Sumter."

That got Jean's attention, and Captain Miller saw the reaction.

"Jean, I thought you said your friends were trying to locate a boat that lays power cables. Does that have anything to do with Fort Sumter?"

Jean wasn't ready to make decisions about what could or could not be said about the locations of shelters, but the cat was out of the bag. If this was any other military officer, she might have played dumb, but this one owed his life to the Chief. She decided to at least neglect to mention that there were over thirty of them, but when she thought about it for a second, maybe it wouldn't be a bad idea to have Army friends running the show from there.

"Captain Miller, I haven't had radio contact with my friends in days, but I can tell you this much. Someone with guns and control of Fort Sumter shot at us when we tried to enter Charleston harbor the last time, and we figured they had to be dealt with before a line laying barge could be liberated from the harbor. We had reason to believe there might be a shelter like ours under Fort Sumter."

"Reason to believe?" Captain Miller smiled at Jean's discretion, which obviously meant they had reasonably good intelligence about where shelters might be located, but right now he was only interested in one shelter.

Jean tried to hide her own smile, but couldn't help herself.

"Okay, so let's just say we found out there was a shelter under Fort Sumter, but the cretins who controlled the top of the fort weren't likely to know what was below them."

"Why's that? Is there an impenetrable door like yours?"

"I don't know, Captain. Like I said, no radio contact, but if you're wondering about how a small group like ours could consider taking a fort away from someone, we also knew where the back door was located."

A Corporal approached and told the Captain it was mandatory exam time. Jean suggested they set up at the showers and let everyone get clean at the same time. The men and women under Captain Miller's command were more than glad to accept, and they eagerly lined up at the entrance to the shelter.

19 HOME

It was supposed to be a celebration of a job well done as we gathered at the end of the dock, but we were a somber group as we left for the final part of our mission. The Chief was in the wheelhouse of the Cormorant with Kathy at the remote controlled guns. Tom was their lone deckhand who would help attach the towing lines.

The outboard boat was mine to drive, and Chase was with me. The plan was simple. I would dock with the line laying barge and release it from its moorings. If it had an anchor, I'd raise it. Then I would toss over the towing lines, and we would be on our way.

Bus had the best job. We decided he could do a quick pass over the harbor in our newly acquired Beaver, and he would just see if there was any trouble waiting for us at the barge. The Chief was obviously wanting his turn flying the powerful bush plane, but he reluctantly agreed Bus should continue back to Mud Island. Bus had been able to establish radio contact between the plane and the Coast Guard ship, so we were all hoping he could make contact with Mud Island and then relay information back to us. It would be nice to know Jean was safe. I had connected the wires to the radio I had gotten at the marina and wanted the opportunity to test it.

We didn't have any trouble persuading Olivia to stay at the shelter with Sam and Whitney. All three of them were still badly shaken and were in no shape to go along for the ride. We considered shipping them out with Bus in the plane, but in the end it was decided that we should just keep them inside. The Chief locked the elevators and the stairwell door for their peace of mind.

We launched the Cormorant first so Bus would have plenty of room to taxi away from the dock. When he took off, we were all impressed by the sound of the engine in the Beaver. It sounded like it could tow the barge by itself. Bus headed off in the direction of the barge, and as we approached in our boats, we saw him make several passes before he turned in our direction.

As the Beaver roared overhead, Bus radioed and said, "Be advised the barge is clear of activity, but the surrounding area has multiple infected, over."

That was no surprise to any of us, and we had hunting rifles with scopes with us this time. If we could reduce the number of infected dead in the area by shooting them at a distance, it would make life a little easier.

I keyed the microphone and said, "Roger your last, Bus, and have a safe trip home, over."

The Chief came over the radio and said, "Thanks, Bus. Let us know what's happening back home if you can. All of us want to know how Jean and Molly are doing, over."

"Will do, Chief. Can't wait to park this baby next to the dock at home. Maybe I'll let you take it out for a spin, over."

The Chief kept the microphone button keyed up, and we all heard him say, "Kathy, target the Beaver."

We heard Kathy say, "No."

Then we heard the Chief say, "Please," in a really sweet voice.

Kathy said, "No," again, but we could tell she was trying not to laugh.

The opportunity to improve our collective mood was needed, and we seemed to be at our best when we joked a bit. Not one of us forgetting that we had lost a good kid today, but we had to put it behind us.

As we cruised past Castle Pinckney on the way to the barge, I wondered if Tom realized how close he was to where Allison died. I knew that I would be thinking exactly that if it had been Jean. I could see him on the deck of the Cormorant, but there were no outward signs giving me a clue about how he felt.

It was only a matter of minutes before we were at the barge. I tied us off at a cleat on its flat surface and climbed aboard. Chase handed a rifle up to me and then climbed aboard.

"I'll get the lines and the anchor," said Chase.

I gave the Chief a thumbs up as the Cormorant began to rotate its stern toward us. As I was sighting in on the infected that were milling around on the dock, I thought to myself there was no doubt about it I had come a long way from that first day when I went into town for some video games.

******

"Beaver to Cormorant. Over."

"Cormorant here, Beaver, how's everything at home? Over?"

I had to admit, it seemed like the brightest, prettiest day ever when Bus said he had a visual of Mud Island, and the US Army has set up a large safe zone on the entire northern end of the island. He said Jean and Molly had spoken with him by radio, and they said it was the Chief's friend from Fort Jackson. They were outside waving at him as he made a pass, and he would be landing in seconds. Then came the really bad news.

The Oconee Nuclear Plant in the far northwestern corner of South Carolina had a meltdown. He didn't have many details, but radio contact with someone broadcasting near Charlotte said a radioactive cloud was drifting roughly in the direction of Mud Island.

The Chief relayed the message down to us, and the obvious question was how much time did we have. If that cloud dropped on us we would be forced inside, possibly for years if the fallout came down heavy in our area. My first thought was Jean, and whether or not it would have an effect on her pregnancy.

Once we got the towing lines in place, the Chief began to ease the barge away from its berth. The Cormorant wasn't really designed to tow something the size of the line laying barge, but there were two things working in our favor. The current was so strong in the passage between the mainland docks and Castle Pinckney that the barge moved practically on its own. The second thing was the open stern of the Cormorant. An extra line was tied straight through the back of the ship, and it gave us more pull where it was needed the most.

We had a hard time stopping the forward motion of the barge as it began to swing like a pendulum when we made our turn around Castle Pinckney, but the Chief managed to get it going in the right direction by using the current from the Ashley River. Once he had it moving in a straight line, he just let the barge keep moving out of the harbor into the open sea.

As I watched the progress of the barge past the jetties, I worried about how much time we had. We didn't have accurate weather reports, so we didn't know how fast radioactive fallout would reach us. We also didn't have enough information to know exactly how bad the accident was. Like most people my age, I was too young to remember Chernobyl, but I knew enough about it to know it was bad. I had seen statistics that said over four thousand people would die over the years from illnesses related to the accident.

There was one big difference with this accident besides our lack of information. At Chernobyl they buried the reactor under a mountain of concrete. At Oconee no one was doing anything to stop whatever was happening. We might never know when the accident was really done doing damage.

I pulled the boat up to the dock at Fort Sumter, and Chase tied us to the posts. We were moving much faster now that we had to worry about getting the power cable in place before fallout could reach us. I contacted the Chief one last time before he would be out of range and asked for an update, and he said we had about a day before we had to worry.

The good news was that we had a doctor to help us survive this latest problem. He sent a message that the Mud Island shelter had a large supply of Potassium Iodide, and he had already started dosing everyone. He explained that it would block the absorption of radioactive iodine by the thyroid gland. He had already quarantined Jean and Molly to the shelter.

I didn't flunk Chemistry 101 in college, but I came close. All that mattered to me was getting the job done so we could get inside. The clock was ticking as Chase and I ran into Fort Sumter. We made our way through the familiar tunnel and through the hidden door. We were in the control room within minutes, and found Olivia, Whitney, and Sam at the monitors. None of them had any gear packed and ready to go.

Our questioning faces were enough, and they seemed uncomfortable as we waited for them to give us an explanation.

"We don't want to leave," said Olivia. "We have everything we need here. In time there might even be others living here with us, but for now, this is where we want to live. Besides, you guys have always said Mud Island would be crowded."

I couldn't help thinking Molly could use Sam's friendship. He was only a couple of years older than her, and they would find a lot of things they had in common. Tom might not appreciate some of those things, but it was part of growing up, and dads needed to go through those pains, too. I started to say something to him, but Whitney gently cut me off.

"Ed, we know you've been talking about Molly getting to meet Sam, but Perry was like a brother to both of us. We need to be here for now. Maybe later we can work something out."

"There won't be a later for a long time," I said. "The Oconee Nuclear Plant has had an accident. It's the farthest reactor from here, but the fallout will be here in about a day. When we get back to Mud Island and connect the new power cable, we plan to close ourselves inside for however long it takes to be safe to come outside again. If you stay here, you'll have to do the same thing."

They weren't nearly as fazed by the news as I had expected. As a matter of fact, they just shrugged it off.

Olivia said, "Maybe that's a good thing, Ed. I know there are still a lot of survivors out there who will get caught in the radiation, and they will die because they don't have a safe place to go, but a lot of bad people will die too. And maybe...just maybe it will destroy the infected. Wouldn't that be great?"

Chase had been as surprised as I was when they said they weren't going, and maybe Olivia knew all along what his reaction would be. He listened to us just long enough to be sure, then he said what Olivia hoped to hear.

"Ed, you found Jean because the world as we knew it came to an end. Things have worked out for you and your group, and because of you guys we can live too. What if you guys hadn't come along? Olivia and I would have been dead at the hands of those crazies up there. You know what they would have done to us. It's sad about Allison, and it's sad about Perry, but you guys did good. After this reactor thing blows over, your group is gonna hit the road again, and someone is going to be better off because of it. In the meantime, I'm staying here with my new family."

The tender expression on Chase's face made tears begin to stream down Olivia's cheeks. I couldn't say that I blamed him or the rest of them, and as long as they had each other and a lifelong supply of food and water, they could live here forever.

I could see it was a closed issue, so I gave each of them a hug and said goodbye. It wasn't as sad as I expected, and that was probably because they were all so happy. They were all smiling as they escorted me to the tunnel and watched me go up the ladder.

"One last thing," I called down from above. "Follow the advice of my Uncle Titus. Don't open the doors for any reason. Think like survivors."

We all knew that wasn't going to happen, but it was advice I hadn't followed from the start, and it had worked out well.

******

I caught up with the Chief about five miles up the coast and radioed the news that the others had chosen to stay behind. He said he wasn't surprised, and then gave me his own good news. Captain Miller had used our two boats to begin clearing a perimeter around the hidden cable on the mainland. We would be able to work faster without interference from the infected. He also had several people trained in the use of SCUBA gear, and they were clearing the moat in the path of the new cable. It was tricky work, but they were making progress, and everyone was being closely screened for bites when they came out of the water.

The Chief said there had been no Electro Magnetic Pulse associated with the accident because nuclear accidents weren't the same as thermonuclear explosions. In my mind I was thinking, "Whatever," but when the Chief explained it meant our electronics weren't fried, I understood it was a good thing.

The clock was still ticking when we were in view of Mud Island, but I had to appreciate the view. It was a beautiful sight, even though there was a tent city on the beach side of the island. There were also guards everywhere, and they were waving at us as if they were welcoming home heroes. I didn't know yet how many of them were with Captain Miller at Fort Jackson.

The Chief passed the island and then gently let the current pull the barge into the northern entrance to our moat. The waterway had always acted as a natural river with the water entering at the north and exiting to the south. The current would pull the barge right to the dock where the backup cable was hidden.

As I passed the southern exit, I saw scores of infected being washed out of the waterway. The Army had managed to free the nets from their attachments at the mainland and the island, and the trapped infected were being flushed out. It was good timing because we needed to get inside.

I was greeted at the dock by a large number of men and women in Army uniforms, all thanking me for what we had done. I kept trying to tell them it was the Chief, but then I learned it was also the hospitality of Jean that had given them hope. Hot showers and hot meals had made us all heroes.

It was roughly a mile to the shelter entrance, but I made good time because I didn't have to worry about any infected dead. I was told to expect the entrance to be open because there was a bite inspection in progress. I wasn't sure what that meant exactly, but when I saw an inspection included a hot shower, I could understand people were glad there would be a bite inspection. I had to squeeze through about two dozen naked people waiting for their turn, which was interesting, but I had to see Jean.

I found her in the kitchen with her little companion, Molly, and both of them tackled me. It was the best welcome home I had ever gotten, and I was loving it. Then I got bummed out because Molly was happy, and I didn't think she knew about her mom.

They saw my expression change, and Jean said, "It's okay. Bus told us, and Molly was happy to find out Allison was a hero."

I didn't know what Bus had told them, but I would have to find out so my story would match his. He apparently said something to make Molly feel like her mother had done something good for the group.

Jean said, "It was so awesome what she did for the Chief when the plane crashed." She managed to give me a quick wink over Molly's head.

"Yes, yes it was incredible," I said. "Hey, I need to get back out there, but I just had to see you two first. I'll be back as soon as I can."

Jean was as pretty as the day I met her, but time was running short. I had something tugging at the back of my mind, and I had just figured it out. I couldn't take my eyes off of her, but reality was hitting me like a ton of bricks.

I thought to myself, "Where are we going to put about a hundred more people if we have to seal ourselves inside Mud Island until the effects of the radiation are known?"

One more quick hug and kiss, and I was running for the door again. I practically ran over Bus as I reached the outside, and he was happier than I had ever seen him.

"We did it Ed. We pulled it off. They're rolling the power cables onto the barge and should have it across within the hour. All the prep work done by the Army made it a breeze. If not for them, we would've been shooting the infected all day while the Chief, Tom, and Kathy did the cable."

He was so happy he didn't see that I was concerned about something. When he did, he thought something bad had happened to someone, and when I told him what I was worried about, he was amused.

"Ed, I'm sorry. No one told you. We have that all figured out," he laughed.

******

It was only a couple of hours later. The tent city was gone from the beach, and besides the trampled sand there was no sign it had even been there. The soldiers worked efficiently to even drag driftwood into place to make it all appear more natural. Part of the reason Mud Island was a successful place to hide was because it gave the impression that it wasn't a nice place to live. Hidden among the trees with the cameras were radiation monitors. We didn't have a clue how bad it would be, and we couldn't risk going outside for measurements of the radiation levels.

The power lines were connected, and Mud Island was no longer using reserves. The work had progressed quickly because the moat was more clear than it had been since the infection started. They had even been able to lay the cable on the bottom of the moat, so it was unlikely to ever become disconnected again by something landing on top of it. Without the nets and the hundreds of bodies filling the moat, the current was moving more swiftly, and the barge was easily towed to the northern dock. We placed it where the houseboat had been originally parked on the side facing the ocean. If nothing else, it would block the plane from the harsh winds if there was a storm.

Once the barge was tied up at its new home, the Cormorant was literally packed with soldiers. Every square inch had someone squeezed into it for the ride to Fort Sumter. They only brought their weapons and ammunition plus gear they could probably use to restore communications.

Olivia, Chase, Whitney, and Sam didn't know they were going to have company yet, but none of us doubted they would mind. They would be getting the best protection in the world, and Captain Miller would be getting the forward base he had been trying to establish. He said more than once that our small group of friends had been able to accomplish what an entire command structure had failed to do. Maybe that was the answer. Keep it small at first and give it a chance to grow.

The Chief was at the helm of the Cormorant. It was decided the faithful Coast Guard vessel would stay with Captain Miller at Fort Sumter. It was too big of an advertisement to be parked at Mud Island. Besides, it wasn't going to be of much use to anyone until the radiation levels dropped, and even then, it would be contaminated. They planned to disable the machine guns just enough to keep them from being used against Fort Sumter.

Tom stayed behind to spend some much needed time around his daughter, and he planned to have a talk with her about Kathy to see how she would feel about how close they had become. From what we had seen in the last few hours, Molly was smart enough to have figured that out for herself, and she was okay with it.

To ease the surprise at Fort Sumter a bit, Kathy and I were flying back with Bus in the de Havilland Beaver. It was bulkier and noisier than the Otter, but someone had put a lot of love into furnishing it. We had a comfortable ride back to Fort Sumter that seemed to be over too soon.

Since the clock was still working against us, we surprised the others by dropping in and quickly explaining what we were doing, and they were absolutely delighted. To have that many soldiers with them meant they wouldn't have to be afraid of the lower levels, and they would have plenty of company. They were especially excited to learn it was likely that communications would be restored, and they would be able to talk with Mud Island whenever they wanted.

The Cormorant docked at its new home not long after we had arrived, and we all went down to greet them. The men and women who climbed from her decks were smiling, and as each one passed our new friends that we were leaving behind at Fort Sumter, they took the time to say hello and give out big hugs. Olivia gave Chase an elbow and reminded him he was spoken for. He gave her a kiss on the cheek and told her he would have to do that a lot so she would remember she was spoken for, too.

The Chief took Captain Miller ahead of the rest of the troops so he could give him a quick tour of the shelter. He gave him the codes to the doors and showed him how to find the back door in case they ever needed it. The Captain wanted to spend as much time around the Chief as he could since this would be the second time that the Chief and his friends had saved their lives. Of course the Chief wasn't big on taking credit for anything, but he allowed the Captain and his people to give their respects.

We only had a few hours to spare when we pulled away from Fort Sumter. The Chief was behind the controls of the Beaver, and he had a grin on his face like a kid with a new toy. He circled around the stern of the Cormorant, and gave her a salute. We all saw that someone had hung an American flag on the mast, and we were all aware that another flag had been raised on the main flagpole inside Fort Sumter. Someone had found the blue and white state flag of South Carolina and raised it on another pole. As we took off I could see them both, and it felt like the right thing to do.

Kathy said, "It seems ironic that we have a foothold at this place again. It was the symbol of this country's division at one time. The country is divided again, but we have to start somewhere."

It had been a long day, and we were all tired to the bone. When it would all be done, it would be back to the way it had started when the power line got disconnected. Allison was gone, but new families were starting. We had a new plane, and we could do no more than hope the fallout from the Oconee Nuclear Plant didn't mess things up too badly, but hope was what kept us going.

We practically had to make the Chief land the plane when we got back to Mud Island, and Kathy had to keep herself from laughing when she told him he couldn't go out and play after the rest of us piled out on the dock. We had carried back as many cases of MRE's as we could to replenish some of what we had shared with Captain Miller's people, and it would take a couple of trips to haul it in, but it would be worth the labor.

Everything was restored to the way we had left it, and we had to remind ourselves that even in the short time we had been gone the infected could have washed up on the beach and wandered into the dense bushes and trees of the island.

We took the time to disable the boat and the plane using the Chief's creative wiring skills. Then we used tarps we had found in huge supply at Fort Sumter to cover them both. Our hope was that decontamination would be easier if we only had to remove the tarps. We wished we could cover the houseboat, but we were running out of time.

The sky to the west had taken on a strange color, and we didn't think it was just the sunset. It was dark and ominous as the cloud grew, and it was so odd to see the western sky grow darker than the east at this time of day.

I was facing east as I pulled the door shut on Mud Island, but it already felt different outside, with one exception. An infected dead was stumbling along the edge of the trees in my direction. I wondered if it would survive the radiation, and as the light from the outside disappeared around the edges of the door, I could only wonder how long it would be before we could open it again.

ABOUT THE AUTHOR

Bob Howard (1951-) was born in New Jersey to an Army Sergeant from Ohio and a mother from Romania. He was moved from one Army base to the next, and before he began high school in Huntsville, Alabama he had lived most of his life overseas in Germany and Okinawa with brief stays in Maryland and North Carolina. He credits his imagination to his exposure to different cultures and environments at an early age. He began reading science fiction and fell in love with post apocalyptic novels. He still has an original copy of the first one he read in 1966, The Furies by Keith Edwards. He joined the Navy after high school and continued to move from one base to another, including a submarine base at Holy Loch, Scotland. He eventually stayed in one place when he got stationed in Charleston, South Carolina. He graduated with a BS in Psychology from the College of Charleston and married his wife of 31 years. His son still lives in Charleston, but his daughter has married and made a home in Ohio where the Howard family has its earliest known roots. Through the years he has had one burning passion that he has wanted to fulfill, and through Alive for Now he is getting to live that passion. Creating a book is something so many people want to do but never have the opportunity, and after writing this book he believes the sky is the limit. He plans to write for the rest of his life because it is enjoyable beyond his wildest dreams. As for the zombie genre, he saw Night of the Living Dead when it originally hit the theaters, and until recently it didn't receive the attention it deserves.

Made in the USA
Columbia, SC
19 April 2023

15140610R00178